SONORA

SONORA

AND THE EYE OF THE TITANS

T.S. HALL

This book was originally published in paperback by New Guy Publishing in 2011

ISBN-13: 9781545591260
ISBN-10: 1545591261

Printed in the United States of America

www.sonoraseries.com

Acknowledgment

So many people have been crucial to the completion and success of this book. First of all, I'd like to thank my mother and father for their unending support in the pursuit of my dreams. I'd also like to thank Clarissa for being the first to read my adventure and giving me the confidence to persevere. Thank you to my amazing brother, Gavin, who gave me the tools to complete the final manuscript. I'd also like to thank Katie, Kyle, Barclay, Rick, Martha, Molly, Jarrod, Taylor, Patrick, David, Paige, and Jenny for helping to inspire and support me in my quest for adventure.

Foreword

Fifteen years ago, the capital city of Titanis on the world of Sonora, came under attack from a power-hungry general. He was a part of a silent majority of Sonorans who were angry with the increased freedoms of humanity, and other species, given to them by laws enacted under the leadership of King Tildar and Queen Kalia. The general infiltrated the highly regarded ranks of the Royal Guard, isolated the king, killed his most loyal guards, and assassinated him while the general's forces took control of the army and air force.

With the help of a few loyal guardsmen, Queen Kalia was able to escape the palace with the last royal descendant of the Zeus bloodline and heir to the throne. Only six months old, this baby girl represented the only threat to the general's claim over the kingdom. General Salazar sent his elite guard after the last of the royal family, cornering them on the outskirts of Titan land near the edges of Crystal Lake.

Surrounded by hooded assassins, Queen Kalia sacrificed herself, enabling her sister and daughter to escape through one of the ancient gateways that ported them to Earth. In order to protect the royal heir to the Titan throne, Kalia's sister changed her name and adopted the baby as her own. With the help of a guardian warlock named Sas, she gathered a contingent of loyal followers and blended into human society by hiding away in the small mountain town of Sandy, Oregon.

One

Tryouts

"Allora…" The dream shook as sleep escaped the prone, brunette sixteen-year-old. She opened her eyelid halfway, unwilling to give up her slumber. "Allora!"

"Five more minutes mom," Allora said in a half-conscious state of annoyance as her mother rocked her shoulder.

"It's six-thirty princess," Milly said, walking to the door. "You're going to be late for soccer tryouts."

Allora's eyes popped wide, and the dark purple bed sheets flew into the air. Scrambling around the chaos of her room, she found the scattered soccer clothes littering the floor of her closet. A shoe flew across the room, as she rummaged through the clutter.

"Where are my cleats?" Allora yelled as she sifted through the funky armoire at the edge of the bed. The piece of wooden furniture had no straight lines, with curves that curled like waves. It sat next to shelves of multicolored gemstones, snow globes, and odd-looking South American dolls that her late uncle had brought back from his trips.

"Ma, cleats, I can't find them," Allora said, tossing all of her shoes out of the armoire.

A blonde girl popped her head around the corner of the bedroom door frame. "You mean these?" Allora rushed across the room and grabbed the shoes, shoving them into her duffel bag. "Have you ever been on time to anything in your life?"

"Shut up Katie," Allora said, smirking at her best friend.

"You kind of look like a goblin."

"You look like a troll."

Allora grabbed a brush from the desk to her right, and stood in front of the mirror pulling the knots aggressively from her long brown hair. Her beauty was subtle, with dark brown eyes, fair skin tone, and long legs with a few scars on her knees due to a childhood filled with adventures in the forests of Oregon.

Milly flipped eggs onto colorful neon yellow plates and placed them onto the kitchen table. "Girls, come eat some breakfast before you go."

Allora threw her duffel bag toward the door, and slumped down at the end of the table. Aunt May sat across the table still in her pajamas, reading the newspaper. She was lean and fit, with short, dark brown hair, green eyes, and a serious demeanor.

"Don't forget—you two need to be at training practice at noon in the outer realm," Aunt May said from behind the paper.

Allora shoveled a piece of bacon and a slice of toast into her mouth. "We have daily bubbles." Katie laughed and spit up orange juice. Allora swallowed. "Doubles."

"I don't care young lady," Aunt May said, dramatically lowering the newspaper. "You are not missing a training session."

"May is right. You four need the practice. You've still got a lot to learn before you're old enough to focus."

"Oh, that reminds me, make sure to tell the boys to show up after soccer practice," Aunt May said, pulling up the newspaper.

"Hey, when is Sas coming back?" Allora asked, gulping down some orange juice. "I haven't seen that big fur ball in forever."

"He's still at Shangri-La for the Guardian's meeting," Milly said, placing another plate down as a young brunette girl hopped into the empty seat at the table. "Probably not for another week or two."

"Sas smells," Allora's sister said, as she shoveled food into her mouth.

Bell was thirteen years old with dirty blonde hair, short in height, with rimmed glasses, and green eyes.

"Can't argue with that," Katie said, sipping down the last of her coffee. "We need to roll."

Allora grabbed a piece of toast and her duffel bag and ran to the door.

The light was just peeking out over the horizon, which was blocked out by the enormous Douglas fir trees that lined her five-acre yard. The morning dew trickled off of the rhododendron leaves, and the birds chirped a song in the cool mountain air. The sun lifted above the eastern mountain, and warmed the atmosphere as they jumped into Katie's red Jeep. Sun rays pierced the thick forest canopy as the car sped through the winding roads. Big block letters of Sandy High School greeted them as the car turned into the parking lot near the base of the field.

"You should've been named captain," Allora said as they gathered their bags and cleats.

Katie slung her strap across her chest. "She scored more goals than I did last season. Besides, you know that Coach Taylor wasn't going to give leadership to a junior."

"And the fact that she's a royal suck-up," Allora added, prompting a giggle from her best friend.

They strolled up to the field where a group of girls were stretching. From the left of the goal, a pretty blonde girl strutted up. Her expression was stern and angry from behind the layer of makeup caked on her face.

"You're late, as always," Jenny said, tersely.

Katie tossed her bag on the ground. "Nice to see you too."

"What are you doing here?" Jenny asked, staring at Allora. "Freshman team tryouts aren't until next week."

"Ha. Ha. You should be a comedian."

"You know that you've got no chance of making this team."

"We'll see about that," Allora responded, flashing a fake smile.

Jenny rolled her eyes and went back to bossing around a few sophomores.

"I really hate that girl," Allora said, unzipping her bag and pulling out her shin guards.

"Yeah, she sucks," Katie muttered, slumping down to stretch her legs.

Coach Taylor arrived a few minutes later and got them going with a few warm-up runs around the field. Wind sprints came first, then suicide sprints,

T.S. HALL

which was followed up by high stepping for the length of the field ten times. By the end of the half-hour speed drills, Allora's legs were burning, and she was out of breath. She had taken a couple fitness classes at the local gym, but nothing could prepare someone for the rigorous daily double practices that are required to make the varsity squad.

After about an hour, the soccer boys started to arrive. Tanner, the junior mid-fielder, rolled into the parking lot in his black Ford Bronco, and popped out of the driver side door. He had short blonde hair, dark blue eyes, and a muscular body that was accentuated by his polyester compression workout clothes. Dax jumped out of the passenger seat, clad in a similar cut-off shirt, and soccer shorts. Katie's twin brother was tall, muscular, with light brown hair, and dark brown eyes.

Allora caught them out of her right eye as she refilled her water bottle from the fountain near where the track met the stands. Tanner sauntered up and smiled.

"I thought you said you weren't going to run the gauntlet this year," Tanner said.

Allora topped off her bottle and twisted the cap. "Katie talked me into it. Besides, it'll keep me out of doing workouts with my mom, who insists that I stay in good running shape. I'm guessing that she thinks I'm fat."

"Well, you're definitely not fat," Tanner said, pinching her side playfully.

Allora scrunched her abdomen and smiled. Her expression reversed when she saw Jenny stomping over from across the turf field.

"I gotta go," Allora said, taking a swig out of her water bottle and running over to Katie who was scolding her twin brother over taking her earphones.

Allora ignored Jenny's glare. Glancing back, she saw Jenny cross her arms and glare at Tanner.

"Scrimmage time," Coach Taylor yelled, prompting everyone to meet in the middle of the soccer field. The coach split up the groups to make them even, and tossed one team a few yellow bibs.

Allora watched as Jenny began whispering something to her friends Nancy and Tanya, two girls who were notoriously mean.

"Watch yourself out there," Allora said to Katie who was adjusting her jersey.

"Against the bruiser squad? Please. I can run circles around those idiots."

The scrimmage began. Allora was playing midfield, and finally got an opening, passing it cleanly to Katie, who took off like a cheetah. She maneuvered around a defender, leaving her wide open to take it toward the center. Nancy was cross field and made a quick step towards the oncoming player. There wasn't much room to get in front, so Nancy slid from behind, taking out Katie's legs. Blonde hair snapped forward, and she hit the turf with a thud. The slide tackle was highly illegal and prompted everyone to head to that side of the field. Allora clenched her fists and grit her teeth. She sprinted to Nancy and shoved her to the ground. A fight broke out. Coach Taylor screamed as the guys in the locker room flooded the field to watch.

"Catfight!" Dax yelled.

Allora felt a hand grab the back of her hair, pulling her along the ground. Instinctively, she pivoted her foot, and through the mask of matted hair, she swung a fist, connecting with a jaw. Someone screamed and fell backward as the coach pulled the girls apart. With a flick of her brown hair, Allora noticed that the girl she had punched was Jenny. She was lying on the ground glaring and holding her cheek. The blonde captain got to her feet and stared Allora down.

"You're going to pay for that, trailer trash," Jenny yelled, getting really close to Allora's face. Some of the other girls were fighting, occupying the coach.

"Nobody pulls my hair."

"Your daddy never taught you manners, did he?" Jenny said, adjusting her swollen jaw. The question made Allora's emotions boil. The hairs on the back of her neck stood straight, and even the fake blades of grass on the turf stood up. A strange electrical energy permeated the area. "Oh, yeah, that's right, you never had a daddy. I guess that's why you're such a disappointment in life."

The comment hit Allora like a knife to the gut. She was shocked into speechlessness, stunned by an anger and hate she'd seldom felt before. A faint swell of electricity crawled up Allora's spine, moving through her torso and into her arms.

Jenny glanced over to Tanner, who was standing on the track with the other soccer players, then back to Allora. She raised an eyebrow and whispered, "Oh, and by the way, this little thing between you and my boyfriend… that's over."

A pulsating energy flowed into her palms as she extended them away from her body and let out a tormented scream. Her palms burst into purple flames. Only the gawkers immediately surrounding Allora witnessed the spectacular phenomenon, but in mere moments, panic spread among the several dozen surrounding onlookers. Allora's body felt heavy, and the purple light of the fire danced in her peripheral as the world became fuzzy. Devoid of any energy, she dropped to the ground.

Two

CONFUSION

Lying prone on the bleached white linens covering the bed, Allora slept peacefully. A plastic bag of hydrating vitamins hung on a metal rack feeding clear liquid into her veins. The hospital room smelled of a strange mixture of lavender and bleach.

Standing at the foot of the bed, Milly and Aunt May remained steady and silent for a long minute of reflection.

"How is this possible?" Milly asked after a moment.

"Plenty of Sonorans have focused before the maturation age," Aunt May replied.

"Yes, but focused an element? And an element like fire?"

"Well, that is rather rare, I know. You can't be all that surprised given her bloodline though."

"I don't remember her father ever being able to focus an element."

"Ancestral DNA can lock in certain gifts that don't reveal themselves for generations. I can't really see any other explanation."

The faint sound of Allora's breathing echoed against the whitewashed walls of the intensive care unit. The two women stood idly, contemplating their next move.

"We have contingency plans, right?" Milly asked.

"Not for something like this," Aunt May admitted.

Milly's heart began to beat faster and her head throbbed as she thought about the potential consequences of her daughter's tragic event.

"Do we need to be worried about being compromised?" Milly asked.

"I don't think so," Aunt May said, staring down at her niece. "The energy signature would have been strong, but they would need to have someone close by to detect it."

"And the humans?"

"I'll come up with a logical reason for the fire."

"We also need to increase the security personnel. Can you get a hold of Baymar? I want him stationed at the summer camp just in case."

"What about Sas? Should we get him back here early?" Aunt May asked.

"No, he's got to finish that meeting. It's going to be even more paramount that the Guardians are prepared for the inevitable. When Titanis finds out that a living royal exists, all hell will break loose."

"We need to increase the training regiment immediately," Aunt May said, her tone filled with concern and dread.

"We should get out of here," Milly said, eyeing the door. "If she is an Elemental, her dead skin will peel, and those burns will heal fast. Not exactly something that the doctor will understand."

"Wh-what's going on?" Allora asked, perplexed by her abnormal surroundings. As she scanned the room, Allora's memories slowly surfaced. She eyed the tightly wrapped dressing on her hands and remembered the horrifying fire that had engulfed them. Not entirely awake, Allora rubbed her eyes. A strange energy filled the room.

Milly knelt beside the bed, and placed her hand on Allora's bandaged arm. They held each other's silent gaze.

"Honey, I'm so, so sorry about your... uh, accident. Are you okay?"

With her defiant teenage pride on the line, Allora replied, "A little sore, but I'll be all right."

Milly gave her younger sister an ominous nod and excused herself from the room. "Aunt May, what's wrong with Mom?"

Trying to mask her concerns with a smile, a weak, "Hello, darling," was all Aunt May could muster before her eyes began to well up. She sat down on the bed. "Your mother is just worried about you, that's all."

The medication was wearing off, and the throbbing pain in her hands and forearms felt as if she'd stuck her fingers into a light socket.

Milly charged back into the room. "Get dressed, Allora. We have to go home right now."

Aunt May helped Allora with the arduous task of exchanging her hospital gown for her everyday clothes. Adamant about getting out of the hospital, Milly hurriedly undertook the discharge process.

On the ride home, Bell educated the passengers of the car on the different treatments for severe burns and the various antibiotics to fight infections and anti-inflammatory creams used to decrease swelling and pain. "Some of the quacks say you can even put mustard or butter on it, but who wants to do that?"

Allora was rather impressed by how much her sister knew about the subject, but everyone else in the car remained silent.

The minivan took a left at the wooden mailbox and headed between two large pine trees. The long gravel road curved to the left, then opened into a large meadow. At the end of the driveway, a rectangular, one-story log cabin sat in the middle of a field, surrounded by trees. The roof angled down on either side of a large brick chimney.

Milly pulled the van into the garage and turned to her daughter. "Lora, I want you to go straight to bed. You're gonna need plenty of rest."

"Yeah... and some mustard!" Bell said with a giggle.

Spent from the afternoon events, she nodded.

Inside, she closed the door to her room and leaned against it. Glancing around her sanctuary, Allora saw only what she had always seen, yet the room somehow felt unfamiliar. The assortment of random gemstones on her shelves, the imaginative drawings of fantastical creatures on her wall, and even the funky armoire. Allora fell down on the bed and looked up through her skylight at the bright stars. Her mind raced between the tryouts, the fire, and her mother's strange behavior at the hospital.

How did my hands catch fire?

None of it made any sense, and obsessively reflecting only left her feeling more fatigued. Like the shades of a window, Allora's eyelids fell down, and within minutes, the girl fell into a deep, deep sleep.

* * *

A pounding headache greeted Allora when she awoke. As she sat up, her back became extremely itchy. She ran into her sister's room, crashed through the doorway, and jumped onto Bell's bed. "It itches so bad!" Allora wailed, dancing up and down, unsuccessfully reaching for the itch with her wrapped hands. "Please, Bell. Help!"

Bell was bouncing on the bed from her sister's frantic footwork, but she finally got to her knees and used both hands to scratch her sister's back.

Allora exhaled in relief.

"Can't you get some sort of back scratcher?" Bell asked, yawning from her interrupted sleep.

Allora raised her white bandaged stubs. Bell stopped scratching, crossed her arms and rolled her eyes, then left the room without a word, heading for the shower.

Allora hurried down the hall, still wearing her tank-top and purple polka dot pajama pants. When she found her Aunt May in the living room, reading the newspaper, Allora ran to her and begged for relief from the discomfort. Aunt May folded the newspaper and instructed her niece to sit down next to her.

"So, my hands produced fire. You never mentioned those abilities."

"That is because it is extremely rare."

"So, what does this mean?"

Aunt May grabbed her hand and began unwrapping the gauze. After a few spins, she pulled back the layer covering her palm, which pulled off the dead pink skin. Allora cringed, thinking that her hands were going to be grotesque. Opening her eyes, she saw that the skin underneath the peeling wound was completely healed. She unwrapped the other hand to see the same result. Twisting her torso, she stared up at her aunt in astonishment.

"This means that your body has the ability to harness hadron energy at a whole different level, and your body is able to manipulate the molecular structure of fire," Aunt May said, with a proud smirk. "The heat from the flames doesn't harm your body's cells. It's a rather fascinating ability."

"What about the other people who saw what happened?" Allora asked.

"The fire was caused by a firework prank that went wrong. That is the official story, and you must be convincing. We can't have any of these humans prying into our lives."

"Seems like a flimsy story."

"Got a better idea, girl?"

"Not really," Allora muttered. "What's next then?"

"We need to make sure were prepared for anything," Aunt May said, getting up from the couch, heading for the kitchen. "It also means that your training regimen just increased ten-fold."

"Saw that coming."

"I think that you'll have time now. Not sure that you're making the soccer squad darling."

"Yeah, no kidding," Allora said, dropping her head in disappointment. "Where is mom?"

"She's out checking the security protocols around town with Sheriff Newton," Aunt May replied, pouring herself some coffee. "Make sure that you feed the animals."

"What about summer camp next week?"

"Yes, you'll still be attending. We have to act like everything is normal."

Allora stood and walked out the backdoor to the greeting of two extremely excited Labradors. She fed Rex and Cody, then went to the chicken coop to throw some grain. Upon throwing a handful in the far side of the coop, the grains slipped down through the cracks. She walked over, and saw the slightest tint of something reflecting from down below the floorboards.

"Hey," Aunt May said, sticking her head into the coop, and rousing Allora from the curiosities below. "Can you let your posy know that we are going to be training early tomorrow morning? We are starting a more advanced training session since your incident."

Allora nodded, and then left the coop to finish her chores.

That night, Allora lay in her bed, staring up at the skylight, wondering about which star held the secrets to her other life. Sonora was somewhere out there, beckoning, calling for her.

Feeling anxious and overwhelmed, she decided to get some fresh air. She rolled off the bed, lifted the window sash, and squeezed through the opening. After circumventing the rhododendron bush at the base of the window, Allora quietly crossed the field, escaped the property, and headed east down the darkening road, a route she'd taken many times before.

With her home behind her, she walked a mile before turning left on Norman Court. At the end of the cul-de-sac, a trail zigzagged down a steep hill. The sun was going down, which made the trek over tree roots and uneven terrain far more difficult, but even in the fading light, the trail was so familiar that Allora didn't so much as stumble or trip once. After several hundred feet, she walked out of the woods, into a rocky clearing.

It was quiet, except for the rushing water that grew louder with each step. The flowing river glistened against the day's last beams of light, and water tumbled over large rocks, into a pool at Allora's feet. The sound of the rushing river was soothing, almost a lullaby, as Allora sat on a flat rock by the pool and recalled the odd series of events. She stared up at the full moon, the silvery orb inching its way up into the indigo sky as the brilliant sunset exhausted its splendor in the western hills.

A cracking noise reached across the rocky riverbed. Startled, Allora jumped backward, losing her footing on the slippery rocks. When she managed to pull herself upright again, she scurried across the rocks and propped herself up against a sizable boulder. She fell silent, listening for any sign of movement as her heart thumped loudly in her ears, her panic increased with each passing second.

There was no time to reflect. She grabbed a large, smooth rock from the creek bed. A quick glance around the side of the boulder didn't reveal anything, but the sound of pebbles grinding under the weight of a foot reverberated on the opposite side. When more footsteps followed, Allora squeezed her fingers around the rock in her hand, ready to strike. The sound stopped, and she knew her would-be assailant was directly to the right of the boulder.

Beads of sweat trickled down her forehead, and a chill crawled down her spine. The footsteps started again, and a dark figure glided past. She made her choice in an instant and leapt onto the intruder, knocking the body to the ground, then raised the rock over her head.

As the figure turned over and screamed, the light of the moon revealed a familiar face.

"Tanner?" Allora asked in disbelief.

"Allora?" Tanner answered, equally shocked.

She threw the rock down, pushed off of Tanner's chest, and stood over him.

He gradually got to his feet and brushed off the dirt from his shirt. "Are you crazy?" He asked, still shaking from the surprise attack.

Allora wasn't about to take the blame for the situation. She glared at Tanner and said, "Yeah, well, what are you doing sneaking up on me like that?"

"What? I wasn't sneaking up on you. I didn't even know you were down here."

After a few seconds of silence, Allora decided to give in. "Sorry. I guess I've just been paranoid lately. What are you doing down here anyway?"

"I come here a lot, whenever I need to think." Tanner lowered his shoulders, releasing his tense muscles. "Are you all right?"

Allora lowered her chin, uncrossed her arms, and walked past Tanner to the water's edge. She picked up a smooth, flat rock from the creek bed and skipped it across the water, trying to think of what to say. "You mean my hands?" she said, holding them up.

"What the...?" Tanner grabbed her hands. "There's not a mark on you. How... what—"

"I know," she said. "Weird huh?" Noticing Tanner's bewildered look, she pulled her hands away from his judging eyes. "Don't look at me like that."

"I'm sorry. I don't mean to. It's just... well, what happened that day?"

"Your girlfriend decided to say a few things that got my blood boiling," Allora said. "Next thing I knew, people were screaming, and I was on fire."

"Oh. I had no idea. I'm so sorry. She can be pretty mean sometimes."

"Mean? That's the understatement of the century."

Tanner rubbed the back of his neck and blinked in the semi-darkness. "I know. I'm not even really sure why I date her."

The impromptu confession caught Allora off guard, and they stared at each other for a minute in awkward silence. The moonlight softly illuminated Allora's natural beauty as they unconsciously inched ever closer, until their bodies softly touched. Just as each felt the other's heat, Tanner's cell phone rang.

Allora stepped back while Tanner awkwardly searched his pocket for the beckoning device.

He flipped open the phone. "It's Dax," he said, giving an awkward half-smile.

Allora watched Tanner's face. He seemed relieved for the interruption, happy to be saved by the bell. She decided to act accordingly and ignored their previous exchange. After a few grunts, he said, "What time are we training in the morning?"

"Aunt May said five-thirty so that you guys can get to tryouts."

"You get that?" Tanner asked over the cell phone. "Alright, we'll see you guys at Allora's house."

Tanner hung up the phone after a few more grunts, and they left the creek bed, heading up to the road.

"Dax said that Katie decided to quit soccer."

"Why?"

"She said that she wanted to train with you more, I guess."

"I have a feeling that we might need it."

They said goodbye at the crossing, stealing a few glances back as they headed home under the light of the moon.

Three

TRAINING

The next day, Milly shook her daughter awake. Allora looked through the slits of her eyelids at her clock.

"Ugh," she groaned, rolling to the other side and flinging the sheets over her head.

"Rise and shine. Training day," Milly announced, pushing her daughter's limp body. "Come on, honey. Take a shower and get dressed. Tanner, Dax, and Katie will be here in a half-hour. You don't have much time."

Reluctantly, Allora slid out of bed and stumbled to the shower like a zombie. Mornings were never pleasant. The alarm was a relentless enemy. After putting on a tank-top and shorts, there was a knock at the front door.

"Your friends are here," Milly yelled from the living room.

Allora lumbered toward the front of the house, turned the corner of the hallway and saw her friends standing in the front entryway.

"Hey, how you doing?" Tanner asked, moving up to look her over.

"I'm exhausted."

"Yeah, tell me about it," Tanner replied, his bright blue eyes staring down at her with affection.

"OMG, your hands are completely healed," Katie said, grabbing Allora's palms. "So, it is true. You're an Elemental!"

Milly gathered the group and explained, "We've created a protected path to the portal. A little extra precaution. Just take the normal path through the back meadow. Don't deviate. May will be waiting for you there." Milly then hugged her daughter and kissed her on the cheek.

Allora and the others walked out the back door. Outside, the sun was inching above the horizon as the four teenagers made their way through the back yard. Morning dew covered the grassy field, and the birds chirped as the group reached the forest path.

A mile up, there sat a large boulder, oddly placed in the middle of a recess in the hillside. Allora walked up to the seemingly solid rock, placed a hand forward, and then pushed through the liquid barrier. The portal pulled the body like gravity, then a flash of light appeared and she was standing on grass. Enormous oak trees situated in a perfect, grid-like pattern surrounded them. Each tree had been planted in a line, as if in an orchard, yet it seemed too perfectly designed to be real.

"This is new," Allora said, glancing around.

Aunt May stood in the middle of a round gravel pit in the middle of the orchard.

"I've changed our outer realm simulation to a more advanced environment. This is a replica of the same facility that myself and Milly used when we got to the point where we could harness hadrons, such as you did at tryouts Allora. And what are hadrons again?"

In unison, and with monotone voices, they said, "energized molecules that can be focused into your body's cells, and projected out in different ways."

"That is correct." Aunt May gestured to her left. Several colored robes were folded neatly on a small wooden bench. Allora grabbed a purple robe, Tanner chose blue, Dax preferred green, and Katie selected pure white.

As soon as they were appropriately dressed for training, Aunt May asked them to line up. She smiled. "Do you all know why you chose the robes you did?"

The four glanced down at their new outfits, then back up at the older woman.

"You all picked a certain color robe without fighting or even realizing they were different." She paused to let them contemplate their actions.

"Sonorans have always embodied a distinctive color based on a number of factors, mostly having to do with emotions. Just like a ruby is red or a sapphire is blue, it is a part of you. This color is also what is produced when you perform a burst of energy. The colors of the fabric of your chosen robes will be the color of hadron you produce when you mature."

"Are you sure?" Dax asked. "We haven't even been able to produce hadrons yet."

Aunt May gave him a knowing smile. "Call it women's intuition."

Before they began their physical training, Aunt May gave them a lesson in hadron focalization. "The manipulation of energy is an ancient practice and requires knowledge, strength, patience, control, and understanding. Hadrons are everywhere, even in the trees that surround us. Hadrons connect every living thing." As she said this, Aunt May closed her eyes, and held out her palms.

Silence was followed by a rustling of the leaves, and then the oak trees glowed with a tint of orange. A small, faint trail of orange light formed on the tree branches, wove its way down the tree trunks, and slithered along the ground like a snake, absorbing itself at the base of her feet, and then winding its way into her palms. Two circling balls of orange energy hovered above her hand. She then opened her eyes, spun around while combining the balls of energy, and sent a hadron burst into a straw-filled dummy that had popped up from the ground behind her. The dummy exploded, sending pieces of wood and straw raining down. The four onlooker's eyes widened in amazement.

Aunt May swung around to face them. "It is essential that you understand your limits. Nature will allow you to use its energy, but do not be greedy." Her tone was soft, but the words were sharp and meaningful in the context of the teachings.

"Why was I able to produce fire? And how, since I'm not even the normal age for hadron maturity yet?"

"It requires a very rare kind of energy focalization, one which only a few Sonorans are capable of. I've never heard of anyone doing it at your age. Allora. There are four stages of hadron development. The first is Beson, second is Meson, third is Baryon, and the last is Fermion. Most don't reach the last stage, but you apparently have. Those special few who do reach it have the ability to produce and manipulate certain elements in our environment. The elements, of course, are rock or earth, wind, water, and, as you found out for yourself, fire."

"I still don't get it," Allora said, staring down at her hands. "How am I at the last stage if I've never even been through the first one?"

"I don't know," she admitted. "I'm as confused as you are about that, and your situation is unique. I've heard of Sonorans being able to focus hadrons at a young age but never at the fourth level. There were stories of young Sonorans with such powers, and some of these stories are supposedly recorded in ancient texts, but not much is known on the subject since most of those ancient texts were burned or lost ages ago."

Aunt May waved her hand, and four fighting dummies popped up from the ground. Each trainee took up a position in front of a plastic fighting dummy. They began with their basic maneuvers, performing a routine of kicking and punching.

After hours of repeating basic fighting moves, Allora rubbed her sore hands, arms and legs. "How much longer do we have to do this?" she complained. "I thought we were going to practice focusing hadrons, or doing some more advanced fighting techniques, not doing the same old routine."

Aunt May glided over next to Allora. "Continue," she commanded.

For the rest of the day, it was the same basic instruction, until Aunt May ended the session and sent her would-be warriors back through the portal. As soon as Allora got home, she iced the bruises on her limbs and crashed on the couch.

* * *

The next morning, Allora felt herself moving. She opened her eyes, and saw the face of an attractive young man staring back at her.

"Hi," Tanner said softly.

"Hi," Allora responded, unsure of what else to say. She began to feel a strange sensation as she stared back at him. Realizing the feelings of the moment, her eyes darted back and forth, searching for a distraction. Awkwardly, she stretched her arms and legs, and winced at the pain in her sore muscles. "I should, uh... probably go get ready," Allora mumbled, pulling off her blanket. Looking down at nothing but underwear, her eyes grew wide. She snatched the blanket, covered herself up, and escaped to the bathroom.

Tanner made a similar embarrassed departure to the kitchen, tripping over one of the family dogs that was lying next to the fireplace.

Katie and Dax arrived a few minutes later, and everyone gathered around the kitchen table for breakfast.

"What's with you, man?" Dax asked, noticing that Tanner seemed a bit nervous.

"Yeah," Katie said. "You've hardly touched your food, and I know you're always hungry."

"Nothing," he replied, casting a cautious glare in Allora's direction.

Allora quickly took a large gulp of orange juice, ignoring everyone and staring out the window.

Every day for two weeks, the four followed the same routine; waking early, eating breakfast together, and traveling through the portal to the orchard for training. Aunt May taught them the vulnerable body locations and how to exploit weak spots in their enemies.

After a couple of weeks went by, Aunt May decided to change the training routine. On the morning of the fifth week, the four arrived to find no dummies. She waited for them to change into their usual robes, and then instructed them to take their regular positions in a line, facing her. They remained still, as they'd been taught, standing at attention with their arms clasped behind their backs.

"Today, your training will require a bit more mobility, as your supposed enemy will be much more interactive, presumably, than the dummies you've faced thus far. You will be partnering up and training against each other," Aunt May said, causing mixed reactions. "Katie, you will be matched up with Allora, and Tanner, you will train with Dax." Reluctantly, they took up fighting positions, facing each other, and Aunt May stood between the two sets of partners. "You have a dual objective now. You must attack, while also blocking your opponent's attacks."

Allora thought about what she would need to do to catch Katie off guard. She knew her opponent was much more skilled, but Allora was ready for it.

"Begin!" Aunt May said.

Katie advanced, swinging her leg upward. Instinctively, Allora swiveled her arms around to deflect, but Katie turned in the opposite direction, launching her fist into her opponent's side. Allora recovered and mounted her own attack, sending a punch into Katie's midsection with a force that expelled the air from the blonde girl's lungs.

Katie hadn't anticipated the swift counterattack. "You've gotten better," she said, standing up straight.

"What's wrong, Master Katie?" Allora responded, with a grin. "Can't take a little competition?"

"Oh, you're going down girl!" Katie dug her foot into the dirt and lunged forward, swinging her arms violently. The confusing move had the desired effect: Allora raised her arms to block a punch as Katie's leg struck her in the shins. Allora knelt down but threw up both arms to block a downward punch. Katie was more gifted in the art of combat, but surprisingly, Allora was able to match most of her advances.

Finally, after about an hour of constant sparring, they all collapsed in exhaustion, their bodies bloody and bruised.

Aunt May stood over them with her hands behind her back. "Since you all have summer camp this next week, we'll have to continue this when you all start school."

Aunt May headed toward the portal exit, stepping through and back into the forest. Allora, Dax, Tanner, and Katie took some time to catch their breath, and then silently left the outer realm.

Four

CAMP

The summer was almost over, but the sun was still scorching hot. Holding a handheld fan in one hand and a glass of lemonade in the other, Allora tried to cool herself. Sweat glistened on her skin as she sat on the hot leather couch. The freezer contained the only solution to her suffering, but when she stood up, her skin stuck to the leather, requiring extra force to escape the insufferable cowhide.

After reaching the kitchen, she pulled open the freezer door and let out a gasp as the cold air cooled the beads of sweat covering her body. The soft breeze from the icy freezer chilled her skin as she leaned farther into the compartment. After getting some ice for her lemonade, she looked out the kitchen window to see her mom coming back in from feeding the chickens.

"Are you all packed?" Milly asked as she entered through the backdoor. Allora nodded, grabbing a cube of ice and pressing it against her forehead. "I've got a few rules that I need you to follow while you're at camp. You must not go out at night, and you must stay in the camp at all times. Got it?"

Allora happily nodded her head and raced off to her room to grab her stuff. Then, they jumped into the minivan, and headed for the school. Hundreds of teenagers lined the bus stop, standing around in groups, huddled next to piles of duffel bags and backpacks.

Katie and Dax stood on the curb with an excessive number of bags in front of them.

Allora glanced around and raised her eyebrows. "Wow. Got enough stuff?"

"Ha-ha. Very funny," Katie said, placing her hands on her hips. "I *need* all these bags. This one has my makeup," she said, pointing to a small brown suitcase the size of a bowling ball. "This one has my summer dresses, this one is my accessory bag, and my workout clothes are in there. Oh, and of course I've got an I-don't-care-what-I'm-wearing bag, which I'll only be using when I'm in the cabin."

"And what's that one?" Allora asked hesitantly, pointing to a smaller bag with a paisley pattern on it.

"Glad you asked," Katie said with a grin. "That's a bag full of clothes for my friend Allora, who never brings enough to wear and eventually has to borrow some." She cocked her head to the side and smiling mockingly.

Allora mimicked the smile but nudged her in agreement.

Just then, Tanner rolled up in his car. "Hey!" he said, waving, only to be smacked by Jenny.

Allora noticed the big blonde hair as her nemesis slid out of the passenger seat. The sight of the pompous soccer captain made Allora cringe. She had almost forgotten how much she despised the prissy elitist. *I'd like to catch her on fire sometime,* she seethed. *I bet her hair would explode with all that product in it.*

Tanner followed Jenny, waved at the soccer players, and then fell in behind his girlfriend.

Jenny strutted up to Dax, gave him a half-hug, and then glanced over his shoulder. Pulling down her designer bug-eyed sunglasses to glare at Allora. "What is the fire freak doing here?"

"Jenny, that was an accident, give it a rest," Tanner said, pulling at her arm.

"No, what I saw wasn't a firework," Jenny said, yanking away her arm, and getting to within inches of Allora's face. "That was some sort of black witch magic. I'm on to you freak."

As Jenny turned around, Allora stomped forward with her fist cocked, but Katie reluctantly grabbed her best friend's body to prevent a fight. The summer training had given Allora a sense of pride and the confidence to defend herself, which was rather useful at that moment.

Jenny was too oblivious to notice the aggressive display and sashayed away to the other side of the parking lot, where her minions, the other soccer players, were congregating.

"She was only kidding," Tanner said, though he didn't look like even he believed that.

"Ugh!" Allora exclaimed, and stomped off in the opposite direction.

Katie glared at Tanner, crossing her arms and shaking her head disapprovingly.

"What?" he asked, shrugging his shoulders with his hands outstretched.

"Sometimes I think all boys are clueless."

Tanner turned to Dax. "What was that all about?"

"Hey, man, don't ask me. I'm clueless, remember?"

Tanner rolled his eyes and stood there confused.

A line of large yellow buses pulled into the parking lot. Everyone grabbed their bags and filed into their designated vehicles. The eagerness was palpable as the youth-filled buses left the safety of the school and formed a long yellow caravan that snaked toward the wonder of the mountains.

Camp Big Lake was located in the Cascade Mountains, near Mt. Jefferson. The camp sat on a large, freshwater lake created from mountain runoff, making the water numbingly cold, but most campers didn't mind the chilly swims, which could be a relief from the scorching summer heat.

The buses pulled onto a gravel road and stopped at a wooden lodge. The old log cabin looked as if it had been built over a century ago. Splintered wood, a stained metal roof, and cracked concrete steps greeted the campers as they filed out of the buses, and camp counselors lined up, ready to meet the arrivals.

As if they'd just arrived at boot camp, the head counselor started barking orders through a bullhorn like a drill sergeant as soon as they exited the bus steps. "Please make sure you have all of your belongings, people!"

"Geesh," Katie whispered. "Next thing we know, he'll be tellin' us to drop and give him twenty. What's with that guy?"

Allora giggled. "Maybe he's been eating the camp cafeteria food for too long. It'll do that to a person," she mused.

"I know, right? That stuff was terrible last year. I had no idea food came in that many shades of green and gray."

The campers found their name on a large list plastered on a wooden post and then line up with the counselor associated with the first letter of their last names. Since Allora's last name was Smith, she searched the group, and found the counselor of Cabin S.

The girls' cabins were located on the east side of the lake, while the boys' were situated on the south. After lights out at ten o'clock sharp, campers were forbidden from leaving their cabins—a rule that was consistently broken every year.

Allora found a suitable bunk and changed into her bathing suit and hiked down the hill to the edge of the lake. The sun was almost at its peak position in the sky. Many of the other girls had the same idea, so the dock and beach were already crowded. Surprisingly, Katie and Allora found a vacant spot on the dock and settled in after applying their sunscreen thoroughly. The peaceful stillness, along with the soothing warmth of the sun, caused both girls to nod off.

They were lying on their stomachs when they awoke to the sound of the dock bending and crackling from the weight of running bodies. They pulled their heads up just in time to feel cold water splashing up from the dock's edge. The frigid wall of water caused both girls to gasp, and they looked around for the perpetrators who had dared to interrupt their cat nap. Of course, the two heads that popped out of the water belonged to Dax and Tanner.

"You're dead!" Allora yelled.

Katie wasn't happy about being splashed either. "Don't you two have anything better to do?" she said.

"Better than messing with you girls?" The boys exchanged sinister smiles. "Nah!"

They soaked the girls from head to toe, sparking a war. The girls retaliated by leaping forward, trying to jump on top of the boys, but Dax and Tanner somehow managed to swim out of the way. They splashed around for a few minutes, until they heard someone loudly clearing her throat on the dock.

"Having fun?" Jenny said, tapping her foot on the wet wood as she stood there in front of Nancy and Tanya.

All three of them were dressed in their best bikinis, obviously with no intention of getting into the icy water.

Katie and Allora gave one another knowing stares, communicating their devious plan with their eyes. Just as the boys had done to them earlier, they began splashing the pretentious girls on the dock.

Jenny and the rest of her entourage screamed and ran away, soaked from the attack.

Dax, Katie, and Allora laughed uncontrollably and continued frolicking in the water and swimming until their bodies were wrinkled and numb from the cold. At that point, Allora swam over to the beach and got out, while Katie grabbed their wet towels from the dock.

At the other end of the beach, they hopped onto a boat for water skiing lessons. After two hours on the boat, the girls headed off to the archery range, intent on getting some practice in during summer camp. The entire week was most of the same.

On the last night, Allora fell into a deep sleep, tossing in her bunk as her dreams pulled her to an unfamiliar field of soft, green grass. The wind blew down in waves, creating beautiful flowing patterns in the rolling hills. The sun gleamed overhead, the sky was clear, and mountains filled the distant landscape. It was a very peaceful place, but for some reason, it felt peculiar. The ground suddenly began to shake violently. All around Allora, the ground cracked. Chunks of rock fell into a flowing river of lava. The liquid fire burned so hot that she could feel the burning steam escaping from the crevices. The mountain ranges crumbled like dried-out clay, till all that was left was a small slab of rock beneath her feet surrounded by darkness.

She turned and saw an old man. His skin appeared wrinkly, the white hair on his head was thin, and he was hunched over on his staff. Rather than looking at her, he just stared at the red hot, molten liquid below. The most amazing thing was that he was floating in the air, hovering a few feet away. When he finally looked up at Allora, she could see that his eyes were unusually blue, even bluer than the sky had been, with a commanding stare that penetrated to Allora's core.

She could feel a considerable amount of energy emanating from the strange, supernatural man floating in front of her, the same type of energy she had experienced during soccer tryouts. His demeanor became somber as he floated closer. "They are coming. Allora. You are the key, and they know it. You must find that which they seek. They are coming!"

The words struck like a sword, piercing her thoughts and bursting into her imagination with ominous images of death, destruction, and pain. There was no time to analyze what the man had said or the horrifying feelings those words had created, because the ground shook, and then plummeted into the river of fire.

Allora awoke to someone restraining her arms. She tried to struggle, but the figures in the dark were too many. A cold sweat had permeated her skin, and her heart beat erratically against her chest. She tried to scream, but they muzzled her with duct tape. All she could see was the light from a flashlight, shining mercilessly into her eyes.

"Make it tight, girls," a sickeningly familiar voice ordered while Allora's hands, feet and knees were bound with ropes. "I don't want the freak to do her voodoo fire magic."

The voice was one she'd heard many times before, a voice that caused most girls to run and hide. As she was carried out of the cabin, Allora was nauseated by the blank, weak, pained faces of the girls of Cabin S. Much to her dismay, they stood idly by, doing nothing to rescue her. *"What's wrong with you?"* she tried to scream through the duct tape. *"How can you just stand there and do nothing?"*

The camp was quiet except for the sound of bullfrogs trumpeting in the shallows of the lake. She looked up at her captors: Nancy Williams, Tanya Brown, Madeline Jones, Emily Bowen, and, of course, Jenny Thompson, all seniors on the soccer team.

When they stopped, Allora was shoved up against a cold steel pole. The girls tied ropes around the pole to secure her there.

The evil voice took shape before her, wearing a smug look of victory, smiling greedily and relishing in the moment. Jenny stepped in close to her victim, so close that Allora could smell her cherry-scented breath as it wafted over her glossed lips. "I told you that you'd pay." She ripped off the duct tape.

"Untie me, and I'll give you another black eye," Allora replied.

Jenny leaned in close so that the other girls couldn't hear. "Just tell me what really happened that day at tryouts and I'll let you go."

"Bite me," Allora whispered.

"What should we do with her?" Nancy asked.

"We'll just leave her here like this for everybody to find in the morning." Jenny moved closer to her prey. "Next time, I won't go so easy on you."

"I'm gonna kill—" Allora tried to yell, but she couldn't quite finish her threat before Jenny forcefully pressed the duct tape back over her mouth.

"Uh-uh-uh. We wouldn't wanna wake up the rest of the camp, would we?" Jenny said, flicking Allora's forehead. "And if you even try to tell anyone about this, we'll be forced to come after your little friend Katie too. Come on, girls. Let's give Allora some time to herself."

Allora writhed in the restraints as she watched the girls laugh and make their way back up the hill to their cabins. Once they were gone, Allora surveyed the area. She was tied to the flagpole, right in front of the mess hall. Again, she tried to free herself from the rope, but the girls had been surprisingly efficient with their knots, even with their ridiculously long acrylic nails.

After a few minutes of being alone, and allowing for the adrenaline to subside, she noticed how naked she was wearing only underwear. In spite of the Indian summer, the wind blew softly down from the mountain, sending chills up Allora's spine and causing goosebumps to form on her bare skin.

Her mind raced back to the dream she'd had prior to her rude awakening. It had been an incredible nightmare. *What did that old man mean?* His words echoed in her head: *"They are coming."*

About an hour went by before Allora heard something move in the woods. Her heart began to beat faster, and she recalled that her mother had adamantly warned her about not leaving her cabin at night. Allora continued staring at the woods, jerking her head from side to side, trying to search for the source of the sound that grew louder with every passing moment.

Whatever it was, it had made its way to the bushes next to the mess hall, and Allora began to panic. When she heard the same noise coming from right behind her, she pulled violently at the restraints as hard as she could, but they wouldn't budge. She spun her head around, trying to see behind, but the metal supports on the flagpole inhibited her movement. The rope burned her wrists, creating lines of red skin. Suddenly, the sound changed to swishing water, as though someone was moving in the lake.

A cold fear enveloped her body as wet footsteps closed in. The muffled sound of her struggle reverberated in her ears as she thrashed against the steel flagpole. Drops of water splashed against the hard dirt. Allora's conscious mind couldn't grasp the idea of death and soon released her from reality. Her eyelids dropped, and the floor gave way as she fainted to the cool, damp ground.

A deep, soothing voice called out her name. "Allora."

A soft, wet hand pulled at the ropes on her back, till she suddenly fell forward, causing an impact that roused her awake. Between fuzzy blinks, she saw a humanoid figure, clear blue and tall, disappear into the moonlit lake. An apparition of sorts, the creature dropped into the depths, as if disappearing in a dream. Allora lay there for a confused moment, unable to comprehend the strange occurrence. *Was that a hallucination?* Finally, she got up from the ground, dusted the dirt from her body, and slowly tiptoed back up the hill, periodically glancing over her shoulder at the dark, still lake.

During the walk back, she talked to herself quietly, wondering if what she had seen was real. She was almost to Cabin S when a bunch of boys popped out from around the corner of the cabin. One of the boys smacked into her, and she looked up to see Tanner. At that moment, she realized she was only in her underwear, and she hurriedly tried to cover herself with her hands, to little avail.

All of the boys were surprised to see Allora and even more surprised—somewhat pleasantly—that she was half-naked.

"What are you doing?" Allora and Tanner asked at the same time.

"Why are you out so late?" Allora jumped in.

"I was about to ask you the same question," Tanner said, trying to look at Allora's eyes while he talked to her. "A moonlight skinny-dip?" he said, pinching her bare shoulder affectionately.

The boys around him weren't trying so hard to avoid looking at her, though, and Allora noticed.

"Hey! Up here," Allora whispered harshly, pointing to her face, even though she was really too tired and upset to care whether or not they saw her in her underwear. She had way too much on her mind to even explain any of it. She deduced that the boys were out to play a prank on the girls. "I'll kill each and every one of you if you step foot near my cabin," she threatened, then stormed off.

Tanner couldn't help but watch her walk away, and none of the other boys could either.

Dax smacked the back of his head. "Hey, snap out of it. We're on a mission, Romeo, remember?"

Tanner turned around and tried to focus on the task at hand. "Uh, okay. Right. Well, you guys know what to do. Let's get it done as fast as we can, then make a break for our cabins. If you get caught, you're on your own. Nobody throws anybody under a bus. Ready?"

"Yeah!" chanted all the boys.

"Break!"

They dispersed quietly through the camp and seamlessly carried out the tasks they'd meticulously planned the night before.

"Mission accomplished," Dax said, giving Tanner a high-five when they returned to their cabins.

* * *

The girls woke up bright and early in the morning, as usual, and were busy talking and making their usual trek down the hill toward the cafeteria. All of them filed behind the senior girls, who filed behind the soccer team. As they walked down the small hill from the girls' cabins, there were a few points where the steps dropped and they had to jump down.

Allora hung back for a little while, still reeling from the trauma of the night before, and also still unsure of what the boys had done. She found Katie and told her to wait as well. Just as they did every day, the soccer girls jumped down the exaggerated step. This time, though, the ground gave way, and they were submerged in mud.

The boys had dug a large hole in the ground and had set up a garden hose to feed water into it from the bottom, creating a giant mud bath. Screams echoed through the camp as filthy faces popped up from the pit. This continued until the girls at the back of the line heard the screams and stopped.

The boys jumped out from behind the bush where they'd been waiting and watching and literally rolled on the ground laughing, in absolute hysterics.

Jenny looked over to where the laughter was coming from, her whole face covered in mud. "Tanner!" she screamed. "You are so dead!"

Dax leaned toward Tanner and whispered, "Maybe this is what the girls of Sonora look like?"

They both burst out laughing.

Allora and Katie ran around the other direction, toward the lake, to see what was going on. They stopped after turning the corner and put their hands to their mouths with bug eyes. Both of them chuckled slowly, then burst into laughter. Everyone who wasn't drowning in mud was cackling at those who were.

"This isn't funny!" Jenny yelled, trying to get out of the mud pit, only to slip and fall back in.

The counselors overheard the commotion and ran over from the mess hall. Holding back laughter of their own, in an effort to be adult about the whole thing, they pulled the girls from the mud-filled hole. The head counselor wasn't happy with what was going on, but everyone could tell that even he was trying to hold back a smile.

Allora spent the trip back with Katie, Tanner, and Dax, sharing stories and reflecting on how much fun they'd had. The one story Allora didn't tell was about the incident at the lake and the strange creature that untied her from the flagpole. There were far too many eavesdroppers on the bus, and she thought it was best to save that story for when they were alone.

The bus drove on as the excited teenagers quieted down, exhausted from the week, and several dozed off. Before they knew it, they were back in Sandy, heading home where they'd sleep safely in their own warm beds again.

UPPERCLASSMEN

At the edge of the driveway, Bell's bright yellow bus disappeared over the distant hump in the road, heading off to the first day of school. Left waiting, Allora reflected on her summer and the harsh reality of her life. She felt confused, scared, and unable to comprehend how to deal with everything. Strange, almost alien feelings were waking, churning and stirring up a cocktail of questions for which she had no answers.

As Allora stood alone in a confused state of emotional turmoil, a distant blurry figure appeared, maneuvering through the trees like a surefooted predator on the hunt. She felt an unfamiliar, cold breeze fill the air. The hair on the back of her neck rose. Allora clenched her bag, unsure whether she should stay still or run for her life. After looking around frantically for something to defend herself, she picked up a stick from the side of the road as another cold chill blew through. For reasons she couldn't explain, the wind didn't feel like a mountain breeze.

Twigs and branches snapped under the weight of the oncoming figure.

"Whoever's there, this isn't funny!" she said, gripping the stick tighter.

Something blurry streaked between the tree trunks, accompanied by the sound of more breaking twigs, so close that Allora could almost see the shape of a human.

She dropped her book bag, put her right foot back, and took a batting stance with the stick clenched tightly in her hands like she was ready to knock it out of the park. "Show yourself!" she demanded.

A car flew over the bump in the road, pulled over, and stopped. "Practicing for softball season already?" Katie joked, not noticing Allora's fearful stare.

Allora threw the stick into the ditch, grabbed her bag, and leapt into Katie's Jeep Cherokee.

"Whoa! I don't think I've ever seen you *this* excited to go to school before."

"Just go!" Allora said.

Katie slammed the accelerator, causing the Jeep tires to spin out. White smoke and debris blew out from the tires as the car jerked forward and sped down the road. A good distance from Allora's house, Katie slowed the speeding car and turned to ask her friend, "What in the heck's going on?"

Allora spun around, with her fingers gripping into the leather headrest, and stared intently at the forest. No matter how hard she stared, nothing materialized. She spun back around and forcefully put her seatbelt on. "There was…I heard…something in the woods," Allora answered between heaving breaths.

"What?"

Allora controlled her breathing, trying to negate a panic attack. "Watch out!"

Since Katie was paying more attention to her friend than the curving road in front of her, she was forced to slam on the brakes to avoid hitting a tree. Smoke from burnt rubber billowed on both the sides of the car, and the pungent aroma of worn brakes filled the interior. The girls breathed heavily, trying to regain their composure.

"Whoa," said Katie. "Sorry."

"Yeah," Allora answered, painfully aware that they could have met their demise right there on that road.

They both took a minute to catch their breathe, then Katie said, "Now… what just happened?"

"I saw… no, I *felt*, uh… something." Allora couldn't really articulate it, because even she wasn't sure if any of what she had experienced was actually real.

Katie lifted her eyebrows and cocked her head.

"I don't know, all right?" Allora exclaimed in frustration.

Katie put the car in reverse, gassed it out of the gravel ditch, and backed onto the road. "Look, Allora, with everything that you've been through lately, it's normal and perfectly okay to be a little paranoid," she said as she turned onto Main Street.

"Paranoid? It's not that," Allora snapped. "I-I can't explain it. Whatever was in the woods wasn't... natural."

Katie just stared straight forward, and then glanced over a few times smiling.

"What?" Allora snapped again, unsure why her friend was grinning from ear to ear all the sudden. "You don't believe me, do you?"

"No, it's not that. This has nothing to do with what you saw in the woods."

Allora paused, waiting for some sort of explanation. "Well? Spit it out!"

"Okay, fine. I was gonna wait, but I can't." Katie bit her lip and continued, "Tanner broke up with Jenny yesterday."

"What?" Allora exclaimed, then pursed her lips together, trying not to show any emotion. "Why? What'd she do?"

Katie could see the giddy struggle playing out in her friend's mind. "Look, don't be mad at me, but... well, I kinda told Dax what Jenny and the other girls did to you at camp," she admitted. "And well, Dax told Tanner, so—"

"So much for keeping it a secret."

"I know, I know, but you shoulda told him yourself. He needed to know what that heinous, evil troll did to you," Katie said. "Tanner had a right to know what he was dating."

Allora sat back in the seat, deciding there was no use fighting with Katie about it. Secretly, Allora had hoped Tanner would find out, as long as she didn't have to be the one to tell him. "You're right," Allora admitted, "but why now? It's not like she hasn't done worse things to other people."

Katie thought for a minute. "I would say that tying you to a flagpole in the middle of the night in the mountains is pretty high up there. You could have been eaten by cougars or bears or something even worse."

"I guess."

"Then again, it might have had more to do with the fact that Tanner totally has a major crush on you."

"He does not!" Allora said softly, turning several shades of red.

"Right." Katie shook her head. "And you obviously have a crush on him."

"I do not!" Allora snapped.

Katie laughed. "Why do you think Jenny has it in for you?"

Then, all of a sudden, as if something Katie had said had sparked her memory, Allora remembered what had happened to her that night. "Oh my god! I totally forgot to tell you," she said, then told Katie about the odd creature who'd released her from the flagpole. It was difficult to explain what had happened since she hadn't seen who had untied the ropes, but Allora filled her in on as many details as she could just as Katie pulled her Jeep into a parking spot.

As soon as they walked up to the grey double-doors of the front entry way, Allora could feel the eyeballs staring at them. Rumors of her incident at soccer tryouts had obviously spread amongst the student body. The quiet snickering kept up for the short walk to the class schedule table in the main lobby area. Allora and Katie ignored everyone, and compared schedules.

"How did I get into Swan's AP History class?" Katie asked. "I suck at history!"

"Good question," Allora said.

She had a lot of questions, and she hoped Mr. Swan could answer a few. When they got to the door of Room 202, though, they found a lady with curly, short hair and glasses surveying the students as they lumbered into the room. Allora double-checked the room number, and after confirming that she was in the right place, she took a seat in front of two familiar faces. "What are you doing in here?" Allora whispered to Tanner and Dax, who slouched in their seats with their legs extended out.

Tanner didn't know how to answer the question because he hadn't even signed up for the class. He only shrugged his shoulders as a response.

The curly-haired lady walked to the front of the class. "Good morning, students. I realize some of you may be confused, since you were expecting Mr. Swan. My name is Ms. Benfield, and I will be your substitute while he is away,"

Allora wasn't satisfied with the vague explanation. "Away? Where is he?" she blurted out without being called upon.

"Miss, you will raise your hand in my classroom," Ms. Benfield ordered, pointing aggressively with a pen.

Allora rolled her eyes and put her hand up.

"Yes, Ms. Smith?"

"First of all, it's 'Allora,' and second, I don't think I should have to repeat my question since you obviously heard me the first time," Allora snapped back.

"Young lady, I don't know what you're used to around here, but I will not tolerate rude behavior," Ms. Benfield replied. "You will repeat your question, and you will show me some respect and use manners."

The abrasive retort piqued everyone's interest. Allora hated when authority figures tried to control her.

She took a deep breath and asked with a scowl, "*Please* tell me, where the hell is our *real* teacher, Mr. Swan?" Allora said, leaning back and smiling.

The whole class erupted in laughter.

Ms. Benfield, on the other hand, found nothing funny about it. She marched down the aisle to Allora's seat, grabbed her by the ear, and dragged her to the door.

"Hey, you evil witch!" Katie said, standing up in protest. "Let go of her right now!"

Ms. Benfield maintained her grip on Allora's ear and motioned to Katie. "If you have anything to say about it, you can join your friend in the principal's office," she threatened.

Allora could have easily gotten out of the teacher's grip, but it would have meant possible expulsion or even criminal charges, so she resisted. Ms. Benfield eventually let go and pushed them both Katie and Allora into the hallway, then pointed to the front office.

"I will not be disrespected like that."

With that, she stomped back into the classroom and slammed the door. Allora made an inappropriate gesture with her middle finger in the small window slit, and the students burst out in laughter again, some of them giving her thumbs-up.

Ms. Benfield spun around, but Allora had vacated the window before being caught. The two girls walked in the opposite direction from the principal's office and roamed the halls for the rest of first period, gossiping about the horrible substitute. They had made it around the back of the school to the end of the sophomore hall when they saw three sophomore girls standing around a petrified freshman with glasses, tightly holding her books. As Allora and Katie moved closer, they saw that the young girl against the wall was Bell.

Allora watched as the sophomore girls knocked her sister's books out of her hands. Fueled by anger, Allora ran up and knocked over the first girl. "What do you think you're doing?" she said glaring at the bullies with her fists clenched. "The only person who gets to push my sister around is me."

The tallest of the girls, Suzy Moore, stepped forward. She was on the girls' basketball team and a well-known bully. "Maybe I should ask you the same thing," she said, pushing Allora. "Butt out."

"Hey," Katie said. She stepped between them and placed her hand on Suzy's shoulder. "Trust me, you don't wanna start something with her—not today."

Suzy grabbed Katie's hand and squeezed it, then pushed her into the lockers like she was made of toothpicks.

Allora stepped forward, dodged Suzy's punch, and placed a brutal fist into the right side of the tall girl's lower abdomen. Then she spun around with one leg extended and kicked the girl in the knees, sending her plummeting to the ground. Suzy wiggled on the floor in pain as the other girls tried to sideswipe Allora. Katie deflected the attack and moved to exact her own vengeance.

Before they could do any serious damage, Allora and Katie froze, their bodies tight, unable to move a muscle. The sophomore girls knew they were outmatched and took the opportunity to quickly retreat. Allora's eyes darted back and forth, trying to find the reason for her immobility. Aunt May had demonstrated a similar trick. No matter how hard she tried to move, her muscles would not respond. All of a sudden, Katie and Allora fell to the ground. When they were finally able to move their limbs again, they looked at each other in confusion, trying to figure out what had happened.

When they saw two black stilettos step onto the carpet in front of them, they both turned their eyes upward to see a figure standing there, rigid and stern, with hands on her hips.

"Uh… hi, Principal Winters," they said in unison, their monotone voices revealing their guilt.

"Bell, go on to your class," Mrs. Winters said to the frightened freshman who was still pressed against the lockers.

Bell looked at her sister and moved her lips to silently apologize, then scurried down the hall.

Allora picked herself up, followed by Katie. The two girls were embarrassed, not because they'd been beating sophomores up, but because they'd gotten caught.

Mrs. Winters directed them to go immediately to the front office. Once they got there, they sat in seats facing Mrs. Winters's desk and waited for the angry principal to join them.

Mrs. Winters sat down in her chair, placed her arms on the desk, and clasped her hands. Wearing a look of disappointment, she said, "You two have been busy today. The first day of school, and you've already managed to get kicked out of class and beat up some underclassmen, and it's not even second period yet!" She sat back in her chair and took a deep breath. "Do you have anything to say for yourselves?"

The two girls remained silent.

"What did I tell you about staying under the radar?"

"But they were picking on my sister," Allora argued. "I had to do something."

"Yes, but you could have used diplomacy. I get that May is training you in combat, but the word is far more powerful than the fist."

"Didn't really see it that way Principal Winters," Katie added.

"Considering your lineage, I wouldn't expect so," Principal Winters responded, prompting Katie to cross her arms and lean back in the chair. "Look, I get that you two are under additional stress, but the situation in town has gotten a little more serious."

Principal Winters continued to lecture them on the importance of discretion. Silently, the girls listened to every word their principal said, but they didn't quite understand all of it. Nevertheless, they nodded their heads in agreement to satisfy Mrs. Winters, then quickly made a break for the door.

Just as they were about to run off, Mrs. Winters halted their escape. "By the way, as punishment, you both can plan on volunteering to set up for the soccer games all season long. I'm sure Mrs. Mondrach can use your help."

They nodded their heads, accepting their punishment, and hurried to their second-period class.

After fourth period, Tanner, Dax, Katie, and Allora met in the middle of the hall.

Allora turned to Tanner. "I heard you broke up with Jenny," she said, looking to make sure the evil soccer captain wasn't around.

"Yeah, well, I heard what she did to you that night at camp," Tanner said, causing Allora to blush a little. "Why didn't you tell me?"

"It wasn't that big of a deal. I'm fine," Allora responded. Even though she was trying to play it cool, part of her took some delight in the fact that she was the reason Tanner had come to his senses and gotten rid of Jenny. "It was just a stupid prank."

A serious look came over Tanner's face, and he softly took hold of Allora's shoulder. "You could have been seriously hurt. What Jenny did was inexcusable."

Allora gazed up into his eyes, and in that moment, she felt completely at ease. Her heart felt like it had fallen into the back of her body. Her limbs were numb as she stood there, paralyzed.

Tanner was inches away from Allora's lips when both of them caught a glimpse of someone out of the corners of their eyes. Tanner let go of Allora and pivoted toward the front double-doors, and Dax couldn't help but follow his line of sight.

A long-haired, beautiful brunette with sparkling blue eyes entered the school, someone they'd never seen before. The wind pushed through the heavy metal doors behind her, tousling her hair. She was dressed scantily in a short denim skirt and a white tank-top. Her long legs were accentuated by her black heels. She walked by, glaring at Katie and Allora, as if trying to project her dominance. Then, she winked at the boys, whose mouths seemed to have fallen to the floor. Dax and Tanner dumbly smiled back and stared at her as she strutted to the front office.

Seeing the boys' hormonal reactions led Allora to slap Tanner on the back of the head, while Katie hit Dax. The girls left, rolling their eyes as they walked away, and the boys remained perplexed.

"Hey! What was that for?" Tanner asked as Allora exited the school.

"Yeah," Dax added, rubbing the back of his head.

Allora spun around. "For being an idiot," she said.

"I just felt like smacking you!" Katie added as the doors closed.

Ignoring his sister, Dax walked up next to Tanner. "I got dibs, man."

"What? You can't call dibs when you haven't even met the girl," Tanner replied.

"Guy code says if you see a girl and claim her, she's yours," Dax rebutted, grinning emphatically.

"Maybe in the Neanderthal days," Tanner said, shaking his head. "What do you plan to do, club her and drag her back to your cave by her hair?" He grinned when Dax couldn't think of a suitable comeback.

Outside the school, Katie said, "She must be new," as she climbed into the driver side of her car.

"Did you see the way she was dressed?" Allora said.

"I wonder if she's good at soccer."

"Sure. I bet she's got some great ball-handling skills."

They looked at each other and laughed.

"I guess we shouldn't judge her though. I'm sure she's a nice girl," Allora said, not really believing it herself.

"Right," Katie said. "Nice girls in black heels? Gimme a break."

After Katie dropped her off, Allora went inside and waved goodbye. She grabbed a cold soda out of the fridge, flopped down on the couch, and spent the rest of the night alone, reading a book in her room, happy to have some time to herself in a safe, quiet place.

Six

Girl

The following day, Katie and Allora arrived at school, dreading the eventual confrontation with Ms. Benfield. The thought of having to apologize was revolting.

Much to her relief, though, Allora walked into her history class and saw a different substitute teacher putting her name on the chalkboard. "I wonder where Benfield went?" she whispered to Katie as sat down.

Tanner leaned forward from his seat behind the two girls. "Principal Winters fired her."

"Really?" Allora asked, enthusiastically spinning around in her chair. "But why? I mean, I liked her so much. We were just getting to know each other," Allora said sarcastically, drawing a smile out of Tanner.

"Well, I'm pretty sure that you can't physically abuse your students," Katie said.

"Good morning, students," The pretty brunette woman said. "My name is Ms. Norman, and I will be your substitute teacher until Mr. Swan returns. I don't know when that will be, but let's hope we can get through as much material as possible before he gets back."

Someone opened the classroom door, and a familiar-looking girl poked her head in and then swung the door open. "Uh… hi. I think this is my class," said the new girl, looking just as beautiful and confident as she had the previous day.

"You're a little late, darling," Ms. Norman said.

"I know. I'm so sorry. I'm new here."

"Well, what's your name?" Ms. Norman asked.

"Kim."

"Well, Kim, I'm Ms. Norman. Your schedule may say something about Mr. Swan, but he's going to be out for a while. Please have a seat so we can get started," the teacher said, directing her to an open desk near the front.

Kim strutted over to Allora's row on the other side of the classroom, as if she was some kind of princess about to address her court. She was an obviously audacious individual, and Allora felt strange as she watched the new girl take her seat.

At the beginning of history class, they watched a documentary movie about the Roman Empire. Then Ms. Norman conducted a lecture on Gaius Julius Caesar and his military victories in Gaul.

"In the Battle of Alesia, the Romans were outnumbered five to one and still came out on the winning end of the confrontation by erecting fortifications and traps to slow down the attacking Gallic army. Soon after the victories in Gaul, Caesar was ordered by the senate to disband the army and return to Rome. Does anyone know who was leading the Roman senate at that time?" Ms. Norman asked the class.

Allora was about to answer the question when Kim interrupted her without even raising her hand. "That would be Pompey, Ms. Norman."

Allora glared at Kim, unhappy with being upstaged. History was *her* subject, and she'd always been the top gun when it came to history trivia.

"Good job, Kim," Ms. Norman said, then continued with the story. "Caesar chose to take one of his legions and march with them to Rome. This ignited a civil war, since no Roman army was supposed to be there. Does anyone know what happened to the Roman senators who defied Caesar?"

Again, Allora was about to give the answer, but Kim blurted out, "Most of them were pardoned, ma'am, but a few of the traitors were killed."

"And what happened to Caesar?" Ms. Norman asked.

Kim smiled. "He became a great Roman dictator."

Allora jumped in, "Actually, he was a tyrant who wouldn't give up his power over the Roman Empire, which was probably why he was assassinated."

Kim glared at Allora. "An obvious tragedy."

"A tragedy? What about the thousands of people who were oppressed, killed, and raped by the Roman Empire? The Romans burned, pillaged, and murdered their way across Europe."

"A necessary evil, if you think about the barbaric weaklings the Roman Empire destroyed," said Kim. "In my opinion, they did this world a great service, a sort of taking out of the trash, if you will."

"A service? What gives you the right to call people trash and—"

Kim was, quite literally, saved by the bell when Allora's tirade was interrupted by the end-of-class buzzer.

"All right, class," Ms. Norman said, cutting off the argument, "great discussion today. I'll expect those papers on the history of Caesar on my desk on Monday."

Allora marched across the room, eager to confront the new girl, who was busy putting her notebook away. "How can you possibly think it's a good thing for one man to have absolute power over so many?"

Kim continued putting her things away and didn't even give Allora the courtesy of eye contact. "Because it's an efficient system when one man, one mind, is making all the decisions. Look at what he was able to accomplish in such a short amount of time. The Roman Empire controlled half the world," Kim said, putting a glittery red pencil in the zipper pocket on the front of her designer bag.

"Yeah, but in the process, they killed thousands, if not millions, of people," Allora argued.

Kim moved closer to Allora and shrugged. "For the greater good," she said.

Katie walked up as soon as Kim exited the classroom. "What's with her?"

"I'm not sure. The one thing I do know is that I don't like the new girl very much."

* * *

On Thursday, the soccer team began their last full practice before game day. Tanner and Dax stretched on the field, while loudmouth Jenny led her underlings in wind sprints near the track. As Allora descended the stairs toward the equipment room, she noticed Jenny's subtle teary eyes. Upon seeing Allora, Jenny wiped her face with a towel and ran back onto the field.

In the equipment room, Allora and Katie received an extensive tour from Mrs. Mondrach, the parent volunteer for the Pioneer Club. Most of the funding for equipment, uniforms, and setup for the games came from the club's fundraising efforts. "So, uh... well, this is where you can make signs. You should make a big one that the players can burst through when they run onto the field for the season opener," she instructed.

"I thought the cheerleaders would do that," Katie said. "Isn't it sort of... their job?"

"Not this time," Mrs. Mondrach replied. "They've got a competition in California that they have to prepare for."

As Mrs. Mondrach explained where to place the long tables, Kim walked out of the girls' locker room, dressed in very short tight shorts, and a loose tank-top with shin guards.

"Mrs. Mondrach," Allora said, yanking Katie by the arm in the direction of the field, "we're gonna go, uh... get some water from the fountain."

"That's fine, girls, but make it quick," Mrs. Mondrach replied. "I still need to show you where the chairs go."

Allora and Katie hurried down to the field just in time to hear Coach Laurent introducing the new girl to the rest of the soccer team. "Everyone, this is Kim, a transfer student from Florida. She's been a varsity soccer since her freshman year, so I am sure she'll be an asset to our squad."

"An *asset*, huh?" Allora said, rolling her eyes. "Well, she's half-right."

"I hope ya'll will welcome her with open arms," Coach Laurent announced.

Jenny pushed her way through the crowd, which parted like the Red Sea to make way for their fearless leader. "But, Coach, she wasn't even here for tryouts," Jenny said. "She shouldn't just automatically be given a spot. That wouldn't be fair to all the other girls who tried out."

"Fair?" Katie whispered, nudging Allora. "Since when does she care about fair?"

"Since somebody hotter and more talented came along to upstage her," Allora said.

"It also wouldn't be fair for us to rob her of her senior season," Coach Laurent said. "Besides, Jenny, when you see how talented she is, I think you will change your mind."

"Not likely," Jenny muttered, causing the soccer squad to giggle.

Hearing this, Kim lined up next to the girls, facing the field, and grabbed a soccer ball from the bag. From forty feet out, she struck the ball, sailing it high over the soccer players, and right into the corner of the soccer net.

The other soccer girls stood on the sidelines with their mouths wide open, and a couple of them even dropped their water bottles in reaction to the Olympic-grade performance of their newest senior member.

Tanya walked up next to Jenny. "Wow. She may even be better than you."

Jenny turned, put her leg behind Tanya, and pushed the girl's shoulder, causing her to fall over. "Nobody is better than me," Jenny said.

Allora was as amazed by Kim's talent as everyone else, but her amazement changed to jealousy when she saw Tanner strutting over to the new girl.

"That was unreal!" Tanner said.

"Thanks, hotshot. You're not so bad yourself." As she said this, she gently stroked Tanner's chest flirtatiously. "Good luck tomorrow."

Jenny watched the sensual exchange and erupted like a volcano. Since Coach Laurent was oblivious, too caught up in her chart of soccer drills, the furious captain charged past her and confronted the new girl.

"What do you think you're doing?" Jenny asked, pointing aggressively.

Tanner jumped between the two girls.

"Whatever I want blondie," Kim responded. She put a hand up and turn to walk away.

Jenny reached across Tanner's chest, grabbed Kim's hair, and yanked hard. The new girl didn't move much. She turned around and glared. They stared each other down as a horde of students gathered around the oncoming fight.

"What the hell is going on here?" Coach Laurent said, stomping toward the altercation. "You two, my office… now!"

"Dude, you really know how to incite a riot, don't ya?" Dax teased. "That was the best chick fight I've ever seen! Too bad I didn't have my camera, 'cause that shoulda been on the internet."

"Shut up,"Tanner replied.

"Seriously, dude, you have a gift."

"I hate you."

"I'm just sayin', you might wanna think about calling one of those talk shows—you know, the real trashy ones where the guy has, like, five girlfriends who don't know about each other."

As Dax continued to hassle his friend, Allora remembered an important message she was supposed to pass on to the other three. She grabbed her friends and pulled them to a spot on the green turf where no one could hear. "I forgot to tell you guys something," she said. "Aunt May wants us to head up to the outer realm after were done here."

"What for?"Tanner asked.

"I'm not really sure. She left a note on my bed saying she wants to speak with us."Allora paused for a second. "We should probably meet with her. It might be important."

After practice, they hiked through the forest to the portal and jumped through. The orchard had changed into the interior of a castle. The vaulted ceilings were over twenty feet high with beautifully carved wooden archways spaced throughout long corridors filled with weaponry of every sort. Swords, spears, bows, arrows, and more lined the stone walls. At the end of the hall Aunt May was sitting cross-legged in front of a large fireplace that housed a crackling fire. As they walked down the corridor, flames began to dance out from the fireplace. Each one licked along the stone floor, crawled up one of the pillars, and lit a candle, bringing light to the entire room.

"I get the feeling we're not in Kansas anymore, Toto," Dax joked.

"Shut up,"Tanner said, rolling his eyes, well over his jokes by now.

When the teens were only a few feet from Aunt May, she got up and gazed at them, her eyes glistening orange from the firelight. "Thank you for coming." She then moved away from the fire, walked between the others, and headed out into the corridor.

"Where are we?"Tanner asked.

Aunt May turned around to face them. "This is an outer realm copy of our weapons facility in the guardian base of Shangri-La. The reason I asked to see you all today is because I believe you are ready to be issued weapons. You will pick them from here, and I will get the physical copy from armory."

They made their way to the middle of the grand hall, which split off in four directions. In every corridor, weapons were stacked against the walls, towers of arsenal much higher than their heads.

"Please spend some time with these and find the weapon that fits you best. I'm sure you already have some idea of the type of weapon that best suits you, so go on and take a look."

With that, they all split up. Tanner found the section with the long swords. He walked down the hall and ran his hand along the cold steel blades of the swords hanging on the racks. He went past the Roman spatha, the European rapier, and the Scottish claymore. After a while, he stopped in front of a two-handed German long sword, a zweihander. The double-edged straight blade was forged from steel, and while such a sword would normally be sixty inches long and weigh eight pounds, the one Tanner found was fifty inches long and weighed about five pounds, which made it far easier to use.

Katie wasn't that much farther down the hall, and she'd discovered a Japanese katana. "Aunt May, can we pick out two weapons?" Katie asked.

"Yes, girl," Aunt May said.

Katie pulled two swords from their sheaths. The single-edged, beautifully crafted, moderately curved swords glistened when she swung them in the air. She made fast, swooshing motions and then placed them back in their sheaths.

Dax was in a completely different hallway, looking at staffs. He made a pass through the entire row of them before he chose the one he liked best. When he found the perfect weapon, he picked it up and twirled it around in his hands. The ends of the staff were rounded, and the wood was smooth and surprisingly light. "Cool," he muttered.

"That particular staff is made of a rare type of dogwood," Aunt May said, catching Dax by surprise. Then, she headed toward the ranged weapons, where Allora saw a composite bow that hung out of reach.

Suddenly, the bow lifted itself from the wall and fell into Allora's arms. She looked to her left, then to her right and found that Aunt May was holding up her staff. "Hey! How did you do that?" Allora asked.

Aunt May smiled. "I will teach you when you get older." She waved her staff, and a quiver of arrows appeared from down the hall, flying toward them. "These are especially efficient and strong, and they will fly true. They are made from hickory, and the feathers are that of a Bennu bird. It is said to possess the soul of the ancient Egyptian sun god, Ra. I think they'll be perfect for you."

"Thanks," Allora said and collected the arrows when they fell at her feet.

The teens met back in the middle of the grand hall and excitedly showed one another their weapons. They were all very proud of their choices.

Aunt May let them reflect over their new gifts before she said, "Now that you have your weapons, I must tell you about their power. Each are old and once charmed by an ancient mage. These weapons are imbued with hadrons that will flow through you and back into your weapon. They can be very powerful, so you must use them wisely." Aunt May walked over to a wide circle in the middle of the hall. "I will be gone for a little while, but you must continue your training without me. I will assess your progress when I return." Then, just like that, she disappeared through the portal.

Seven

GAME

The first game of the season was always crazy. The entire town was quite fanatical when it came to Pioneer soccer, and everyone dressed from head to toe in the school colors, so the bleachers looked like a sea of red and white. The soccer players always had their jerseys on, and the cheerleaders wore their uniforms to school. The previous year, Sandy High School had made it to the semifinals of the state championships, only to be beaten in the last quarter by Lake Oswego.

Allora found Tanner in the parking lot leaning against his car and staring into the sky. "Hey, got a big game tonight."

"Yeah, I guess," he said, seemingly aloof.

"What's going on?" Allora asked, leaning up next to him. "You're usually ecstatic for game days."

"I just don't see the point," he said, pushing off from the grill of the car, and shoving his hands in his pockets. "Before, our lives were much simpler, I guess."

"You mean before my hands exploded."

Tanner pressed his lips together and nodded.

"But now it's different," Tanner said. "It made me think that there are more important things in life than kicking around a soccer ball."

"I hear ya. I felt the same, but for some of those guys, this is the most important thing in their lives right now, and you're still their captain."

"You always did have a way with words," Tanner said, putting his arm around Allora's shoulder, and walked towards the field. "Heard you got setup duties. Beat up a few sophomores?"

"Yeah, Principal Winters wasn't exactly understanding of the whole situation."

They descended the concrete stairs next to the gym and stepped down onto the track. Large trees surrounded the field, giving it an enclosed feel, and the far end was a slope of matted grass and dirt.

Katie was waiting for Allora down at the equipment closet next to the bleachers. She watched as Allora walked by with Tanner's arm wrapped around her neck, before Tanner ran off to join his team for a pregame talk.

Allora didn't smile back at her friend, who was giving her a huge grin. "Not a word," she said, pointing at Katie.

Katie shrugged her shoulders. "What? I didn't say a thing," she replied, unable to wipe the know-it-all smile from her face.

The two of them went through the entire checklist Mrs. Mondrach had given them so they could fulfill the community service requirements of their punishment. She had gone over everything twice so they wouldn't have any excuse for missing something or messing it up.

When Mrs. Mondrach showed up an hour before the game, she was surprised and glad to see that they'd accomplished everything to her exact specifications. The signs had been made, the tables and chairs were placed perfectly, and all of the decorations hung in their correct places. "Wow, girls, you did a great job. I'll be sure to let Mrs. Winters know how fabulous you are," Mrs. Mondrach said, then left to perform her pregame duties.

Allora and Katie found seats in the student section of the stands, at the edge of the running track. Students and parents filled the stands as the soccer players took up their positions on the field and the game started.

At halftime, Allora stood, eager to find something else to do while the cheerleaders did their dance routine. "I'm going over to the concession stand for a drink. You want anything?"

"No, I'm good," Katie responded.

Allora walked down the track, past the rambunctious junior high kids. Memories of being fourteen circulated through her mind. Her life had been so carefree back then, so much simpler, even if it had all seemed so important and significant while she was living it. She ordered a soda, paid for it, then moved to the exit, where a group of kids came screaming out of the woods, toward the stadium. Their parents rushed down the hill from their seats. Allora slowly walked past them so she could hear what they were saying.

One of the girls was crying uncontrollably, absolutely terrified, as she told her mother about a monster in the woods. Between gasps of fright, she kept repeating the same two words. "Red eyes, red eyes! It... it ha-had red eyes!"

As her mother tried to calm her down and carried her away, Allora thought about following them to find out more, but she figured that it might have just been a prankster with a halloween mask. She rushed back to her seat, spilling soda all over her arm as she ran, and told Katie what had happened. As soon as she finished the story, the cheerleaders lined up, and the soccer players jogged out onto the field.

Tanner walked past her, looked up, and winked.

Allora giggled.

"Geesh. When are you finally going to admit that you like him?" Katie asked.

"Huh? I don't know what you're talking about," Allora said.

Katie crossed her arms, leaned sideways, and raised her eyebrows. "C'mon, Allora! I'm not blind. I see the way you two look at each other. It's so obvious. He's single now, you know. You should go for it before somebody else snatches him up."

Just then, as if to prove Katie's point, Tanner kicked a sixty-yard pass to Dax for a goal. The crowd exploded, but the two girls remained seated.

"Well?"

"Well what?"

"When are you gonna stop lying to yourself and admit that you like him?"

Allora contemplated Katie's words for a minute. *Am I just lying to myself?* She cared about him a lot, but she wasn't sure if those feelings were changing into something more. All around her, people were cheering, but she hardly noticed because she was so entranced by her thoughts of Tanner.

"I know that I have feelings for him, but I'm just scared to get hurt, I guess," Allora admitted.

"So, you'd go toe-to-toe with an ogre in a fight, but you're scared of rejection?"

"I don't know. Maybe I'm just scared that if I tell him the truth, then I'll lose him."

"Obviously you don't see how he looks at you girl," Katie said, standing up after noticing her brother grabbing a drink at the water cooler. "Nice goal, Dax!"

"Thanks, sis!" he yelled back, grinning.

At the end of the game, Allora and Katie stood in the middle of the field to wait for Tanner and Dax to come out of the locker room. The Pioneers had managed to secure the win in the fourth quarter, so the boys were exuberant as they strutted out onto the turf.

"See? I told you there was nothing to worry about," Allora said.

Tanner gave her a half-smile. "Yeah, I'm just glad Dax didn't go offside this time."

Dax shoved him playfully.

All of a sudden, the stadium lights shut off. The four jumped, then laughed at each other for doing so. Darkness set in as the bulbs dimmed, the light turned orange, and then faded away. The entire field was empty of people, other than the four. A *snap* echoed from the woods surrounding the field. Sweat rolled down Allora's back and her throat tightened. The four young Sonorans stared toward the edge of the trees.

Nothing happened for about a minute, but then two dark red eyes appeared between the trees. The eyes gradually grew bigger as their owner creeped to the edge of the field. When something grabbed Tanner by the shoulder, causing him to spin around to attack, the other three screamed and took up their own battle stance, ready to pounce on the intruder.

In the next second, a dim green light flickered on, revealing that it was Kim. She had her cell phone out and was clutching it to her chest. When she finally caught her breath, she said, "Oh my god! You scared the crap out of me."

"What are you doing here?" Allora demanded, swiveling her eyes back to the forest.

The red eyes were gone.

"I need a ride home, and everyone else already left to go up camping I guess? I saw you guys down here and thought maybe you could help me out."

"We were actually heading up towards the mountain ourselves to camp on the quarry. It's kind of a Pioneer tradition to have a school campout for upper-classmen after the first soccer game. You wanna join us?"

Allora nudged him slightly, forcing a smile at Kim.

"I appreciate the invite, but I'm going to have to pass. I should be getting home."

They all turned back around to see if the red eyes were still there, but they had vanished.

"Yeah, uh… I'm thinkin' we should all probably get outta here as well," Tanner said with a bit of urgency in his voice.

They all stole a few glances behind them while they walked to Tanner's car. Dax called shotgun, as usual, which meant the three girls had to squeeze to-gether in the back. Allora wasn't too happy to be so close to Kim; she felt a weird vibe whenever she was around the girl.

Tanner pulled out of the school lot and onto the main road. "Uh, where do you live?" he asked a bit nervously.

"River Road," Kim replied.

"That's really close," Tanner said.

"Yeah, like close enough to *walk*," Allora snapped. She didn't bother looking at Kim's reaction to her comment.

Seconds later, the car pulled onto River Road, and Tanner drove all the way down to the end of the street. "Which one is it?" he asked.

"Stop," Kim said when he approached a yellow, two-story house with hedges surrounding it. "We're here."

"Hey, isn't this the Nelsons' house?" Allora asked.

"Yep. They're my grandparents," Kim said, opening the car door, "on my mother's side. Mom's in Europe for work, so she asked me to stay with them for a while and take care of them. They're kind of… old," she said, then closed the door without even bothering to thank Tanner. She remained in the driveway and stared as the car rolled back toward the main road.

"That girl is strange, really strange," Allora said.

"I wouldn't say that," Tanner defended. "She's just new. I kinda like her."

"Right," Allora said. She wasn't too happy with that, of course, but she didn't want to argue with him. Instead, she changed the subject. "So... what the hell was that thing in the woods?" she asked, lowering her voice as if mentioning it might somehow summon it to them.

"What about camping then?" Tanner said. "Not sure if its a good idea after seeing what we saw."

"What did we see?" Katie asked.

"I don't know, man, but whatever it was, it looked unnatural," Allora said.

"Probably just someone in a mask," Dax said confidently. "Stupid kids pull pranks all the time."

"We should ask Aunt May," Katie said.

"She's gone, remember? And nobody says a word to my mom. She'll flip out and lock me in my room for eternity."

"Actually, she thinks I'm sleeping at Katie's house tonight," Allora said, grinning.

"Oh, you are so dead if she finds out," Tanner added, laughing.

Dax turned around in the seat and grinned. "Oh yeah, we be camping!"

Eight

Tanner veered his black Ford Bronco onto an old, abandoned lumberjack road that stretched high into the wooded hills of Mt. Hood National Forest. After a jarring ten-minute drive through the thick woods, they finally came upon an orange light glowing in the darkness. A large bonfire illuminated an expansive abandoned rock quarry. Flames licked ten feet into the air, sending embers rocketing skyward, and the orange-red light danced against the rocky, half-bowl-shaped hill.

Allora looked out over the edge of the quarry, down into the valley below. Dots of yellow sparkled in the distance, and something about them reminded her of home. A fight with her mother seemed inevitable.

As Tanner pulled up beside Katie's vehicle, Allora noticed the infamous, bright yellow Volkswagen with "Pioneer Soccer" plastered all over the rear window. She cringed.

Tanner noticed too. "Sorry. I really had no idea she was here." Allora raised an eyebrow, questioning his remark without saying a word. "We can go if you want."

Allora let out a sigh and shrugged. "Meh. I'm gonna have to see her at school anyway." She opened the door, stepped outside, and warily walked toward the bonfire.

As soon as Brandon saw the foursome, he strutted over. "What up peeps!"

"Hey, Brandon," everyone said with hint of antagonism. Brandon Stringer was a forward on the soccer team. He was short, with dark skin and short, black hair.

"That was a sick game bro, you killed it." Brandon pulled Tanner in for a half-hug, pushing Dax playfully. "You were alright as well."

Dax crouched down, trying to take out Brandon's legs, but just ended up in an arm lock for a few seconds.

Jenny stomped over with her posse right behind. "What the hell are the freaks doing here."

"Chill, girl," Brandon said. "I invited them."

Jenny pushed past Brandon and marched toward Allora.

Katie stepped in front and raised her chin, stopping Jenny in her tracks. "Go ahead, Jenny. I dare ya."

Jenny was intimidating, but she didn't stand a chance against Katie. The two stared each other down like gunslingers, each waiting for the other to draw. Jenny clenched her fists but kept them stiffly by her sides as the standoff and stare-down continued.

Suddenly, a loud rustling of branches interrupted the confrontation. The sound came from the tree line at the top of the rock quarry, drawing attention upward. The group fell silent. Nothing moved except the shadows from the dancing flames.

Out of the darkness, a deafening screech pierced the silence. It echoed into the quarry, where the petrified teenagers stood motionless, grasping one another for some sense of security. Allora turned toward the twins and found Dax and Katie scanning the tree line like two sentries.

"That did not sound friendly," Tanner said.

Katie grabbed her brother's arm. "Did you pack the weapons?"

"No, did you?" Dax responded.

"I've got my throwing knifes," Katie whispered, barely lifting her shirt to showcase the band of steel blades around her abdomen.

"I forgot mine as well," Tanner added.

A foreboding air surrounded the quarry.

"Shut up!" Jenny whispered loudly.

Katie ignored her and turned to Dax. "Did you bring anything?"

"Actually, I might have stuffed my staff in my bag," Dax replied as he hastened toward the bronco.

"What the hell was that thing?" Allora asked, scanning the woods.

"This is messed up," Brandon said. "Shouldn't we get outta here?"

"Katie, any ideas?" Tanner asked. "It didn't sound like anything I've heard before."

Katie ignored the interrogation and ordered, "Tanner, Allora, if something comes out of those trees, you need to run as fast as you can into the forest. Head east… and don't look back."

"What? I'm not going anywhere. I've got to—"

"Allora," Katie snapped, "we don't have much time. It's imperative that you follow my directions." Her eyes were wide and confident, as if a military commander had taken over.

"I can't find it!" Dax said, frantically throwing junk out of the back of the Bronco.

"Shut up, shut up, shut uuuuuuuuuup," Jenny seethed.

A dark, shadowy figure leapt from high above the crowd and landed right on the hood of Jenny's car with such force that the windows exploded outward like a bursting bubble.

"*That* is a rover!" Katie said, charging toward the strange creature.

Allora squinted in the firelight to get a look at it. The rover was small, only a few feet high, with scaly, dark, greenish-brown skin, like a reptile's. Its eyes were golden with vertical, cat-like irises. After briefly surveying the chaotic scramble of humans, the creature grinned, baring sharp, pointed teeth.

Before Allora could move, Jenny knocked her over, attempting to escape. From the rocky ground, Allora noticed Katie pulling knives from her waist as she charged the creature. Dax found the handle of a short stick and pulled it from the bed of his pickup just as the creature sprang forward and hit him in the chest. Dax flew limply across the quarry, into a pile of dirt.

Before the creature could mount another attack, Katie pulled back a knife, gripping the steel blade with her thumb and forefinger, and flung the weapon toward the rover. With a glistening flash, her blade slashed through the crisp air, striking the creature in the side, sending it flying off the gravel lip at the quarry edge. A high-pitched squeal trailed into the night, followed by a chorus of ear-splitting screeches from the valley depths.

Suddenly, an identical creature flew over the line of cars. It sprang forward and struck Jenny in the back with such force that it propelled her forward, hurling her into the road, where she crashed headfirst into the hard dirt, knocked unconscious.

The creature crawled along her back, maliciously pulled her head by her hair, and placed its palm on her forehead. The firelight revealed a lanky, reptilian creature with a long, skinny torso, razor-sharp teeth, and five locks of hair pulled back against its flat skull. Unhappy with its prey, the creature picked up a rock and raised it above Jenny's head.

Allora's fast-moving foot clipped the rover's side and sent it flying into the fire. The creature hit the logs and screeched in vile desperation as its scales were scorched, then ran around the quarry, trying to put out the fire. Allora turned around to see a larger creature charging at her.

There was no time to mount a defense. Just inches from Allora, the creature yelled when one of Katie's knives lodged deep in its side. The monster pulled the weapon from between its scales and dropped it, allowing a fountain of green ooze to spurt from the wound. The rover then cried out in pain and ran toward the parked cars. Upon reaching the quarry edge, it let out another deafening screech, causing the other creatures to abandon their attack and follow it into the woods.

"Nice kick," Katie remarked, placing one of her throwing knives back in her belt and glanced at the unconscious blonde sprawled on the ground. "A little surprised that you didn't let the thing whack her on the head."

"No way! If anybody's gonna whack Jenny on the head, it's gonna be me."

Tanner and Dax ran up.

"Where were you two?" Katie asked.

Tanner pulled a tire iron from his side to prove that he was ready to fight, even if he hadn't gotten back in time to do so. "Sorry," he said, wearing a guilty half-grin. "Guess I missed the party."

"And what about you?" Katie asked, putting her hands on her hips and cocking her head.

"That thing knocked the wind out of me."

"Where's your staff?"

Dax pulled a handlebar from his waist. With a flick of his wrist, the short handle extended out from both sides to a length of five feet.

Katie continued collecting her throwing knives and placing them back into the sheaths secured around her waist.

Allora grabbed a burning stick from the fire. "Okay, so what is that thing?

Katie opened her mouth to explain, but she wasn't able to give an answer before Jenny began to stir.

"Hey, you all right?" Tanner asked, wiping the dirt from her face.

"All right?" she questioned between sobs. "That stupid animal attacked me! Where were you?" she demanded to know, jerking herself out of Tanner's concerned grasp.

The rest of the students were already running down the dirt road. They had abandoned their cars and were trying to make it to the freeway to flag down a ride.

Brandon popped up from behind a large pile of branches. "Is it gone yet?" he asked nervously, walking to the others.

From the depths of the forest valley, another screech echoed, but this sound was different. Much to their dismay, the deep pitch suggested something larger than the creatures they had just fought.

"That's it. I'm leaving!" Jenny said, running to catch up with the others. "Wait for me!" she yelled, but no one seemed interested in listening to her.

Brandon began to jog to his car.

"I wouldn't go over there, man," Dax cautioned.

"Why not? There's no way I'm leaving my car here," Brandon said. "I just got it detailed."

Allora and the others watched as Brandon frantically searched his pockets, trying to locate his keys among the random debris that filled them. He fumbled through receipts and coins, becoming increasingly frantic when no keys presented themselves.

"Brandon!" Katie yelled.

Just as he got to his car, a shadowy, humanlike figure appeared, backlit by the moon.

Brandon finally pulled the keys out of his pocket but dropped them. His hand shook as he picked them up and shoved them into the keyhole on his driver side door. The others watched in horror as he froze, then reached up to touch a spot of moisture that had appeared on his shoulder. He slowly twisted his neck around to look directly into a face full of jagged teeth and dripping saliva.

A gut-wrenching scream followed when the creature picked him up and threw him at least twenty feet. Brandon was unconscious as soon as he thudded to the ground in a heap. Next, the sinister beast moved toward the fire where Allora, Tanner, Dax, and Katie prepared their stances for an attack. Despite their fear, they stood their ground.

"You two need to get outta here," Katie wailed. "Head east, like I said."

Allora moved forward with the torch, her only weapon, held high. "No way! I'm not leaving you guys."

As the figure moved closer, they could distinguish some of its features. Like its smaller counterparts, it had reptilian scales and no hair. Its beady, catlike eyes flickered, glowing gold. A slithering, snakelike tongue slipped in and out with every step it took.

Dax placed his staff in the ground like a vaulting pole and skillfully pulled his body up as the creature sprang forward. As he came down, Dax swung the staff around, twisting his body and striking the rover with the blunt end of the wooden staff.

The rover shook off the pain like a dog in the rain, then positioned itself on all fours like a lion, ready to pounce. Hissing and staring intently, the beast pushed off, moving rapidly. Katie pulled back, launching a barrage of knives. The creature was surprisingly agile and flipped, dodging the flying silver blades. It snapped around and kicked Dax firmly in the chest. He flew backward, flailing and just missing the dying bonfire. Catching Katie's flying kick, the rover twisted around, blocking another strike from the quick blonde. The rover made an offensive downward thrust, but Katie blocked it and pushed her hand forcefully into the creature's chest. It cringed, reclaimed its balance, and spun around.

The glow from the end of Allora's weapon lit the dark battle as the other three took turns attacking. The rover easily blocked and countered every strike. After throwing Tanner onto a car, the creature struck Allora in the gut, pushing her along the ground. Dax joined his sister, swinging his staff into the rover's side, then twisted and tried to catch the back part of its knee. It did little good, for the rover jumped high and twisted downward, landing on Dax's collarbone.

Katie tried to thrust her knife into its abdomen, but the creature arched his back, grabbed her wrist, and smacked the steely blade from her grasp. She tried to counter, but the rover had the upper hand, quite literally, and flung her into the air.

Katie's body crashed into the windshield of the yellow Volkswagen. The rover leapt high, ready to exact a final blow as the other three tried to regain their composure, sprawled sporadically on the ground. Katie screamed as the creature was a second from smashing her skull. A green surge of light crashed into the creature's upper back. The explosion of energy forced it over the quarry edge and into the forest valley below.

All four teens managed to stand, holding the various aching, bruised, and bleeding parts of their body where the creature had struck them. They looked up to the top of the quarry, the place where their saving green light had come from, but nothing was there. Upon meeting next to the fire, they all checked each other's wounds.

Suddenly, an enormous creature almost eight feet-tall and covered in brown hair emerged from the shadows. He had beady brown eyes, lanky limbs, and a funny quaffed hair cut that stuck out in different directions on top of his pointed skull. A brown leather sash was slung across his chest tightly, with a sheathed sword running diagonally across his back, and a brown belt around his waist. A black sheathed dagger was strapped to his thigh, and he had black metal bracelets on both wrists.

"Sas!" Allora screamed, running to the hairy creature and hugging him profusely. "Where have you been?"

"Oh hey, hold your bears, I gots to go after that rover."

"Its 'hold your horses' you giant fur ball," Katie yelled, as Sas leapt over the parked cars into the forest. "I swear, he is awful with Earth sayings."

"Now what?" Tanner asked, as an eerie silence enveloped the quarry.

The dying fire crackled in the dead of night. They stood motionless, without speaking. Then, a shadowy figure sprang from the bottom of the forest, landing hard near the fire.

"Pesky, smelly little rover be fast," Sas said, cracking his back and stretching his torso. "We need to get out of here though."

"We're not going after that thing?" Dax asked.

"No, we're going to my cave."

"Sweet! Wait. Don't tell me were porting there." Allora asked, slouching down in protest.

"You want to be walking the ten miles in the woods?"

"Ugh, I suck at porting."

Sas pulled in the hadrons around, began swirling his arms in a clockwise pattern, moving the dirt and gravel around the ground. A green glow lit the quarry as he pushed downward with both palms, shaking the earth below. The ground turned to liquid, swirling magically in the ground like looking into a blender. Dax went first, followed by the others. Allora reluctantly jumped into the portal, pulling her body forward like jumping through the outer realm, and popping them out in the bushes near Sas' cave. Allora's balance shifted, spinning her wildly as she exited the port. She landed in a bush with her feet in the air, and her face in the dirt.

"You really are terrible at that," Tanner said, laughing as he pulled her out of the bush, and saw her dirt covered face in the light of the moon.

"Shut up," Allora replied, stomping off up the hill towards the entrance to the cave.

Nine

Sas popped out of the portal with ease, and led them over the edge of the rock embankment and onto a large stone outcrop. They proceeded slowly along the wide slab to the mouth of a cave. A natural archway of thick vines lined the cave rim. Sharp, jagged rocks protruded inward in several rows, like the teeth of a great white shark. On either side, moss-covered trees hung low, slightly inhibiting the movement into the cavern. As they moved down into the darkness, they kept bumping into walls.

"You really need to get better lighting in here," Katie said, pushing off the damp rock.

"Sas, you never answered my question," Allora said, her voice echoing slightly.

The path became slightly illuminated from the faint moonlight shining through the cracks overhead.

"You mean the rover?" Sas said over his shoulder as they continued. "Right, well, rovers are reptilian creatures from Sonora, as you might have guessed," Sas explained. "They be breaking apart their arms and legs which can change into smaller creatures." Sas went on to explain the creature's distinctive and unforgettable features, a biology lesson that had Allora shuddering. "The trick is to be finding the main body when the limbs be separated, because the torso can't move very fast. It can only extend four very short legs making it pretty vulnerable. When the rover puts itself back together, it is very quick and strong—not someone you wanna be messing with unless you know how to defend yourself."

Sas stopped at the end of the path staring intently at the rock wall in the corner of the cave chamber. There appeared to be nothing special inside. It was a hollowed-out moist cave, with no distinctive character to suggest that anyone lived there. Sas faced the far wall and swung his arms in a strange, circular motion, expelling light from his palms.

The gritty stone wall glowed as Sas repeated his circular motions in different patterns. When he stopped, light shot out from the wall. The piercing beam imploded into the stone, which then formed an almost fluid exterior that shimmered strangely. "This way," the tall, furry beast directed before he sank into the wall and disappeared.

Allora followed, moving through the swirling liquid, and stepping into the interior of Sas's home base.

Upon reaching the other side of the mysterious wall, they walked into an intricately designed cavernous chamber, lit by large, glowing orbs that hung from the ceiling. Along the walls lay a myriad of trinkets, knickknacks, and various objects commonly found in rubbish. The junk seemed to be purposely arranged in a peculiar manner, forming a vast, eccentric sculpture. Soda cans, metal spatulas, barbecue grills, tent poles, magnets, car doors, hats, lighters, water bottles, and other objects had been placed together to form an array of grand art that lined the path into an elaborate hall full of cascading waterfalls.

"I'm pretty sure that you are a hoarder, Sas," Dax said, picking through one of the piles of camping chairs.

A shadow moved across the expansive rock ceiling as Sas moved out from behind a strange, aqueduct-type system. Made of sheets of aluminum cans, it started at the top of a small waterfall and ended in a luminous aluminum bowl. He motioned them over and smiled. "I'm sure you're all thirsty. This is a natural spring. It is safe to drink, if you wish, and you can wash up over there." He pointed down the path toward the back of the cave, where the water emptied into a large, crystal-clear pool.

"Yeah, but why would that rover go after us?" Allora asked, prompting Katie to try and stop the response.

"Probably because you're a royal, Allora."

"Sas!" Katie yelled, provoking Allora to raise her eyebrows at her best friend.

"Wait…" Allora said, moving toward the blonde with her finger pointed. "You knew?"

Katie bit down, showing her teeth as she backed up toward her brother.

"Smooth move ya dumb ape," Dax added.

"Oops," Sas said.

"You knew too?" Allora said, crossing her arms and glaring at Dax. "What about you?"

"I have no idea what's going on," Tanner replied, shrugging his shoulders.

"I can explain," Katie said.

"Your mother told us that we had to keep it a secret," Dax said, placing a hand on his twin sister's shoulder. "She's the one that ordered us to remain silent."

"Milly. Yes. I should go get her," Sas said, swirling the ground into a portal, and quickly escaping the cavern.

That left the four friends to an awkward silence, as Allora tried to come to terms with the term, 'royal'. The slight trickle of the waterfall echoed in the cavern.

"So, how about that fight earlier?" Tanner said, trying to break the tension.

"Look, I'm sorry for not telling you," Katie interjected.

"You should be! We promised not to keep anything from each other."

"Yeah, but this was an order. Milly would have crucified us!"

"So then, do you two know who my father is?"

"No, all we were told was that he was a part of the royal family, and that you had blood rights to the throne of Titanis," Dax said.

"That is heavy," Tanner added.

"Not helping," Allora replied. "Anything else you want share with me?"

"Our father is alive," Katie said. Allora's eyebrows lifted. "He's a general in the rebellion. Jarrod and Maureen adopted us in a way, but they were originally our security personnel, working under our father's command."

"Fantastic," Allora said, throwing up her arms in protest. "You guys have been lying to me this entire time?"

Suddenly, the ground near the water's edge swirled, opening up. Sas sprung out, followed by Milly, May, and Bell.

"Mom!" Allora yelled and ran to hug her.

Milly grabbed her daughter, held her close, and sighed with relief, but in the blink of an eye, the reunion turned ugly. "How could you sneak out like that?" Milly scolded.

Allora crossed her arms and lifted her eyebrows. "And how could you not tell me about my royal status?"

"You told her," Milly said, eyeballing the twins. They reacted quickly, both pointing directly at Sas who bit down trying to maintain a smile while fumbling around awkwardly.

"Allora..." Milly paused for a few seconds, staring directly into her daughter's eyes. "Our family came to Earth because we were being systematically exterminated. General Salazar, assassinated the royal family, along with most of the leadership in Titanis that had the means to confront him. We were barely able to make it out of the city. Your father was a direct line to the throne, which means that when you turn eighteen, you are the rightful ruler of Titanis and most of Sonora. That makes you the ultimate threat to Salazar's grip on the kingdom. That is why we have kept you here, and it's why we've had you training for all these years."

"And keeping this all a secret was supposed to help me?" Allora said, leaning forward with her arms outstretched.

"I didn't want you to have the burden of knowing. I just wanted you to be able to have a normal life here on Earth. A normal childhood."

"Mom, I hang out with an eight foot tall Sasquatch, train in a magical realm, and can shoot fire from my hands. How is any of that normal?"

"Good point," Milly said.

"So, that is why that creature attacked us tonight?" Allora asked, prompting Milly to glance over at Sas.

"A rover. We be having at least one agent in the area. My guess would be that more will come."

"Did it identify any of them?" Aunt May asked.

"No, I got there first," Sas replied.

Milly walked across the room. When she tripped on a broken hubcap, she winced and said, "Couldn't you invest in a housekeeper, and get rid of some of this junk."

"Hey!" Sas replied, grabbing the hubcap and placing it back in the pile. "None of this is junk!"

"You will watch over these four. If they are not at school or home, you need to keep an eye on them."

Sas nodded quickly, giving her no debate.

Milly's order was direct and forceful, as if spoken by a military officer. Even Allora knew when not to rebel against her mother. The sound of cascading waterfalls splashing into the blue pool filled the empty silence of the cave.

"Were you able to track it?" Aunt May asked.

Sas shook his head. "I lost the trail."

"Isn't that good?" Allora inquired.

"Right," Dax agreed. "It must mean the thing's not around if old smelly, here, can't smell it."

"We need to leave," Milly ordered.

"What!? But I wanna know more. What about——" Allora protested.

Milly grabbed the hand of her other daughter, who had remained speechless the entire time, and gestured for the others to follow. She made a circling motion with her hands, opening a portal into the ground. Swirling light escaped the vortex.

"Seriously, you have to teach me how to do that," Allora said.

Milly and Bell disappeared into the ground. Meanwhile, May whispered something into Sas's ear. Then she winked at Allora and followed the other two into the quicksand-like portal. The others followed, jumping one-by-one through the portal until only Allora and Sas remained. He grabbed her wrist, and closed the portal. Allora glanced up at the tall hairy warlock, questioning his actions.

"I need to give you something," Sas said, wandering off into the stacks of junk, and flinging stuff across the room.

He rummaged through a potato sack. "A-ha!" he said, pulling out a rolled-up piece of beige parchment. He handed the document to Allora, his face somber as he placed it in her hands. "Ben asked me to be giving this to you when you were ready for it," Sas said, unable to hide his grief. "I believe that time is now."

At the mention of Ben's name, Allora began to tremble, and tears threatened to gush from her eyes. When she was ten years old, her mother had arrived home one night with bloodshot eyes and had broken the news that Ben, her uncle, had been killed in an avalanche on Mt. Hood. Holding back her emotions, Allora said, "You've never mentioned him before this."

"He be a friend, and one of the bravest, most selfless individuals I've ever had the privilege of knowing," Sas said. "Ben made me promise to be giving you this parchment when you became of age."

Allora stared down at the foreign object in her hands. It felt light and worn, and the edges were uneven and torn. She slowly unrolled it, exposing a sequence of numbers: "8 5 3 2 1 1 0."

On the other side, a poem was delicately inscribed. The writing was intricately done but barely legible. At the bottom, it read, 'The Eye of the Titans'. Four lines of script filled the middle of the parchment. Allora read the poem out loud:

> *At last you come to the cavern of gold*
> *Grand monuments to the gods of old*
> *The Eye reveals for those who believe*
> *Be wary of greed in the path you weave*

"The Eye of the Titans is an ancient artifact that Ben and Swan were searching for, and this be one of the clues to its location."

"Swan, like my teacher Mr. Swan?" Allora asked.

"Yes," Sas said, nodding his head. "You may want to ask him about it because he's been trying to find the other two pieces of the parchment." Sas swirled his hand, opening up the portal leading to Allora's home. "Now, I be needing to go patrol the area for that rover."

Allora hugged the furry creature tightly, and then jumped through the portal, landing upside down on the couch in the living room. She swung her feet around, and stared down at the piece of old parchment, wondering about its secrets.

An overwhelming feeling of trepidation engulfed Allora's mind. The faces of the people she held closest revealed a quiet unease, one she'd never experience before. In that moment, she felt a kinship to Pandora from the Greek story. Her episode at soccer tryouts had opened up a box of untold evils on the world. *Did anyone bother to ask Pandora why she opened the box? She's been known throughout the centuries as the woman who brought evil to all humankind, but was it really even her fault? Am I somehow to blame for all this?*

In a heartbeat, Allora's curious excitement about her special abilities turned into angst. Nothing could free her from the responsibility of her new life. A powerful burst of emotion had opened a box of evils, and Pandora's guilt was now her own.

Soon, she'd have to make a dreadful decision to either wither before the overwhelming obstacles ahead or fight back. With that grim thought on her mind, she stood up and went to her room, finding a discreet spot in the corner of her armoire to place the piece of parchment, vowing to find the other pieces of the puzzle.

Ten

SWAN

"What's going on?" Mrs. Ferris demanded, perplexed by the sudden departure to the dank, secluded high school basement. The eerie echoes of old pipes softly clanked and clamored on the ceiling. An ancient furnace filled the air with a pungent burning odor.

"I found the second piece!" Mr. Swan whispered.

"Really?" Mrs. Ferris exclaimed enthusiastically. She then gasped at the sight of a rat that scurried along the edge of the concrete floor. "Couldn't you have told me this upstairs?"

"That's the problem." Mr. Swan inched closer. "His agents are getting closer to the truth. They may even be here already. It's no longer safe to talk about it in school."

"How do you know?"

"They somehow *knew* I was going to Peru. There was a Chenoo waiting at the base of Manchu Picchu when I arrived."

"How'd they find out?"

"I've got no idea. I was able to fight the rock man off, but I'm almost positive I was followed when I came back here," Mr. Swan said, grinding his teeth. "It was most likely a—"

"No..." Mrs. Ferris pulled back and again whispered in the darkness. "Where's your proof?"

"I ported back, and the residual of someone else came through only minutes afterward. It's got to be an agent."

"You ported? Why the hell would you do that?" she asked.

"I had to. It was the only way I could get out alive, with the…" Mr. Swan trailed off and paused, his senses picking up on the muffled sounds of voices. Out of his peripheral vision, he caught a shadow dance along the wall, near the doorway. He grabbed Mrs. Ferris and moved toward the back corner, barely making it around a stack of milk cartons before two individuals turned the corner.

Footsteps grew louder as two sets of feet walked up only a few yards away. One pair of feet stopped on the other side of the crates, followed by eerie silence. Electricity sparked from the edges of Mr. Swan's fingertips as he moved to get a better line of sight.

Then one of the individuals spoke. "We only need two crates of milk, right?"

"Yeah. I don't think the kids will drink any more than that."

Mr. Swan let out a sigh of relief, realizing it was only the cook and the custodian. The two left with their supplies, leaving Mr. Swan and Mrs. Ferris in the dark, catching their breath.

"Why in the hell do they keep milk down here in this dungeon?" Mrs. Ferris asked.

Mr. Swan ignored her question and went back to their discussion. "It's imperative that we get our hands on that last piece."

"Do you know where it is?"

"I think so, but I can't get to it," Mr. Swan said, glancing back at the metal basement door. "If I was followed, my identity has been compromised."

"And you want me to go after it? Not exactly in the best of shape here, Swan."

"Well, we can't ask Milly or May. They haven't been supportive of this quest ever since Ben." Silence ensued as they both pondered what they had to do. It was an important task, but it was also a dangerous, risky one. "There is one other option…"

"That ain't happening," Mrs. Ferris snapped quietly.

"Do you have a better option?"

They stood for a moment in quiet contemplation.

"No. It has to be them, I guess, but how will you ever send them without Milly knowing?"

"You'll see." Mr. Swan grabbed the door, then remembered one last thing. "Oh... you should give them a lesson on glues. They're gonna need it." With that, he left the room.

Another rat scurried across the floor, causing Mrs. Ferris to quickly follow behind him. "But I hate making glues!" she muttered. "It's almost as bad as... rats!"

* * *

"Do you know what The Eye of the—?" Allora asked.

Mr. Swan turned pale, yet his body suggested an odd fervor. He leaned forward. "Where did you hear that name?"

Allora was about to speak, but Mr. Swan pressed his finger to her lips.

"Wait," he cautioned. "We're not safe here." He glanced over his shoulder at the open door, where screaming students zoomed past as they socialized before their next classes.

"Bring the other three to my classroom after fourth period. We'll talk then."

As she left the classroom, she sensed something strange in the hallway. Allora tried to make sense of it. She joined the herd of students, while deep in thought. *Why is everyone so freaked out about this Eye of the Titans?* She thought to herself as she arrived at English class.

Allora didn't hear a word her teacher said as she waited anxiously for fourth period to tick away. As soon as the clock struck the hour, she grabbed Tanner, Katie, and Dax and led them to Mr. Swan's room.

"Close the door and sit," Mr. Swan said as they entered.

They did as instructed. Mr. Swan put a finger to his lips, then placed a round, white, gel-like ball on the table. The four of them crowded around, trying to get a glimpse of it. The ball had a strange metallic tint and seemed to swirl with an odd, flowing glint against the light of the dim room.

When he pointed his finger, a green spark shot out and struck the peculiar white ball. It exploded, and a layer of clear goo covered nearly every surface in the room, including the curious individuals standing bug-eyed in a circle around the desk. They tried to speak, but no sound came from their mouths, and no one could hear anything.

Mr. Swan pointed his finger, sending green sparks toward each student. The clear goo fell toward the floor, collecting into a small ball at each of their feet.

"What was that?" Allora said, not at all happy with the teacher's weird, slime-shooting contraption.

Mr. Swan collected the small balls and put them together to form one medium-sized, clear ball. "This is silencing glue," he said, gently placing the ball in his desk drawer. "It coats an interior area and creates a soundproof space." As he explained it, the clear gel formed to the walls and disappeared. "Mrs. Ferris is still trying to perfect the formula."

"So we can say whatever we want, and no one will be able to hear us?" Katie asked.

Mr. Swan put his hands on his hips and smirked. "Exactly."

Katie went up to the wall to see if she could feel anything, but it felt normal. "That's so cool," she said.

"Why is all of this necessary?" Allora asked.

Mr. Swan became uneasy and leaned against his desk to explain himself. He took a moment to collect his thoughts, wondering which parts he should refrain from mentioning.

Allora bent her knee, crossed her arms, and raised her eyebrows. "Well?"

"Allora, I… it's complicated."

"I'm pretty sure 'complicated' is pretty freaking normal from here on out. Now, stop treating me like a baby and tell me what the hell this thing is!"

The other three chuckled at Allora's sarcasm, and even Mr. Swan smirked.

"Fine. I'll fill you in the best I can, but this has to be our little secret, even from your mother."

"My mom?"

"Milly will kill me—perhaps literally—if she finds out."

After receiving reassuring nods from each of his four students, he walked past them and stopped at the back wall. He placed an open palm on the wall and began rotating his hand. A green glow escaped the edges of his hand while he continued rotating it clockwise, then counterclockwise.

Green lines dissipated on his palm, and a green, glowing circle formed on the wall. A bright flash burst out from the green lines, then pulled back inward. Mr. Swan reached his hand into the wall, just as they had done at Sas's cave. From the depths of the liquid wall, he pulled out a rolled parchment.

With her eyes wide, Allora shoved her hand into her bag, wondering if he had somehow stolen her copy. The familiar sheepskin she had received from Sas was still safely tucked inside her book bag. Puzzled, she moved closer to look at Mr. Swan's copy, then anxiously waited as he unrolled the ancient beige parchment.

After it was entirely unrolled, Mr. Swan placed a book on the top to keep the parchment flat.

"That looks just like mine," Allora said, yanking the parchment from her school bag.

Mr. Swan didn't seem surprised. "I figured as much. Ben gave that to Sas for safekeeping, and I was sure he'd pass it on to you when the time was right. I've been trying to find the other two pieces to complete the riddle." He slowly unrolled his copy, but there wasn't any writing on it; in fact, it was entirely blank.

"I don't get it," Allora said. "What good is a blank piece of paper?"

"Just because we can't see something, that doesn't mean it's not there," Mr. Swan said with a smile. Again, his hands began to glow, filling the room with a green hue. A soft light escaped his palms and covered the seemingly blank page, and a moment later, ink appeared on the parchment, slowly forming intricate, artistic lettering that spelled out four lines of words.

"Whoa!" Tanner said. "I don't think I'll ever get used to that."

Mr. Swan stared at the writing, grinning with excitement. "I've waited decades to look upon this script," he said. "We exposed the other parchment when the first one was discovered. The ink reacts to hadrons, some pretty unique stuff." He moved back, allowing the others to take a glance. "Allora, would you like to do the honors and read it?"

"Uh… sure." Allora inched forward, still feeling uneasy.

Heed the warnings of the route you take,
For one false choice be the last you make
Be careful to step with feathered feet
For one wrong move will send you deep

Allora knew there had to be something powerful about those words, even if she didn't understand what they meant. She glanced up at her teacher with a determined stare. "So what is it? What is this Eye of the Titans?"

Mr. Swan leaned against his desk and took a deep breath, as if he had a long, difficult story to tell. "Do you all know the story of the Titan Wars?" he asked.

Recalling the story of Greek gods and Titans, Allora asked, "So it's not just mythology?"

"It is discounted as that now, yes, but the war was very, very real," he began. "The Titans were and still are the rulers of Titanis, the capital of Sonora. Back when the gateways to Earth were discovered, the Titans treated humans as slaves and Earth as its own colony. That was at the time of the initial evolution of humans as intellectual creatures, when humanity began to think on their own.

"Several Sonoran colonies formed in different areas of Earth, and wars were fought over that land, because each place offered its own unique resources. Before long, the rulers of these colonies became entrenched with the thinking humans. They taught them their ways, educated them in technology, religion, math, science, and language. The Titans of Sonora became infuriated with this, fearing that the humans would become too powerful and attempt to overthrow them. Since the gateways were permanently open, a large Titan army invaded Earth, starting one of the largest, most devastating wars for either world."

The four leaned forward, hanging on every word their teacher spoke.

Mr. Swan continued, "To quell the onslaught of the invading army, the Sonoran colonists formed a secret army, the guardians."

"Like Sas?" Allora asked.

"Well, Sas is a guardian, yes, but these were different. If you paid attention during your mythology lessons in school or have watched some movies, you might know them better as Zeus, Hera, Hermes, Aries, Poseidon, and the rest of the so-called 'Greek gods,'" he said, placing mocking quotation marks in the air around the term.

"Why were they called 'gods' if that is not what they were?" Tanner asked.

"That was the acronym for the organization."

Allora's eyes grew wide, and she leaned over the table. "Wait, so you're telling me that all of Earth's historical religious icons are based on an acronym?"

Mr. Swan smiled to one side of his mouth and nodded.

"They were originally known as the Guardians of Delphi or G.O.D., because most of the support for the uprising came from the capital city of Delphi on the western continent of Sonora. The Sonoran colonists of Earth joined the guardians to battle the Titans for the freedom of Earth and the freedom of humanity."

"And who won?" Allora asked.

"The Guardians won, I guess, but we believe it came at an extreme cost. No one knows what happened for sure, because all the historical records of the stories were destroyed or hidden away in secret locations to preserve the truth. I've been trying to locate them, but I haven't been successful just yet. Most of what is known was passed down through verbal telling of the stories, all those mythological stories of the war and the leaders of the rebellion, as told from a human perspective."

"And the Eye of the Titans?" Allora asked. "What is it, and what does it have to do with any of this?"

"Well, The Eye is said to be a myth, but we know better. It was one of the artifacts used to defeat the Titans and bring order to the two worlds," Mr. Swan said with authority and exuberance. "It is said to be more powerful than any known artifact. I believe it is real, and those pieces of parchment are my proof."

Allora's mind began to spin as she imagined an ancient item of great power that could protect the people she loved. She knew that the artifact could be the solution to those who sought to do them harm, and it could help others who might be in a similar predicament. The threat of constant danger was exhausting, and now she knew The Eye could be her saving grace. "So how do we find this thing?" Allora asked, thoroughly intrigued.

"Well, that's the problem. We need to find the last piece of the puzzle. It's the most important piece, because it explains the geographic location of The Eye."

"Do you know how to find the last piece?" Tanner asked.

"No," the teacher admitted. His four students faces became sullen and defeated. "However, I believe I know who might have a clue."

"Who?" Allora asked eagerly.

"Sas."

Allora raised one eyebrow. The creature was friendly enough, but he was a hoarder and sometimes somewhat of a bumbling klutz. Besides that, she wondered why he would have given her the parchment but forgotten to tell them this crucial piece of information. "Sas? Are you sure? What makes you think he knows where it is?"

"Because his father was the one who found the first," Mr. Swan said, pointing to the parchment lying on the desk. "According to transcripts that I found, Sas' father was investigating the existence of the Eye within the old ruins of Shangri-La, and eventually found the first parchment. Only problem was that there was a leak within the organization, which led to his death."

Even though they were curious, none chose to inquire further. Instead, Allora remained focused on finding the last piece of parchment. "So you believe Sas's father told him where it was hidden?"

Mr. Swan reverted back to the moment, shaking off the pains of his past. "Not necessarily," he answered. "I believe the location of the last piece is exactly where Sas's father died."

"Sounds like a suicide mission to me," Katie remarked.

"Wuss," Dax murmured, nudging his sister.

"This artifact could be the key to everything. We must convince Sas to tell us the location."

"If you think he knows, why haven't you just asked him yourself?" Allora inquired. "He seems like a pretty talkative guy to me."

Mr. Swan fidgeted around. "Let's just say the big, hairy one and I haven't really seen eye to eye on this," Mr. Swan said in a vague tone that Allora found most disconcerting. "He's been on a witch hunt to find his father's killer, and won't disclose any information because of the traitor. I can't convince him to tell me."

Allora closed her mouth and swallowed the numerous questions she'd intended to ask.

After rolling up the precarious pieces of parchment, Mr. Swan moved to the back of the room and faced a blank space. He motioned his hand in circular patterns, twisting his open palm as though opening a safe. A green glow shot forward, spreading into a large, liquid circle upon the wall. He placed the documents into the liquid, then sent another open-palm spark into the wall, solidifying the area. "There," he said as he made his way back to the front of the classroom. "I've created a safe to protect the directions to The Eye."

"Whoa! Brings a whole new meaning to 'wall safe,' huh?" Dax joked. "Do we get to learn how to do that?"

"Perhaps when you're able to focus hadrons," he answered. "For now, I need you four to talk with Sas. That last piece is critical." He then sent a wall of green throughout the room, pulling the silencing glue from walls and collecting it into a ball again. He motioned for them to go, then sat down at his desk and began grading papers like a normal teacher.

Before Allora left, she glanced through the small door window to see Mr. Swan staring blankly out the classroom window. His distant gaze was eerily emotionless. He remained still and silent.

Allora walked away from the window, wondering whether she would ever find out the truth to the past that they seemed to all share; a past she wasn't sure she would ever understand.

Eleven

Glue

An arrow sliced through the air, leaving a faint glow as it shot from the end of the bow. Allora saw the trail of clear violet and reveled in her new abilities. The steel-tipped arrow penetrated its target with extreme precision. The tail end protruded, still wobbling up and down, indicating the powerful force of the hit on the six-foot, straw-filled dummy that Allora was shooting at with her composite bow.

The trail of light dissipated, leaving Allora in awe at the wonders of her new life. While amazing, her new life presented overwhelming complications that made those incredible moments of magic seem infinitesimal. Part of her wanted to give it all up for the normalcy she'd had before the incident at soccer tryouts. For weeks, she'd suffered from a severe identity crisis.

As she watched her closest friends sparring with inanimate dummies, she realized that the potential consequences of their new lives were inescapable. *What will I do if one of them gets killed?* The grim and terrifying thoughts made her sick, so ill that she almost keeled over.

"Hey, you all right?" Tanner asked as he noticed Allora turning pale and wobbling on her usually steady feet.

Allora shook her head, unable and unwilling to discuss her thoughts.

"Looks like we've got our first puker!" Dax said, laughing and sparring with a fighting post called a muk yan jong. "Don't be embarrassed, Allora. I can't tell ya how many times I've barfed during practice, especially when Coach Hale makes us do suicide runs."

"I'm fine," Allora said, backing away from Tanner, trying to act tough. "I'm just not feeling very well."

Katie placed a hand on Allora's upper back. "Maybe we should call it a day."

"No way! We need to be prepared," Dax insisted. "I'm pretty sure that red-eyed creep in the woods isn't gonna call it a day."

Reminders of the beast were unwelcome, but they couldn't deny it or take it lightly.

"I hate to say it, but Dax is right," Tanner admitted. "I've got a creepy image of those red eyes plastered in my brain right now."

"Look, I've got physics homework, *and* I have to find a Halloween costume before Friday, so I need to call it a day," Katie said.

"Oh yeah! Halloween!" Tanner said, as if he'd forgotten. "Are you guys coming to the party?"

Allora shook her head, but Katie jumped in and answered for both of them. "Of course we are!"

"Katie, I..." Allora began. She was reluctant to participate in the popular social event, which most had been looking forward to for weeks because of the absence of Robert Mondrach's parents. Katie ignored her best friend and insisted they'd be there.

After placing the equipment in a large wooden shack, they went through the portal and down to Allora's house.

"Don't forget about Mrs. Ferris's room after school tomorrow!" Allora yelled before the others pulled out of her driveway.

* * *

The next day, they all met in the junior hallway and looked around to make sure they hadn't been followed to Mrs. Ferris's room, which appeared to be empty when they opened the door.

Suddenly, a lady with curly red hair and wearing a long, white lab coat popped up from behind a counter. Mrs. Ferris was a short, stocky woman with large, thick spectacles that seemed to devour half of her face. She was holding a glass beaker in one hand and bottle of some sort of liquid in the other, humming as if she didn't realize she had company. When Dax closed the door with a loud *bang*, Mrs. Ferris jumped and let go of the glass beaker, which flew into the air and shattered on the tile floor.

"Sorry, Mrs. Ferris," Dax said, pressing his teeth together and scrunching his nose. "Didn't mean to startle you."

"No, not your fault. I put up the silencing glue before you got here," Mrs. Ferris said, walking over to them. "As a matter of fact, I believe I owe you an apology for getting goop all over you. I got the kinks worked out though. The new formula with skip biological signatures," she said, lifting the broken glass with a wave of her hand and gesturing the floating pieces toward the trashcan.

"Man, you've gotta teach me how to do that!" Dax said.

"Maybe then your room wouldn't be such a pigsty," Katie snapped.

Dax sneered at his sister.

"You'll get your chance, young man." Mrs. Ferris then pointed to the back of the room, where four pots had been placed on the burners in the lab. "For now, though, you'll each be making your own batches of silencing glue."

The exuberance was palpable, yet Dax's excitement suggested something more mischievous. Allora could almost imagine the pranks he was coming up with.

Mrs. Ferris led them to their stations, and then walked to the shelving on the far side of the room. She pointed to the wall, and a small yellow spark shot forward. All of a sudden, everything on the shelves melted into the wall. Containers of ammonia and vinegar disappeared, as if consumed by small black holes.

The four teens stood there in shock, watching as strange contraptions, bottles, cauldrons, potions, human skulls, rolled parchment, animal skins, and odd, colorful orbs materialized from inside the wall.

Next, Mrs. Ferris grabbed a handful of items, and as soon as she walked away, the weird objects were absorbed back into the wall, and the regular lab material reappeared.

Allora picked up one of the bottles and read the label out loud, "Balumar Family: Signature Slug Sauce." She wrinkled up her nose, shrugged, put the bottle down, and picked up another, a very small glass bottle with tiny writing that couldn't be read with the naked eye.

Seeing Allora uncork the container, Mrs. Ferris yelled, "Stop!"

Allora froze, unsure why her teacher had snapped. "Uh… sorry. I was just—"

Mrs. Ferris carefully took hold of Allora's wrist and, like a puppeteer, directed her hand to place the cork carefully back into the top of the walnut-sized glass bottle. A hard sigh followed.

"That is Tiranis extract," Mrs. Ferris said. "It is made from the Tiranis plant and is the stickiest substance on Sonora. One drop can deform the skin and you could possibly lose a finger or hand. If you are going to handle it, you must do so with extreme caution and only with gloves."

Allora slowly lowered the bottle to the linoleum countertop and inched away as if it were a ticking bomb.

Mrs. Ferris neatly arranged the necessary items on the rest of the stations, then made her way to the blackboard. After she carefully wrote the instructions on the board, she said, "Please begin."

Allora started by boiling two cups of slug sauce, then slowly poured in a half-cup of liquid spider web, followed by two teaspoons of crushed lilac powder and a tablespoon of dragon blood. She let the mixture cook for ten minutes, until a shallow film formed on the top.

"Um… Mrs. Ferris?" Dax said as the liquid boiled over the rim of his pot. "I think there's something wrong with my recipe," he confessed as an extremely large greenish-yellow bubble grew from the pot.

"Oh no! Don't touch it!" Mrs. Ferris said, sprinting to the back shelf and extracting a potion from the inner wall.

The bubble grew larger, engulfing the lab station. In mere moments, it ballooned so big that it hit the ceiling.

Mrs. Ferris pulled out a smoky liquid from the potion bottle, like a rabbit from a hat, and magically pushed the contents toward the monstrous bubble. It exploded, covering everyone with a slimy film of greenish goo. "How much lilac powder did you put in there?" she asked.

"Two tablespoons," Dax replied, wiping the slimy goo from his face.

Mrs. Ferris shook her head and grabbed several towels from a drawer.

"Teaspoons, you moron!" Katie yelled, aggressively swiping the slime from her shirt and pants.

Dax apologized profusely, all while trying to stifle a laugh at his sister, who had slime dripping from her bangs.

Mrs. Ferris threw each of them a towel. "It's all right. You're not the first to make that mistake. When the lilac powder mixes with dragon blood, it causes a reaction with the slug sauce."

Katie bent down with arms outstretched and a look of disgust. "Ew! You mean I'm covered in slug boogers?"

Everyone laughed at Katie's discomfort, watching as she aggressively wiped the green goo from her clothes.

"How were you able to do that?" Allora asked, referring to the potion retrieval.

"I just used a small amount of hadrons to counter gravity and raise the molecular contents of the bottle. It's simple really." Mrs. Ferris almost laughed at the confused faces of her goo-covered students. While they waited for the glue mixture to settle, Mrs. Ferris gave them a more advanced science lesson. "A hadron is essentially a wave particle."

"Like electricity or light?" Tanner asked.

"Well, in some ways, you could make that comparison, but hadrons are far more complex. They grow inside of us as we get older, in our blood, cells, brains, and organs. When we choose to, we can absorb them, move them, focus them, and expel them, depending on our level of ability. Sonoran scientists are still trying to understand what they are, so I don't expect you to develop a complete understanding. Nevertheless, you should have a general idea of what's going on inside of you." She paused for a moment, washing the green goo from her towel. "Human scientists mistakenly refer to hadrons as dark matter or dark energy."

"So humans know about hadrons, at least to some degree?" Allora asked.

"The humans have been studying them for some time, but they have only a basic understanding at the moment."

"If humans know about hadrons, how's come they can't focus?" Tanner asked.

"I'm afraid someone much wiser than me would have to answer that question, my boy. Humans do possess a small amount of hadrons in their bodies, but they can't conceptualize them yet. Do you remember when I told you human beings only use ten percent of their brains?"

They nodded their heads.

"Due to that, human minds are not ready to process the power that is associated with the synaptic electrical connections needed for hadron focalization."

"Huh?" Dax said.

Tanner laughed uncontrollably. "I have no idea how your going to be able to focus hadrons."

Dax sneered and shoved him into a chair.

"Any chance you could use some of those hadrons to get this horrible stuff off my clothes?" Katie said, scrubbing her jeans with a towel.

"You're such a drama queen," Dax said.

"These are designer jeans. If I can't get this stuff out, you're a dead man."

Mrs. Ferris ignored the sibling rivalry and inspected the other pots. "Allora, it seems you are the only one who was able to mix a sufficient batch."

Katie continued to wash her clothes in the sink, while everyone else crowded around Allora's pot. A soft white, creamy layer had settled at the top of the liquid.

Mrs. Ferris carefully scooped the white foam off and placed it into four Petri dishes. She handed out goggles and gloves and instructed Allora to gently pick up the Tiranis extract.

Allora uncorked the bottle, holding it out in front of her with her arms straight.

"Hold it very steady," Mrs. Ferris said, her body tense and her hands follow every movement a few feet away.. Then a slight wave of energy escaped her fingertips and an invisible force slowly pulled the weird, thick liquid from the bottle. She magically separated it into four parts and gently lowered each part an inch from the four foam-filled Petri dishes. With a flick of her fingers, the Tiranis extract dropped into the foam, and four enormous plumes of sparkling smoke exploded up to the ceiling.

Filling the air, the smoke smelled of lilac and skunk, an odd aroma that was delightful and vile at the same time. The thick cloud gradually dissipated, and the four Petri dishes came into view. The liquid swirled around, forming four small white, sparkling balls.

Mrs. Ferris took them and placed one in each of the students' hands. "Use these whenever you are compelled to discuss anything about Sonora. You never know when someone might be listening in on your conversations. They are reusable, but if you need more for some reason, come find me."

"Got any more cool things on that crazy shelf of yours?" Dax asked.

"Not for you, young man. Who knows what you'd do with some of that stuff?" Mrs. Ferris said, pushing them out of the classroom and into the hallway.

The four of them decided they'd use the extra time to go get costumes for Mondrach's Halloween party. Even though Allora didn't really want to go, the prospect of just being average teens for the night was exciting.

Before they left, Allora went to the bathroom. She opened the door and heard crying sounds. Quietly, she peeked around the corner and saw a blonde girl slumped over the sink. The crying girl's mascara was running down her face in gray-black rivers, dripping into a puddle in the white porcelain sink. Upon hearing Allora walk up, she wiped her eyes with a damp towel and turned on the faucet.

"What are you looking at?" Jenny sneered, still trying to clean the raccoon mask from around her eyes. Allora pulled her head back, unsure about what to say. "I bet you're enjoying this, huh?" Jenny said, leaning back over the sink. The sounds of her sniffles echoed in the tile bathroom around them.

"Actually, I just wanted to apologize," Allora said, even though she wasn't sure why those words came out of her mouth.

She stood up straight, looking defiant. "What? You're sorry? Why the hell would you apologize to me?"

"I'm sorry because I know what it feels like to lose someone you love."

At the sound of the sincere and sympathetic confession, Jenny eased back down, letting go of her aggression.

"You mean your uncle," Jenny said, her facial tension eased and her eyes dropped down to the floor. Allora gave in to her own vulnerability, unsure why she was discussing one of the most painful times of her life to the one person she hated most. Her eyes began welling up with tears, her body remembering the emotions as if it had all happened yesterday. "Allora, I'm so sorry for what I said earlier about—."

"It's ok," she replied, wiping her eyes. "Water under the bridge."

Jenny put her arms around Allora, pulling her in for an embrace. Shocked by the oddity of the moment, Allora wasn't sure how to react, so she allowed the girl to hug her and said nothing. In fact, she eventually gave in and reciprocated the hug, and the two held each other as if they were long-lost friends. After they pulled apart, neither girl said a word. Jenny half-smiled at Allora, an unspoken farewell, then left the bathroom.

Allora stood there for a while, reflecting on the peculiar and unexpected exchange. Shaking her head, she walked out of the school and onto the pavement of the parking lot.

"What took you so long?" Katie asked.

"I'm fine," Allora said, walking up to the car.

"Give her a break. She was probably just taking a big Number Two," Dax said, causing Tanner to crack up laughing. "We can stop at the store if you're all stopped up."

"Do you have to be so gross all the time? Grow up."

Dax leaned against Tanner's car, crossed his arms, and smirked. "Hey, sometimes I take longer than Allora did, especially when the cafeteria feeds us those tacos with the mystery meat in 'em."

Tanner laughed even harder as they jumped into his car.

"You know, sometimes I wonder how it's possible that we're actually related," Katie said to her brother.

The car pulled away and headed toward Ruth's Costume Shop.

Twelve

Halloween

Fall had arrived, and the trees were blanketed with a vibrant variety of beautiful, autumn colors. A flurry of brown, orange, yellow, and red littered the ground and sky. The smell of freshly fallen leaves, pine, and moss permeated the crisp air. The sun pierced through a hole in the overcast sky, illuminating the beauty of fall. Allora took some time while she fed the chickens to notice the landscape, a nice break from the flurry of activity in her home.

Halloween was in full effect, and the house was covered in decorations. Fake cobwebs were spread across the walls, cauldrons of dry ice boiled in near the fireplace, and plastic skeletal bones were scattered all about. Trays of candy corn, creepy monsters, and other elaborate decorations finished the look. Milly and May had been busy all week preparing the house for their most celebrated of holidays.

"Human Halloween traditions have their roots in Celt and Irish origins from thousands of years ago. Supposedly, on October 31st, the ghosts of the dead would return to Earth." As Milly told the story, she began to laugh. "Of course, humans didn't realize those so-called ghosts were just Sonorans, playing tricks on them. Trick or Treat was invented because if a Sonoran wasn't able to scare the human, they had to give them a treat," Milly explained. "Over time, humans took it over as their own tradition, and now little ones go out with bags on Beggar's Night, asking for candy and other goodies."

"I know mom," Allora said, rolling her eyes. "You tell us this story every year."

May yelled from down the hall, "Milly, I need your help putting up this large plastic spider."

"Well, did I tell you the story about the tooth fairy?" Milly said with a smile, and turned to help her sister in the living room.

"I didn't know fairies live in Sonora," Katie said, putting her witch cape around her shoulders.

"A tooth-stealing fairy. I knew there was something fishy about that," Allora said, placing her pointy black witch hat on her head.

"Girls, it looks like Tanner's here," Milly yelled, holding up the plastic spider decoration.

Allora and Katie looked in the mirror one last time to review their outfits, identical except for their shirts, a white tank-top for Katie and a purple one for Allora. They both had short black skirts, long capes, and pointy black hats. They'd spent hours working on their makeup, and their thick, black eyeliner in a perfect cat eye made them look even more exotic. After a quick application of lip gloss, they were ready for Mondrach's party. Allora finished touching up and walked into the living room with Katie right on her heels.

Tanner was standing next to the fireplace, quite literally dressed like a knight in shining armor. He looked comfortable in his costume, a plated metal suit that looked rather authentic. He was carrying the sword he'd received from Aunt May, hanging in a sheath on his back. The outfit was masculine and eerily familiar to Allora, even though she couldn't understand why.

"You're smart to bring your sword, Tanner," Milly said. "You must all be very careful tonight. Halloween is off limits when it comes to acts of aggression, but the Royal Guard rarely plays by the rules."

"You mean the Royal Guard that is supposed to protect the heir to the throne?" Allora asked, crossing her arms.

"Yeah, well they purged the guards who were loyal to the rightful bloodline," Aunt May said while securing a fake spiderweb onto a nail in the corner.

"There are going to be extra personnel out there tonight watching over you," Milly said, then returned to helping her sister with the decorations.

Allora's eyebrow raised as she thought about the odd change in subject. She ignored it, said her goodbyes, and then they all headed out the door to Tanner's car.

"Where's my brother?" Katie said, looking around for a guy dressed in a Merlin costume.

"Boo!" a voice said from behind the car.

A man with a fake beard and a blue hooded robe popped around the corner. Katie swung around instinctively and hit her brother on the side of the head, sending him to the ground.

Dax couldn't help but laugh as he held his bruised head. "I guess all that training has really paid off. You should have seen your face though. Priceless!"

Katie responded to her brother's comment by kicking him in the stomach. "Do that again, and I'll aim a little lower," she threatened, stepping around Dax to get into the car.

Allora followed, laughing as she jumped into the passenger seat.

Dax slowly picked himself up. With the wind knocked out of him, he opened the car door and inched his way into the seat, all the while glaring at his sister.

"Next time, maybe you'll think before you act."

"Oh yeah? Next time I'll use a cattle prod," Dax replied.

Allora rolled her eyes at Tanner, who had to suppress his laughter as he pulled onto Greenburg Road. The conversation continued all the way to the Mondrach's house.

There, a multitude of cars lined the driveway. Robert's parents were in Hawaii and had left him alone for a week, giving him the perfect opportunity to throw a relatively unauthorized Halloween bash with no adult supervision. He'd made a guest list, but the word got out. Luckily, his house was large enough for everyone, and it was secluded from his neighbors, back in the woods.

The four teens jumped out of the car to the sound of muffled music, bumping from inside the two-story home. Through the living room window, they could see the house packed with their classmates. They moved through the crowd to find Robert in the kitchen.

"Dude, I thought this was supposed to be a small get-together," Tanner said, walking up to their host.

"Yeah, well, so did I!" Robert responded, shoving plastic cups into a trash bag. "Not so small, huh?"

Truth be told, almost the entire school had shown up for the party. Princesses, comic book heroes, M&Ms, and even a Bigfoot show up. The Bigfoot took off his mask to reveal Brandon. He had a jug of red punch in one hand and playing cards in another.

Mondrach's house was filled with amazing artwork, tapestries, and sculptures. They had six bedrooms, a game room, a swimming pool in the back yard, and a weight room. Allora, Tanner, and Katie weaved through the crowd to the game room, while Dax sauntered out to the pool to shamelessly hit on unsuspecting sophomore girls.

"I think you've got an unfair advantage," Tanner said after losing at darts for a third time. "Maybe you should give me a handicap."

"I can't help it if you suck with ranged weapons," Allora said, jabbing Tanner playfully in the side.

"Maybe you should give me some pointers…in private," he said, pinching her side playfully. When she didn't answer, he said, "Hey, I'm gonna get a soda. You want anything?"

"Sure, grab me one as well."

Tanner left the room and worked through the labyrinth of people to get to the coolers where the drinks were held.

Katie came up behind Allora. "Heads up. Crazy blonde just got here," she whispered.

Allora jerked around to see Jenny strutting down the hallway with Tanya and Nancy trailing behind her. They were all scantily clad in bright pastels, with fake wings attached to their backs. Glitter sparkled on their skin, eyeliner was heavy, and their lips were covered with the same bright red lipstick.

"They look like butterflies on drugs," Katie murmured.

Robert walked over to his giggling, girly guests and asked, "What are you guys supposed to be?"

"Pixies," Tanya said, moving in closer and touching his biceps flirtatiously.

Robert just smiled and backed away. "Sorry," he said. "I just don't wanna get glitter all over me."

Jenny found her way to Allora and stopped in front of her.

The room fell silent. Gossip from the incident at camp and the soccer try-outs had circulated through the entire student body, and everyone assumed, with eager anticipation, that a pixie-on-witch brawl was inevitable.

Jenny's cheeks lifted, as if she was breaking into a smile, a rare expression for her. "I like your costume," she remarked, confusing the curious spectators who'd been eagerly watching, hoping for a dramatic fight. "It suits you."

"Ditto," Allora responded, smiling to one side of her mouth.

Someone in the back began to applaud, and the girls turned to watch as a petite, beautiful brunette slid from behind a zoot suit-wearing gangster. Kim was dressed in skintight, almost painted-on black leather, with tall boots that went past her knees, a long, flowing cape, a pointy witch hat, black eyeliner, and bright red lipstick. "How precious," she almost hissed, slowly moving toward the center of the room. "The pixie and the witch." she said, now within a foot of Jenny, "sounds like a great love story."

Jenny turned to face Kim who stared her down with an evil grin.

Just then, Tanner walked back into the room. "Did I miss something?" he said to a quiet but giddy crowd that was excited to be getting their drama fix.

Kim turned toward Tanner, placed her hand on his chest, and smacked a long, wet kiss on his mouth. "Nope, you didn't miss a thing," she said and sauntered toward the kitchen.

Jenny stormed off in the opposite direction, followed by Nancy and Tanya.

Allora stomped over to Tanner. "You're unbelievable," she said, forcefully jerking the Diet Coke from his hand. Then she took off toward the door, pushing Dax out of the way.

Tanner just stood there dumbfounded, completely confused.

"What just happened?" Dax asked, stopping next to his friend, who was just as confused. "I always miss the good stuff."

"I've got no idea. One minute I was getting a soda for Allora, and the next thing I knew, I was being kissed by the new girl, then yelled at by everyone else."

"Wow. Tough life, bro."

Allora was fuming outside, though she wondered why she was so upset. Tanner wasn't her boyfriend, and she knew he was allowed to kiss anyone he wanted to. *Maybe I'm just angry because he had the nerve to kiss that little witch while Jenny's in the room. How rude!*

Then again, it didn't make sense that she would care about Jenny getting hurt. She had apologized, but one apology certainly couldn't erase all her evil deeds from over the years. Her inner debate raged on, taking so much of her attention that she stepped right off the edge of the porch, only to land on the side of the house, next to a rose bush.

"Pssst!"

Allora jumped back.

A furry head popped out of the top of the bush.

"Sas!" Allora exclaimed, putting her hand to her chest and exhaling. "What are you doing? You scared me half to death."

"How does someone get scared half to death?" Sas asked.

Allora could only stand there staring at him, and she wasn't laughing.

"Sorry," Sas said, coming out from behind the bush.

"Why are you here? All these people might see you."

"I was going to be asking you the same," Sas replied, raising his eyebrow.

"Please don't tell my mother," Allora responded, grabbing the furry creature by his wrist.

"You four need to be leaving here now," Sas said, looking stern. "I'm tracking a wraith of some kind, and I don't think that he be friendly."

"A wraith? Do they happen to have red eyes?"

"How do you know that?" Sas asked.

Before she could answer, a figure moved out from behind Sas. When the shadow moved into the light, Allora blinked her eyes at the sight of another hairy being, a much shorter Sasquatch that didn't look quite as authentic.

The hairy thing took off its head. "Hey, Allora," Brandon said, moving closer and stopping next to Sas. Brandon looked down at Sas's huge feet, then at his own. "Am I seeing double?" he asked, slurring a bit. He pulled his head upward but had no other reaction to the creature standing next to him.

"Uh..." Allora faltered, not sure what to say.

"Cool costume, dude! We're like twins," Brandon mumbled.

Sas looked very uncomfortable, as if he wasn't sure what to say. "Yeah, well, I got it on the Interweb," he muttered, looking upward and then sideways as he racked his brain.

"Well, it's awesome. It's so much better than mine," Brandon said, pulling strands of hair from the creature's leg. "It looks and feels so real, man. Is it made of yak hair or something?"

Sas winced at the pain, obviously agitated by the pesky human.

Brandon began swaying from side to side. "I'm heading to the barn to find more plastic cups. You guys need anything?"

"Nope," Allora said as he walked off. "Don't you need a flashl—" Allora started to say, but she couldn't get the words out before Brandon stumbled inside.

The sound of crashing garden tools, pots, and broken glass followed.

"Ouch!" Allora said. "You think he's all right?"

"I'm sure he is," Sas said, but then he froze as if he'd heard something else. "I gotta go. Be careful, Allora," he cautioned before he ran off toward the woods.

Kim came hopping down the porch steps just as Sas disappeared behind the trees. She looked around suspiciously. "I thought I heard you talking to someone out here."

"Uh, yeah, well, I was just talking to—"

Brandon fell out of the tool shed. "I'm okay," he said, getting to his knees.

Allora turned to Kim. "Brandon. That's it. I was talking to Brandon." She walked across the lawn and helped Brandon to his feet. She put his arm around her shoulder and dragged him back to the house.

"I'm hungry," Brandon mumbled.

"Let's go get some candy corn," Allora said, dragging Brandon past Kim, who stood by with her arms crossed. Allora left Brandon in the kitchen to gorge on Halloween treats and met back up with Katie in the game room. "I think we need to go," she said quietly to the other three, who were playing pool.

From the urgent, horrified look on her face, they all could tell Allora needed to talk, so they said their goodbyes and left the house.

Tanner turned the key in his car ignition, but it wouldn't start. No matter how many times he turned the key, nothing happened.

Dax jumped out of the car to look under the hood. A few minutes later, he came back to Tanner's window, scratching his head. "Man, you aren't gonna believe this, but your spark plug is just… gone," Dax said.

Tanner jumped out and slammed the car door. He stared down at where the missing spark plug should have been and slammed the hood, causing both girls to exit the car.

"Check the other cars," Tanner said, lifting the hood of a sedan. Dax did the same.

"They're all gone," Dax said, slamming down the car hood.

"What now?" Allora asked.

"Obviously, someone is trying to keep us at the party," Dax said. "I guess we should just walk."

"I don't think that's such a good idea. I just spoke to Sas, and he told me a wraith is on the prowl, looking for us," Allora said.

Everyone just stared back as if they didn't know what she was talking about.

"You know, the red-eyed monster thing in the woods."

"When did you talk to Sas?" Katie asked.

"That's why I asked you guys to leave," Allora explained. "Sas found me outside and told me he's been tracking it. He came here to warn us, and said that we need to get out of here now."

"What if that thing shows up here," Tanner said, pointing toward the house party. "If its after us then we can't put all of our friends in danger."

They stood in silence, wondering what they should do. No one wanted to meet the wraith on their way home, but they had no other choice but to walk. Their parents didn't know they were at a party by themselves, and if they got picked up at Mondrach's house, everyone's parents would know they had lied about where they were going.

"We've gotta hoof it. I have my sword, Dax has his staff, and Allora has her throwing knives," Tanner said, taking off his metal costume and putting it in his car. The noise alone would have attracted attention. "We should be all right."

Allora hiked up her black skirt a little to reveal the leg band she'd hidden, where six small knives hung in sheaths along her thigh. When she noticed Tanner glancing at her bare leg, she pulled her skirt down.

As they hiked along the dark, eerie road, Allora pulled a knife from the band and held it in her sleeve. Tanner gallantly moved ahead, keeping his hand on the hilt of his sword. Dax followed closely, holding his staff in front. Allora's house was two miles away, which seemed much farther in the cold, black night. They walked in silence, periodically glancing at the dark woods on either side. Whenever Tanner heard a noise, he stopped to scan the murky area. Allora tried to peer through the trees, but visibility was poor. The moon was absent, and with no streetlights, the walk home was dark and ominous.

Every step was one closer to her home, but each step felt wrong, as if they were walking into a trap. Allora felt the woods watching their every move. Her intuition pleaded against moving forward. A chill ran up her spine, causing a spasm. Something just didn't feel right.

They had now walked about a mile and a half down the forest road. Tanner stopped and held his hand up for the others to stop behind him.

Allora pulled out her knife. "What is it?" she whispered.

"I thought I saw something move up ahead. It was weird, like a shadow without a body."

Dax walked up to the front. "What's the holdup?"

"I don't have a very good feeling about this," Tanner replied.

"Now you say that," Katie complained loudly.

Allora watched as Tanner's eyes opened wide. His terrified expression caused Allora to quickly jerk around, just in time to see two red eyes speeding toward them. Allora pulled the knife behind her head, then moved her arm forward, but the dark figure was too quick. It hit her side, tossing her into the ditch.

Tanner and Dax ran forward, leaping to attack. Katie tried to spin around but tripped over her own feet and fell backward into the ditch, alongside Allora. The wraith pulled out two swords from sheaths attached to its back and caught both boys' downward swings. The boys stumbled back, finally able to get a good glimpse of the creature.

The wraith was the same height as Tanner and Dax, with human-like characteristics, except for its jet-black skin. It had muscular features and long, pitch-black hair, pulled back in a tight ponytail that flowed in the wind like mist in the night. It wore a tight, military-type black jump suit, with a utility belt, and a gun holster on its thigh.

The wraith pulled back, stepped sideways, and encircled the boys while they mimicked the creature's motions. "Well, well, well. Looks like we have ourselves a couple of warriors," the dark creature said in a deep, condescending voice. "This should be fun."

With that, the boys launched themselves at the creature, swinging their weapons aggressively. The wraith swung his black crystal swords around, blocking every attack. As Allora picked herself up, Tanner was able to knock one sword from the creature's hand, but it motioned its arm forward, sending Tanner flying through the air, as if an invisible force had struck him.

Dax pushed forward, swinging his staff as well as his body. He hit the wraith solidly in the side, knocking it to one knee. Dax pulled the staff over his head, leaving his body open. The wraith punched Dax's chest, launching him into a tree.

Allora had just enough room with Dax out of the way. She held up her knife, and as she did, her body began to tingle. Warm electricity flowed, absorbing into her hand. The weapon glowed purple as she hurled it, and it streaked through the air, leaving a magical trail behind to illuminate the darkness. Seeing the purple streak, the wraith put up his hands, but only in time to create a hadron energy field to block the attack. The knife hit the invisible field and exploded, showering the wraith with purple sparks and knocking it into the trees.

"Gotta go," Katie said, grabbing Allora's wrist and dragging her into the trees as they boys followed.

The adrenaline pumped through their veins, along with the hadrons accumulating inside. They ran as fast as their sore legs would carry them. The woods were dark, but their eyes adjusted quickly, and the fact that they could hear the wraith behind them in fast pursuit egged them on. The sound of crunching leaves and breaking twigs grew louder as they ran. Finally, they exited the woods into a large, grassy field.

"It's gaining on us!" Tanner yelled.

They all stopped, not sure what to do. Allora pulled out another knife, Tanner unsheathed his sword, and they stood side by side, preparing for an attack.

"Guys, we're in trouble," Katie said.

"Yeah, and he doesn't look happy," Dax observed, watching the wraith as he sprinted through the woods, exploding every small tree that dared to stand in his path. His eyes bobbed up and down as he leapt over a log.

"What's that?" Allora asked when she caught sight of a dark figure moving toward them from across the field. She could barely see through squinted eyes, but the figure was covered in fur and moving quickly.

"It's Sas!" Tanner yelled.

Sas leapt over the four and struck the oncoming red-eyed creature as the wraith exited the woods. The impact sent both creatures crashing into a large tree, shattering the trunk, and the huge Douglas fir began to fall toward where the four teens stood.

"Move!" Dax yelled.

Thirteen

FATHER

The four Sonorans ran in opposite directions to avoid the deadly falling evergreen. Allora rolled along the grass just as the trunk crashed into the ground. The branches smashed her into the grass, covering her body. Sharp branches cut into her skin, and pain pierced her body as she pulled herself from the cocoon of needles. Frantically, she scanned the dark for signs of life. A hand reached upward from the ground. Allora grabbed it and pulled Dax out of the tree. In the dark of the night, Allora could see black streaks of blood on his face, neck, and arms.

"Where are the others?" he asked.

"I-I don't know," she said. "C'mon."

Without saying anything, the bruised, broken, and worried duo trudged through the fallen tree, climbing over the trunk to where they assumed their friends would be. They swam through the sea of branches, searching for a hand or foot or any sign of life.

Tanner was barely able to stumble from an avalanche of evergreen branches, and he moaned as he got to his feet, bruised and visibly bloodied.

"Where's Katie?" Allora asked with a fearful pitch in her voice.

A muffled yell came from a few feet away, and the three ran to the area and began sifting violently through the thick undergrowth. When they pulled back a large branch, Katie's face appeared.

"Took ya long enough," Katie said softly. The foliage had slammed her into the ground, leaving her breathless from the impact.

Simultaneous sighs of relief came from everyone.

"My leg is pinned," Katie said, pointing down her body.

"Is it broken?" Dax asked.

"I don't think so," Katie responded

With an admirable group effort, they pulled up on the tree branched and yanked her out. The sound of snapping twigs echoed from across the field. They scanned the forest for the wraith.

"I lost my sword," Tanner said.

"My staff's gone too," Dax added. "We'll have to come back for them later."

Nevertheless, they bravely stood, ready for whatever might spring from the woods. A figure jumped out and landed firmly in front of them, but it was only Sas.

"Where is the wraith?" Allora asked.

Sas looked disheveled and a bit disoriented. It was obvious that he'd been in battle.

"I don't think he'll be back anytime soon," Sas said puffing up his chest, holding his chin high, and glaring into the forest, "but we shouldn't wait around to find out."

He moved his hands in a circle. Green sparks swirled into his arms, focusing at his palms, and he suddenly slammed his hands into the ground. A shockwave of earth flowed outward from the impact point, causing the dirt to push upward. The wave of dirt raised the four momentarily, then dissipated through the field.

Sas stood over a swirling circle of dirt. "Time to go!" he said, motioning to the portal.

"Can't it still track us?" Katie asked.

"Not through this type of portal," Sas explained. "Now please hurry up."

Without hesitating further, they followed his orders and jumped through. Allora tightened her muscles, trying to stay rigid as she shot through the streaking gray portal. When she landed on two feet, she reveled in the successful port. A grandiose cave, sparkling knickknacks, and the sounds of multiple waterfalls gave away their location. Sas had ported them to his cave, and he arrived only seconds after they did.

After landing next to the portal, Sas pulled hadrons from the ground and stuck his arm into the portal. Suddenly, the ground stopped swirling and froze. As he pulled his arms from the cement-like ground, a green light escaped the closing portal.

"What was that all about?" Allora asked.

"Just locking the door," he said, smiling. "It will inhibit anyone from tracing the exit point."

"We learn something new every day," Dax said, shaking his head.

Sas grinned. "We guardians be having abilities that other Sonorans are not privy to," he said proudly. Sas moved around a large pile of pots and pans and took a drink from the natural underground spring.

Following his lead, the other four gulped the fresh liquid as if they'd been lost in the Sahara Desert for weeks. The fight with the wraith had drained most of their energy.

"We need to get you four home and tell Milly what happened tonight," Sas said.

Allora nearly choked on a mouthful of water. She knew she'd be placed under house arrest if her overprotective mother found out about the wraith, and a life of imprisonment would be far worse than any attack from a Sonoran assassin. "Wait!" Allora grabbed Sas's arm before he was able to create a portal to her house. "You can't! My mother will never let me out of the house again."

"Allora, Milly must know. We cannot keep this a secret."

Allora was desperate and decided a guilt trip might work. "Sas, we were in that situation because you told us to leave that house." While slightly underhanded, she intended to make sure Milly never found out about their evening. "Do you really want my mother to know that you were the one who led us toward the wraith?"

"That's not fair, Allora," Sas said with eyebrows furrowed. She kept a thoughtful stare, glaring mercilessly. Writhing uncomfortably, Sas gave in. "Fine, but if that wraith comes back, I'm afraid I'll be forced to spill the peas."

Dax rolled his eyes. "Beans!"

"Sorry. I don't have any, but there might be a deer leg around if you're hungry," Sas said.

"Never mind," Dax said, shaking his head and laughing.

Allora smiled overtly, wrapping her arms around the reluctant creature.

They all called their parents to see if they could stay with Sas for the night. Sas showed them a large pile of sleeping bags, which made for decent beds, and they all settled in and talked quietly about the fight that almost cost them their lives. After a short while, they fell asleep, exhausted from the tumultuous Halloween they would never forget.

An excruciating headache woke Allora in the middle of the night, a sharp pain that felt like a pickax to her brain. Five minutes of throbbing pushed Allora to escape the confines of her sleeping bag in search of relief. Her friends snored softly as she walked through the maze of debris to the dark blue lake at the bottom of the path. In its depths, she could see small, bluish lights swimming through the water. Every few seconds, the luminescent creatures would brighten, creating a sparkling orchestra of blue light.

"Fascinating, aren't they?"

Allora jumped backward and slid on her rear, searching the dark cavern for the source of the voice. Two beady eyes were perched on a ledge behind a large pillar of rock. The eyes darted around the corner and finally became familiar.

"Sorry. I didn't mean to scare you," Sas said, noticing Allora's frightened glare.

"You keep doing that!" Allora said, clutching her head. She didn't mean to be so irritable with the friendly beast, but her headache was becoming worse.

"They're called Botaqua bugs. They clean the water," Sas said, jumping down from ledge to the water's edge. "Great natural filtration system."

Allora ran her fingers across the top of the water, looking intently at the blue glowing bugs.

"What's wrong?" Sas asked, helping Allora to her feet.

"I've just got this horrible headache, and I don't know why."

Sas left the pool and disappeared behind a pile of black inner tubes. He came back a minute later and handed her two white pills.

"What's this? Magic fairy pills or something crazy like that?" she asked, hoping for something powerful.

"Nope, just aspirin," Sas said, moving toward the edge of the glistening pool.

Allora shrugged, took a drink from the waterfall, and swallowed the pills, happy to have something for the pain.

"Sometimes when you expel a large amount of hadrons like you did tonight, it depletes your body of water and energy, resulting in a throbbing head. It's a common side effect," Sas explained.

"Yeah, well, I'm pretty sure headaches are also a side effect of a fifty-foot tree landing on me."

"Right. That could've had something to do with it," Sas said.

They both laughed.

The pool twinkled in the dark cave as they stared at the serene water. A flutter of bats sounded in the dark crevices of the cavern.

As they sat there, listening to nature, Allora's mind wandered back to Mr. Swan's request. She assumed it would take some maneuvering to get the necessary information from Sas. "What was your father like?"

The question caught Sas off guard, and he turned to look at her in surprise. "Why would you ask about my father?" he asked, his tone rigid and apprehensive.

Allora realized she had to choose her next words carefully. She didn't want Sas to become defensive and shut her out entirely, for that would destroy any chance of finding out the location of the last piece of parchment. "I never had a father," she said.

Sas's body language became less tense. "Oh. Right."

"I just figured it was something we could talk about."

"I'm sorry," he said. "I just get a little suspicious of those who ask about my father."

The slight verbal maneuver had worked. Allora felt a little guilty for manipulating her hairy friend, but her mission's success was imperative.

"He was also named Sas. I took his name out of respect, an honor to his legacy. He was an amazing guardian—taller, bigger, and far more skilled than I could ever be. He served as the leader of the Guardian Council during a very tumultuous time. When he died..." Sas teared up, staring at his father's sword that he mounted on the cavern wall. "When he died, it was a great loss for us all, especially for me."

"How did he die?" Allora asked.

Sas lowered his gaze, searching Allora's eyes for malicious intentions, but he could find none. He stared back at the blinking blue lights in the water, which was slightly rolling in the wake of the cascading waterfall at the back of the pool. "As I think I mentioned vaguely before, my father was searching for something," he began. "It was… something of great importance. When he left, he told me he'd found what he was looking for but that it wasn't a safe time to go after it. I never quite understood what he was talking about, and I never got a chance to ask him."

"What happened the day he died?"

"He… I…" He paused and choked on his words. "Allora, I cannot talk to you about this. It's very dangerous. Whatever my father was searching for, it was so important that someone killed him for it."

Allora paced around, racking her brain, grasping for some other way to get the necessary information. "Sas, I think I know what your father was searching for," Allora admitted.

Sas perked up and faced the small human. "You do?"

"That parchment you gave me. The one that my uncle had. There is one last piece, and I believe that your father found it."

"So… this little talk really wasn't about your father, was it?" Sas asked.

Allora put her head down. Dishonesty wasn't part of her nature, and she was overcome with guilt for misleading a friend.

"Allora," Sas said, pausing for a few seconds. "My father was betrayed by someone within the guardian organization. He was ambushed and killed by Salazar's assassins in his quest to find the Eye of the Titans. I just don't want that to happen to you as well."

"I have to find it Sas. It's going to be much easier if you help me."

After a few awkward silent minutes, Allora turned around to go.

Sas said over his broad, hairy shoulder, "Mount St. Helens."

Allora stopped in her tracks and walked back to the water's edge.

"Before he left, he told me the secret lies in the lava tubes."

Allora smiled and hugged her hairy friend. "Thank you."

Fourteen

CAVE

"Mom!" Allora yelled down the hall. "Where is my bow?" Allora rummaged through a pile of clothes in the corner of her room.

"I put it in the garage, honey," Milly yelled back.

"Okay, thanks." Allora made her way out to the garage and began sifting through the boxes lining the wall, and finding her bow in the corner.

"You're not bringing your bow on the field trip are you?" Milly asked, peering around the door frame of the garage. "Not exactly a very discreet accessory."

"No, mom. I just wanted to make sure that Sas had brought it back."

"You're going to stay with Aunt May while you're in the Ape Caves, right?"

"Yes mother," Allora said, rolling her eyes. "You've grilled me a hundred times already."

"I just don't see the necessity in this trip. Can't you kids get a geology lesson while at school?"

"And miss out on the real thing? No way!"

Milly wandered back to the kitchen, leaving Allora to rummage some more in the boxes of old stuff. One of them in particular caught her eye. It had her Uncle Ben's name written on it in big block letters. The box hung out over the edge of the top shelf in the corner, as if it was just asking to be rediscovered.

She stared at the box, touching it, and then pulling her hand away. Milly never talked about Ben and had always changed the subject whenever Allora inquired; the same happened whenever the girl asked about her father.

With her curiosity piqued beyond her ability to avoid the temptation, Allora gave in and pulled the box down from the top shelf. Right before she pulled back the lid, someone yelled her name from inside.

"Allora, Katie's here."

She stopped, staring at the dusty lid for a minute. "I'll look at you later," she said to the box, then shoved it into a discreet corner of the garage.

After jumping into Katie's car, Allora surveyed her friend's outfit. She wore a puffy white coat, tight white jeans, and a pink scarf wrapped elegantly around her neck. "You're really dressed for the occasion, huh?" Allora teased, shaking her head at the ensemble that looked more appropriate for a winter fashion show than a journey to the center of the Earth.

"Who says I can't look good while I go spelunking?" Katie remarked, while driving toward the main road toward school.

"Spelunking?" Allora asked with wide eyes. "I'm shocked you actually know what that word means."

"I know, right?" Katie said, rolling her eyes. "Maureen's been forcing me to study S.A.T. flash cards. Ugh, boring!"

They parked, and walked toward the front entrance. A line of yellow school buses lined the front parking area, ready to ferry the junior class students on the impromptu field trip to the Ape Caves, just south of Mt. St. Helens in the state of Washington. Mr. Swan had arranged the trip after speaking with Allora regarding her conversation with Sas.

Two hours after leaving the school parking lot, they arrived at the national park.

"Make sure you don't forget your jackets," Mrs. Ferris instructed as the large group of students filed off the bus. "It will be quite chilly down there."

The Ape Caves were located just south of Mount St. Helens. Winter had brought with it a sharp cold front, and a thin sheet of white covered the path as the parade of students made their way to the entrance of the caves.

Descending into the dark cavern. As they passed the stalactites hanging down from the cavern roof, Allora searched the area for anything that seemed out of place. "I don't even know what we're looking for," she muttered.

"Where's Mr. Swan?" Katie asked. "I was sure he'd chaperone this little trip."

"Mrs. Ferris said they think he's being followed," Allora whispered. "He thought it would be safer if he didn't go."

Katie locked arms with her, and the two moved together down the narrow path.

"What we have here is quartz," the tour guide began. "This is created when rock, heat, and pressure mix to form small crystals. These lava tubes once had immense heat and pressure."

Katie and Allora stood in the back of the group, snickering at the park ranger's uniform: large hiking boots, knee-high socks tucked into his pants, a dark green fanny pack strapped around his waist, a tight green national forest jacket, thick, horn-rimmed, black glasses, and a highly starched flat ranger's hat that was too tall for his head.

"Now *he's* dressed for the occasion," Allora joked. "You gotta get a fanny pack like that."

"Right," Katie said.

"A Boy Scout troop discovered the Ape Caves, and those boys named it after a group of foresters, The St. Helens Apes. Many believe it was named for the infamous man-ape, also known as Bigfoot or Sasquatch, who is said to have roamed these parts."

"Has anyone ever seen such a creature down here?" Allora asked.

All four became attentive, moving closer to the front.

"Well, one lady claimed she did," the guide said, "but I was told she was a little crazy, so I'm sure she was just seeing things. Now, please follow me, and we'll continue the tour."

"Wait!" Allora yelled at the ranger, who was already moving down the path.

When the yell reverberated against the cavern walls, the ranger stopped. "Yes?"

"I wanna know what she said."

The ranger sighed and walked back up the short incline, laboring with each step as if utterly bothered by the reversal of direction. He stopped short of where the girls stood, pointed aggressively down a narrow cavern, bent down and pushed his horn-rimmed glasses back against his face.

They looked at the black opening and saw a large rope draped across it, along with a "Keep Out" sign.

"Right there missy."

Allora and Katie leaned back to avoid inhaling any more of the aftermath of the tuna fish sandwich the ranger had obviously eaten for lunch. They half-smiled, grossed out by the weird, awkward gestures of the ranger.

The tall, thin man snapped around, as if he were in boot camp, and went back to following the cavern path. "All right, people, let's move along," he barked.

Allora, Katie, and Mrs. Ferris remained behind, quietly moving out of sight against a rock outcrop.

"We've got to move fast, girls," the teacher whispered. "Like he said, there's another tour coming along behind us."

Just then, Tanner and Dax showed up, running, and came to a hurried stop.

"Sorry we're late," Tanner said between gasps after his fast-paced sprint through the underground labyrinth.

"Where were you guys?" Katie asked.

"Our bus got held up because of a car accident," Dax said, looking agitated. "The bus driver assumed the car had hit an animal, but when we passed by, it looked like a crumpled heap of metal. No animal could have caused that much damage."

A bat screeched as it fluttered only inches above the group. A squeal followed, but it had come from the blonde girl all wrapped in pink and white.

"I hate bats!" Katie said, grabbing Allora's arm.

"All right," Mrs. Ferris said, ignoring the girl, "we need to split up."

"We'll go that way," Allora said, pointing to the restricted area.

After the others left to search other openings, Allora and Katie crawled under the rope and ventured into the dimly lit, off-limits cave. Luckily, Allora had remembered to bring a flashlight. The farther they moved, the colder it became. A slight sting formed at the tips of their fingers, and the frigid air numbed their noses. Pretty soon, only the small beam of the flashlight was visible. The only sounds were the occasional drip of water and the deep, smoky breaths from the two frozen girls. As they moved deeper into the cave, the walls began to narrow. Creepy shadows danced along the rock, caused by the flashlight beam casting over the sharp stalactites.

Allora and Katie squished closer together, scanning the area like skittish cats. A quiet scurrying echoed in the dark. Allora frantically swung the light around, feeling her heart beat twice as fast. The beam of light projected a large shadow of a spider, seen on the wall as over ten feet high. Katie screamed, but when their narrowed eyes finally grew accustomed to the dark, they saw a tiny arachnid spider dangling from the ceiling, no bigger than a pencil eraser.

Embarrassed, Katie walked ahead defiantly. "I could have taken that spider!"

Allora squinted in the darkness. Above Katie, something moved against the cavern ceiling.

"They are such awful little creatures," Katie said, shaking with disgust. Above her, a long, thin leg clasped a stalactite, tightly wrapping itself around it. "Their webs are the worst. Ew!"

Slowly, Allora moved the light up, illuminating a grotesque figure. The creature had what looked like three heads joined at the ears, a single cyclops eye in each. Its arms looked like razor-sharp butcher knives, with fingerlike tentacles. The creature's body was thin, covered in short-fuzzy hair, and equipped with more than ten long legs, allowing it to move along the roof of the cave with frightening quickness.

The monster crawled slowly, hanging right above Katie's head. Allora was paralyzed with fear. All she could do was stand there with her mouth open, frozen with fright.

"Not funny, Allora," Katie said. "I'm not turning around, so stop trying to scare me." Katie defiantly stood with her hands crossed on her chest. "This isn't the time or the place for practical jokes, so you might as well—"

Just then, the creature reached out with its butcher claw, and Allora planted her foot and sprang forward with a jerk, a forceful lunge that knocked Katie off her feet. The creature swung its cleaver-like arm downward, missing the feet of the flying teens.

After she rolled to a stop, Katie got to her feet in confusion. "What the hell are you doing?" she asked, shaking the dirt and dust from her white coat. "Do you realize how expensive this thing is?"

Allora crawled on all fours, grabbed the flashlight, and projected it on their attacker. The light shined on the creature as it pulled its arm from the ground.

"Oh... *that*," Katie said.

The creature let out a terrifying screech, arching its back. Allora grabbed Katie's arm and pulled the shocked girl down the only escape. Sprinting through the dark cave, the two girls randomly chose their path. The flashlight bobbed up and down with every step, only illuminating a few feet ahead. Unable to turn around, they heard the creature scurrying quickly along the ceiling and walls behind them.

"What do we do, what do we do, WHAT DO WE DO?" Katie said, frantically waiving her arms.

"How am I supposed to know?" Allora yelled back.

A new smell wafted into their nostrils as they moved deeper into the cave, the aroma increasing in intensity with every step.

Katie glanced over her shoulder just in time to see an arm swinging at them. "Duck!" she said, pushing Allora forward.

The momentum of the creature's own attack knocked it off balance. It slipped from the wall, crashed into the other side, and sent fragments of rock everywhere. It writhed around, giving the girls enough time to get to their feet.

"Damn it! Where'd that flashlight go?" Allora exclaimed.

The creature turned over, shaking off the rocks that pinned it.

Katie grabbed her friend. "Forget the flashlight. There's no time!" She then pulled Allora into the blackness.

Unable to see, their progress was slow as they fished around with their hands to prevent themselves from running into rocks, cliffs, or jagged edges.

"I can't see a thing. We needed that flashlight!"

"Well, excuse me," Katie responded. "Feel free to go back and get it if you wanna be an appetizer for Super-Sized Spidey!"

The path turned abruptly and opened into a larger chamber, illuminated by a small crack in the closed off wall on the other side.

"Now what?" Allora said.

Katie frantically shuffled along the wall, feeling for any kind of hole or crack they could escape through. Unable to find anything, they searched frenetically around the darkness, unsure of their next move. The sound of falling rock and growling echoed in the chamber.

Katie snapped her fingers. "Hadron burst."

Allora calmed herself, breathed deeply, and pulled hadrons from the cave interior. A slow progression of energy surged within her body and focused into her hands. Two purple balls grew and surged with immense power.

The purple glow revealed the creature in an eerie hue as it entered the chamber. It snarled and growled when it saw the glowing girl. Allora pulled her hands to one side, combining the hadron energy. She controlled the swirling weapon, holding her focus intently, making sure maintain the magic until the precise moment. The creature made its move, scurrying along the ceiling.

"Get ready to jump out of the way!" Allora said as she shot her hands skyward.

In anticipation of its victim's move, the creature blocked the hadron burst with its butcher knife appendage. The force from the attack knocked it from the ceiling, sending it crashing to the ground with a rumble. Katie and Allora jumped in different directions as the creature slid along the dirt floor until it hit the wall at the end of the chamber.

An explosion of rock filled the chamber with dust.

Katie pulled her head up and noticed a reddish-orange light peeking through the cloud of particles. It was coming from a crack in the wall, further illuminating the dusty chamber. "You think it's a way out?"

"I don't know, but it's the only chance we've got," Allora replied. The creature was regaining its footing, blocking their escape.

"How do we get over there?"

Allora only had a moment to figure it out, but a childhood memory came in handy. "Do you remember playing dodgeball in the gym?" Allora asked, shaking her hands and dancing in place with a panicked look on her face.

"You're kidding me!" Katie exclaimed as it dawned on her what Allora was suggesting. "*That's* your plan?"

"Got a better idea?" Allora asked with a shrug.

"So I guess I'm the bait, huh?" Katie asked apprehensively.

"Get ready."

The hideous creature spat and growled as it crept closer.

Just as it prepared to lunge, Katie sprang forward, and Allora rolled to her right. Caught unaware, the creature swung at its first target, but Katie rolled left, avoiding the swinging arm. The beast adjusted, moving to its right to counter the evasion. Meanwhile, Allora was able to get a clear shot at the glowing crack, and her hadron burst destroyed the remaining wall. A piercing light blanketed the cave chamber, blinding the creature and causing it to wince and squirm. Furious, the creature swung violently, unable to see.

"Watch out!" Allora screamed as a cleaver-limb crashed into the wall.

Katie jumped out of the way of the falling rock, The violent swinging caused the chamber to become unstable. They sprinted to the opening in the cavern wall as the entire chamber collapsed behind them. A deafening screech echoed into the narrow, dusty rock cavity. The sound subsided and was replaced by a low crackling rumble. They fanned the dust and sighed in relief as the light grew brighter.

"Do you feel warm?" Katie asked, her adrenaline pumping so much that she hadn't noticed the extreme temperature change right away.

"Very warm," Allora replied.

They slowly turned and gasped loudly.

"I-I don't think that was the exit," Katie said.

In front of them flowed a sea of lava, moving like a river within a grandiose lava tube. The red-orange landscape was eerily beautiful, like something on Mars. Along the walls, cascading lava escaped out of holes, erupting in sparks as it hit the flowing river below. The unrelenting heat hit their faces, causing them to sweat. Every few seconds, bubbles of lava would burst, sending a wave of scalding air throughout the cavern.

"I'm almost missing the cold, spider-filled cave," Katie said, sweating profusely, peeling off her filthy, ruined jacket and scarf, unable to stand the excruciating heat.

A reflection from the lava caught Allora's eye, and she focused on a small platform protruding from the center of the river of fire. On top of the platform sat a shiny object. Squinting, she made out a small black orb. "We found it!" Allora said.

"How are you even able to handle this heat?" Katie asked as she hung back in the rock cavity.

Allora moved toward the lava river, feeling the warm energy filling her body's cells. "It might have something to do with my elemental powers."

"Where is it?"

"In the middle of the lava." Allora pointed at the platform. She scanned the area for some way to access it, but she saw no safe route. The platform was about fifty feet away, on the other side of a lake of molten lava.

"Now what?" Katie said, squinting her eyes with a hand in front to block the extreme heat.

Allora noticed large boulders sporadically flowing along, knocking into each other as they floated on top of the lava. "Stepping stones," she muttered to herself.

Katie watched Allora's stare, moving back and forth. "No way," Katie said, shaking her head. Allora smiled. "No, Allora. Don't you even think about it."

Ignoring her friend, Allora jogged up the lava river, looking for the best place to cross, where the rocks were larger and more plentiful.

"You're crazy if you think you're gonna play hopscotch across that boiling river," Katie said.

Still ignoring her, Allora found the perfect path and stopped to calculate the best route that would get her safely to the platform. Every step had to be perfect, or she'd be dragged down the river.

"You don't even know if those rocks will hold you!" Katie continued to fight against it, but her friend's stubbornness was relentless.

"And you don't know they won't," Allora said. She then backed up, got a running start, and jumped forward when she reached the edge. The first rock swayed, pushed through the lava by the force of her impact. It bobbed in the lava but remained safely above the scorching surface.

Katie moved to the edge, but the heat was so intense that she was knocked back. "It's so hot." she asked, following her friend as she floated down the river of lava. "I can't even get close. It burns my skin!"

Allora braced herself and leapt to another rock. "Don't worry, I got this," she said, preparing for her next jump. With every jump, she got closer to the middle, and the platform loomed in her sight. Allora leapt to the next rock, but she slipped on the edge and fell forward.

Katie screamed and cupped her mouth with wide eyes.

Allora quickly grabbed a pointed edge and prevented herself from falling into the boiling red lake. Her hair, however, flipped down close enough to catch on fire. She pulled herself up in a hurry and madly beat the flames.

"You okay?"

Allora didn't have any time to respond. The platform was only a few feet ahead, and she knew if she didn't move quickly, her chance of reaching it would be gone. She hopped nimbly to the next rock. After dancing from one rock to the next, she made a final, desperate leap and clutched the edge of the platform for dear life.

Katie winced, watching as Allora swung her legs, trying to drag her body onto the granite surface.

With her shoes melting beneath her, Allora heaved herself up onto the platform surface. She collapsed, breathing heavily from the physical exertion. She gave Katie a thumbs-up, then crawled up a ramp to the top of the platform. There, in a bowl-shaped granite podium, Allora looked down upon a shiny obsidian orb. It seemed to swirl with motion, but it was made of seemingly solid material.

"Is this it?" Allora asked.

"Well? What's taking so long?" Katie yelled, wondering why Allora hadn't grabbed the thing and returned already. The environment made her anxious, and she was already searching for an exit, eager to get out of there.

"It's too easy," Allora answered.

"Easy!?" Katie exclaimed, exploring the walls of the cavern. "None of this has been easy."

Something was wrong, and Allora knew it. *Why would Sas's father leave the artifact out in the open? And isn't the last piece supposed to be a piece of parchment?*

"Let's go!" Katie yelled, becoming more agitated.

Allora picked up the orb between her thumb and forefinger. Fascinated by the small object, she stared at its mesmerizing surface. The interior swirled with silver-black liquid, yet the exterior was solid obsidian, reflecting the orange glow of the lava. Suddenly, the platform jerked, and Allora fell sideways down the marble. The orb slipped from her grip and plummeted toward the river of lava. She stretched out, dived down the platform ramp, and caught it just in time, grabbing it from the granite rim before it was incinerated.

When the podium descended and the whole chamber shuddered violently, Katie screamed, "Move it!"

Allora leapt to her feet as the walls burst open and a rush of water exploded into the chamber. She placed the orb in a zippered pocket for safekeeping, leapt to a rock, and proceeded to dance across the large rocks, moving fast. The water crashed into the boiling orange liquid, creating a terrifying *hiss* and released hot steam. The cloud enveloped the area, pushing hot air toward the girls. Bobbing on each jump, Allora picked up her speed. An eruption of magma, steam, and rock was building.

Meanwhile, Katie had found a small hole that seemed to extend back into the Ape Caves. "Hurry up!" she screamed.

Erupting pockets of magma exploded toward the ceiling as Allora reached the other side of the chamber. She sprinted to the cave opening and dashed through with Katie right beside her. Behind them, the lava burst over the bank and began flowing into the opening. They turned their heads to see the bright, ominous glow of the pursuing magma. It illuminated their path, but it was gaining fast.

"Look!" Katie yelled, pointing ahead. "Dead end—maybe literally!"

Allora squinted and saw the orange glow shining on a wall, but what caught her eye was the dark contrasting floor only a hundred feet away. Her eyes went wide, but she had only a moment to react. She pulled back her arms, absorbing a purple ball of hadrons within, then shot it forward, bursting the wall and creating a hole.

"Aaaaaaaahhhhhh!" the girls screamed in unison as the leapt over the deep crevice and into the hole Allora had made.

The lava flowed into the depths below, unable to reach the hole on the other side. The girls slid along the smooth cave rock, crashing through a thin shale wall. When the crumpled pile of arms and legs detangled itself, they found themselves sitting in a cloud of dust, breathing heavily. Covered from head to toe in dirt, the girls looked like strange cave creatures. Their clothes were blackened with ash, and their hair was matted, muddy, disheveled, and scorched.

Once the dust settled, a group of onlookers stood with their mouths wide, perplexed by the odd entrance.

Katie and Allora awkwardly smiled at their classmates. Tanner, Dax, and Mrs. Ferris ran down the trail after hearing the commotion and were relieved to see their friends alive.

Allora smiled back at them until she saw a familiar face wedging itself through the crowd of students. "Oh, hi, Aunt May," Allora said, having forgotten her aunt had come along as a chaperone.

"You're in big trouble, young lady."

Fifteen

Conferences

"And in breaking news, Mount St. Helens has come back to life. At 11:38 a.m. this morning, the quiet volcano spewed ash and lava from the interior of the crater. As we can see from a viewer submission, lava escaped the round dome in the middle of the crater. Ash and debris exploded into the atmosphere and is said to be traveling toward the Portland metropolitan area. The last eruption of Mount St. Helens was in 1980. That event was far more extreme than we saw today, but this new eruption comes as a complete surprise."

Milly walked in front of the television screen with her hands on her hips, staring at her daughter with a bewildered expression on her face. "Well, Allora? What the hell happened?"

Allora rubbed her knees while seated on the couch. "Nothing."

"Nothing? The reactivation of a relatively dormant volcano isn't nothing!" Milly said, pointing back to the television.

"With us today is Dr. Alexander Von Derau, of the United States Geological Survey. Doctor, what could have caused this unexpected eruption?"

"To be honest, we're not sure. There was only a slight earthquake prior to it, and there were no signs indicating the sequence of events that generally leads up to such an eruption. In addition to that, Mount St. Helens isn't known for lava eruptions. Like the 1980 eruption, the pressure builds and explodes with mostly ash, but this was different. To be honest, my colleagues and I are completely baffled by this. Something extraordinary happened here today, though, and we will get to the bottom of it."

Milly turned off the television. "I wanna know right now what you and Katie were doing in that cave."

Allora hesitated, knowing her mother would be furious, but she had to give her an answer. "We were searching for a piece of a map."

"A map? What kind of map?" Milly asked, sounding skeptical

"A map that would lead us to The Eye of the Tita—"

"Stop!" Milly yelled to prevent Allora from saying the words.

Aunt May put her head down in silent anticipation of her sister's fury. Milly paced from the front door to bookcase, trying to control her emotions.

"Breath Milly," Aunt May said, motioning her hands and head upward. "You don't want to cause another outburst like before."

After a few deep breaths to calm her rage, Milly addressed her daughter. "How did you find out about The Eye?"

"Mr. Swan said—"

"I knew it!" Milly said, pointing toward Aunt May sharply. "He's never gonna stop this ridiculous quest, no matter how many people get killed in the process! First Ben and now my daughter. How many sacrifices is he willing to make?"

"What does that mean?" Allora asked.

"Your Uncle Ben was killed by a shifter because he and Swan set off a trigger, like the one you found today. When they did it, it sent an extremely strong energy signature, informing our enemies of our location," Milly said, becoming angrier. "They compromised our community then, and you've compromised it now."

Guilt crept up Allora's spine as she realized she'd once again, albeit inadvertently, put her friends and family in danger. An inner argument arose though. Finally, she blurted out, "That's not fair!"

"This isn't a game, Allora. You could have been killed."

"At least I'm doing something," she snapped back. "Maybe if you'd tell me what we're really up against—"

"Trust me, you don't want to know what we're really up against. You have no idea how evil and deadly it is. Don't you see that I'm just trying to protect you?" Milly fired back.

"Protect me?" Allora said. "How? By sitting here and doing nothing? You're supposed to be this brave, legendary leader, yet I haven't seen you do anything." Tears burst from Allora's eyes. The scared girl inside couldn't take it anymore. "I may be young, and I don't understand everything that went on before I was born, but I'm not going to sit around and hide." Tears flowed freely down her cheeks. "I'm scared, Mom. I'm really, really scared, but that isn't going to stop me from fighting." Allora took a deep breath before saying words that she knew would be like a spear to her mother's heart. "At least Uncle Ben stood for something. At least *he* was willing to do something to protect the people he loved."

The comment hit Milly to her core. A lone tear broke from its nearly impenetrable emotional shell and crashed like a dumbbell to the hardwood floor. The weight of guilt upon her shoulders grew unbearable.

* * *

Squeezing into the undersized desk chair, Milly waited patiently at the back of the room. She glanced around at the numerous maps hanging on the walls. When she turned around, she saw a faint discoloration in a small area in the corner, something only a trained eye could decipher. Milly wondered what was in the safe.

The room slowly filled with unassuming parents, waiting for their kids' teacher to arrive. The small talk dissipated when Mr. Swan entered the classroom.

"Welcome, everyone," Mr. Swan began, moving behind his desk to ruffle through some handouts he'd prepared for the presentation. "I'm glad you all made it. For those who don't know, I'm Mr. Swan, your children's history teacher. Before we begin, does anyone have any questions?"

"I've got one," Milly said, raising her hand.

"All right, Milly, go ahead," Mr. Swan answered, trying to sound surprised.

"What, exactly, are you teaching our children?"

Mr. Swan pulled his head back, shocked by the simple, ordinary, almost rude question. "Well, as I said, I teach history. Currently, we're reading Homer's great masterpiece, *The Iliad*, learning a lot about Greek culture."

"Great!" one of the parents interjected. "I loved that story when I was in school."

"So you're teaching our children about Greek mythology?"

Mr. Swan hesitated, wondering what Milly was getting at. He knew how manipulative she could be. Her cunning was legendary, and he could see himself stepping into a trap, but he couldn't just avoid her in front of all the other parents. "Yes, some class discussions focus on Greek mythology, as it does have a historical element."

"Historical element? Mr. Swan, you know as well as I do that there is more to mythology than that. Are you suggesting you have a right to teach religious doctrine in a public school?"

Mr. Swan became tense as all eyes were on him, waiting for his response. "I believe Greek mythology has relevance to historical events," he said, trying to get at the real truth Milly was pushing for, "and it can explain certain outcomes that have implications to modern society."

"So does every other religion, but that doesn't make it right to feed our children these stories just to feed their curiosity and endanger their lives!"

Some of the other parents shuffled awkwardly in their seats. Others crossed their arms and glared at the teacher.

Pulling at his collar, Mr. Swan could feel his blue satin tie becoming tighter. His brow became sweaty as he contemplated an exit strategy. "May I speak with you outside?" Mr. Swan asked softly.

"Most definitely. I think you should." Milly grabbed her coat and marched into the hallway. The two squared off like two boxers in a ring. Mr. Swan shut the door on the curious group, many of whom were leaning over their desks to try and catch a glimpse through the narrow door window.

"What's the matter with you?" Mr. Swan whispered.

"Are you kidding me?" Milly said. "You sent the heir to the throne of Titanis after that stupid artifact. What is that matter with you?"

"Don't you realize how important that *stupid* artifact is?"

Milly shifted her weight in the quiet hallway and looked both ways to make sure no one was listening. "What I realize, Kurt, is that my little brother died looking for that piece of paper, and none of you even know if it exists or what it does."

"It exists," Mr. Swan assured her, "and when we find it, we'll finally have a fighting chance."

"You don't know that," Milly said. "It's too dangerous, too much of a risk, and I will not let someone else die because of it."

"You promised Ben that you would continue the search, Milly. Have you forgotten that?"

Milly's mind burst into a memory of her younger brother dying in the deep forest. A picture of the blackened wound that had killed him was permanently imprinted in her head.

Milly fluttered her eyelids, looking upward to stop the flood of tears that were threatening to break through the dam. "I loved Ben, but Allora's safety comes first. I think even her uncle would have agreed about that."

"And what about the safety of our people? Of our world? The unsuspecting people of this world? Pretty soon, *they* will be at our doorsteps, whether you like it or not."

"The Eye is a myth, a far-fetched idea and an unhealthy obsession that ultimately got my brother killed. That is not going to happen to Allora."

"She is meant for greatness, but you're holding her back."

"Only for her own good. She doesn't understand how dangerous our world is."

"That doesn't sound like the Milly I knew."

"You have no right to judge me for the choices that I've made to make sure that the heir is safe."

"And what about the others? You can't just pretend that a war is going on." Mr. Swan could tell his words struck a chord within the woman's hard exterior. "You took a vow to protect the innocent, remember?"

Milly pulled back like a cobra ready to strike. "Don't you dare lecture *me* on the Code! Not too long ago, your own allegiance was in question, *remember?*"

Mr. Swan bit his lip and stepped backward; she had stabbed at the one part of his life that pained him most.

"Don't try to give me a lesson on my responsibilities to the order. You are only here on my good graces. If you hadn't been my brother's best friend, I would have thrown you out long ago. One more mention of The Eye to my daughter, and I'll kill you myself. Is that clear?"

"Yes, commander," Mr. Swan said, stepping back in defeat. He swallowed hard, fighting back the urge to argue more.

Sixteen

SKI

Allora stared intently at the small black orb she'd pilfered from the cave, as she drove in the passenger seat of Katie's Jeep toward school. As she held it in her palm, the orb pulsated with a light, sparkling glow, as if it had a heartbeat all its own. It was cold, yet it projected small sparks from its interior. She was mesmerized by the crystal orb and couldn't take her eyes off the mysterious, magical object.

Because of the incident at the Ape Caves, Allora had been grounded, forbidden from seeing her friends at all during winter break, so even Katie's incessant rambling was a nice change from the boredom of her home.

"I got these awesome diamond earrings. They're so beautiful. I think I'm gonna save them for prom though. I'm getting a white dress and—"

"Sorry to interrupt your fascinating fashion report," Allora broke in, "but have you seen Mr. Swan lately?"

"Not since school let out," Katie replied, then went right back to her story.

When the girls, Dax, and Tanner arrived in their first-period history class, they noticed an unfamiliar face at the front of the room.

"Where's Mr. Swan?" Allora asked.

The old lady stopped writing her name on the board to address the four young students. "He's been assigned to a different classroom, honey."

Allora wasn't very keen on being called "honey," but she let it slide because of how old the woman was. "Why?" she asked.

"I don't know, darlin'," she said.

"Ugh!" Allora grunted, and stomped out of the room with her posse in tow. "What's with old people? I am not 'sweetie,' 'honey,' or 'darlin'. She's not my grandmother."

"Well, she looks old enough to be," Katie said. "Did you see her shoes? They must have been made a hundred years ago."

"Long break?" Tanner asked, feeling Allora's agitation.

Allora let out a sigh. She'd been cooped up in her house for so long. "Sorry. I guess I'm a little stressed out from being stuck at my house without any answers about this thing." She pulled the small crystal orb from her pocket. "I need to talk to Mr. Swan about it, because it's not parchment like the other two pieces."

"You did find it!" Dax exclaimed.

Katie rolled her eyes. "I told you we did. Why don't you ever believe me?"

"Well, sis, it's just that you also told me you fought off some giant bug and that Allora went lava-surfing."

"We did!" Katie yelled.

A few other students glanced over at the group, causing them to move in closer.

"We shouldn't be talking about this here," Tanner stated. "Remember, it's not safe. Let's meet in the outer realm after school."

Allora shoved the orb back in her pocket, and they all went their separate ways. Allora searched for Mr. Swan but couldn't locate his new classroom. She wondered whether her mother had something to do with his reassignment.

After the last class of the day, the four friends met in the parking lot. From there, they went to Allora's place, hiked up to the portal, and jumped through to the orchard.

"Why are you so obsessed with this Eye thing anyway?" Dax said. "It just seems to be causing more problems than solutions."

"Halloween proved that we are hopelessly outmatched," Allora said. "If this Eye is what Swan claims it to be, than it may give us an edge over whatever is out there."

"She's got a point," Tanner agreed. "If this artifact can help us fight off those stupid creatures, we have to find it."

"And what if one of us dies trying to find that thing?" Dax asked.

"What if one of us dies at the hands of that wraith?" Allora paused. "Or something even worse."

"But you don't really know anything about it," Dax argued, "and neither does Swan. For now, all you've got are a couple old pieces of paper with poems on them and some cosmic-looking golf ball that you stole from a volcano."

"That sounds like the plot to a really funny movie," Tanner suggested.

"Yeah, not that funny when you're outrunning an erupting lava tube," Katie said, sneering at the two boys.

"All I'm saying is that we are risking a lot for something that we have no information about," Dax added. "We are flying blind."

"My uncle believed in the power of this thing," Allora said. "That's good enough for me."

When they jumped back through the portal, they noticed the first snow of the winter season falling through the forest canopy. The meadow behind Allora's house was covered in a thin layer of white, reminding her of a more innocent, peaceful time.

"I realize this year has been stressful for all of us," Katie said, staring from the edge of the forest, "but I think it's time we have a little fun. If we don't let loose and act like normal kids once in a while, we're all gonna go crazy, and that won't do any good for the people of Earth or Sonora. You know what we need?"

Tanner smiled. "A ski trip!"

Allora imagined only one response from her mother. "Milly will never go for it, and you know it. She'll say it's far too dangerous."

"That's why we have to do it on a school day," Katie said, wearing a sinister smile, "when she thinks we're in class."

Grinning profusely, they silently agreed upon the idea. It had been a difficult, different year for the four teens, and since the attacks, their extracurricular activities had been limited to after-school sports, a Halloween party they'd had to sneak to, and nothing else.

"Katie's right," Allora admitted. "We definitely need this. I don't think anything will attack us on the downhill slalom. Besides, we won't tell anyone where we are, right?"

"Right," the other three said, nodding their heads in agreement.

The plan consisted of meeting at the local grocery store in the morning before school, and each would sneak his or her ski gear out of the house and into the car the night before. Since Allora's skis and poles were in the garage, she had to beg Bell to distract their mother, which proved to be difficult because her sister kept asking questions.

"Why?" Bell asked. "Why should I do this for you?"

"Because I said so," Allora said, pushing her little sister toward the living room, where Milly was reading a newspaper. "Just get Mom to go outside."

"Fine," Bell whispered, then reluctantly complied. "But you owe me big time!"

As soon as the coast was clear, Allora went to the garage to find her skis, boots, and poles. She had to make a second trip to carry her ski clothes. As Allora was exiting the garage, she heard her mother and sister coming back into the house. She waved her arms frantically. Bell began dancing in place, giving Allora enough time to disappear around the corner. She threw her supplies out her window, just as her mother was opening her bedroom door.

"Why is your sister acting so strange?" Milly asked.

Sitting back on her bed, Allora shook her head. "No idea," she said, raising one eyebrow.

Milly stood there for a minute, trying to figure out what her daughters were up to. When she couldn't come up with anything, she finally gave up and slowly closed the bedroom door.

Allora exhaled and collapsed into her pillows.

* * *

The next day, Allora bid her mother goodbye after breakfast, grabbed her stuff from the side of the house, and shoved it into Katie's car. They drove off toward the grocery store, and met the boys in the parking lot, as planned. After packing up the Bronco, they headed east.

A few miles up the road, they saw the majestic, white-capped mountain glimmering in the sunlight like an oil painting. It was a beautiful winter day, much better for skiing than for sitting in class.

It was only eight o'clock when they reached the parking lot of Timberline Lodge at the bottom of the mountain. The girls dressed in their ski clothes while the boys went to get passes for everyone. Once everyone was fully equipped, the four hopped onto the chairlift and took off up the mountain.

Allora took the time to close her eyes and relax. The clean, crisp mountain breeze blew through the trees, carrying the aroma of pine. The slopes were pristine white, sparkling in the brightness of the morning sun. The trees swayed as the mountain breeze danced down the canyon below them. The *swish* of passing skiers echoed in the canyon, along with the rumbling of the chairlift as it passed the stands that held it up. Allora was in her own personal heaven, a blissful state of peace, and the worries of the past year seemed to melt away. All she could think about was the feel of the snow beneath her skis. Thoughts of evil creatures were replaced by the anticipation of flying down the mountain with her friends.

When they arrived, they put the support bar up and hopped off the chair. Dax wobbled and caught the front edge of Tanner's board, sending both flying forward. The people behind them tried to ski around but couldn't avoid the collision, and they fell over, smacking into the boys.

The pileup caused the attendant to stop the chairlift. The girls stood a couple of feet away, cracking up with laughter as the boys tried to pull themselves up while still maintaining their pride. On that mountain, not even an embarrassing crash could have spoiled their mood, and Dax and Tanner just laughed along with the girls while they strapped in their back feet.

The first run felt amazing. In front of them, blue sky and rolling white hills lined the landscape. Etched in the valleys were rivers and lakes, glistening against the rays of light. Allora felt the fresh powder beneath her skis as she cruised, side to side, along the run. The mountain was surprisingly empty for such a beautiful day, so when they made it to the bottom of the run, they didn't have to wait in line to hop back on the chairlift.

The rest of the day was even more fun. They traveled around the mountain, making sure to ski on every run, even on the bunny hill. The end of the day was quickly approaching, but they wanted to take one more run.

Allora hadn't had a chance to ski through the trees, so about a quarter of the way down, she veered off the main path, skiing between two large pine trees and slicing through as if she were on a professional slalom course. Allora caught her pole on a branch, which swung her toward the trunk of a tree. She extended her right leg against the snow, turning her body to the left. She missed the tree, but her right ski clipped the trunk, sending her sideways into the powder. She screamed, which caused her friends to stop.

"Allora!" Tanner yelled, hopping up the mountain as fast as he could. He stopped, and starting unfastening his board until he heard Allora yell back.

"I'm fine," she said, pulling herself up and walking up the hill toward her skis. "I just fell."

The sun started its descent along the western skyline, and the air began to get much colder. The light was fading, especially among the trees.

Allora's boot was almost clipped back into her binding when she heard a rustling coming from the trees. Her heart jumped, and a sense of alertness burst from her stomach and into her throat. She quickly put pressure down on her heel, and the sound of the boot clicking securely in the ski caused the rustling to stop. Allora looked through the trees, but she couldn't see anything. She remained still, listening to the wind. Finally, out of the corner of her eye, she saw a large, furry creature peeking around a tree. "Sas?" Allora said in a loud whisper.

The furry creature peeked out from behind the tree to reveal that he was, indeed, Sas. He slowly stepped forward.

"What are you doing here? Someone might see you."

"I'm just checking up on you," he said, uncharacteristically serious.

Allora was puzzled. "How did you know where to find us? We didn't tell anyone where we were going."

Sas moved even closer. "Never mind that. We have an emergency, and I'll need you to give me the map," he said flatly.

Allora inched away, moving down the hill as Sas neared. "Why are you talking different?" She could tell something was wrong, and as he maneuvered through the trees, there was an odd energy about him. Allora pushed herself farther away from the oncoming creature, even though he looked like the friendly beast she knew.

The furry creature bellowed, "Give me the map!"

As he approached, Allora realized his eyes were strangely unfamiliar, and her inner alarms screamed at her to run. "You... you're not Sas!"

Allora quickly pushed her pole into the snow and launched herself to the left of a tree as the creature leapt forward with its arms outstretched. The creature hit the tree Allora had avoided, knocking snow down on its head from the foliage above.

Allora came screaming through the trees, trying to find Tanner and the others. "Go, Tanner!" she yelled. "Go!"

Tanner put his board forward and pushed off.

Seeing that he didn't have any momentum, Allora extended her pole. "Grab it!"

Tanner obeyed and grasped the pole. "What's going on?" he said as Allora launched him down the mountain.

Sas's doppelganger exploded out of the trees, hurling itself toward them. Allora sliced with her ski, changing her direction to the left. She veered back to the right as the oncoming creature leapt to her position. Tanner carved on his board, cutting across to distract the creature. He launched himself over a jump as the creature dived to grab him.

Allora zoomed past the chairlift attendant, who was trying to close up the lift for the night.

"Whoa! Slow down!" He yelled.

Tanner whizzed by at an equal speed, spraying the attendant with snow.

The attendant was about to yell again, but a large, hairy arm launched him into the air, only to land right in front of Dax and Katie, stunned.

"We gotta go... now!" Katie said, throwing her skis on the ground and clipping herself in. Dax took longer because he had a snowboard, so Katie left without him, slamming her poles into the snow to gain momentum.

"Wait! I'm almost in," he said, pulling the strap over his boot. "Hold on, Katie! Wait! Stop!"

Katie didn't listen and just pushed herself past the ski lift and down through the trees, in the direction the others had gone.

Allora was dodging the creature's every advance, and Tanner was doing the same, but they weren't sure how they were going to escape.

Tanner yelled over to Allora, "Can you shoot a hadron burst at it?"

"I don't think I can get a good shot off without falling down," Allora replied, barely missing a tree branch.

The snow beneath them became thicker, slowing their escape and allowing the pursuing creature to gain on them. They darted among the pines, making use of the only deterrent they had. Allora noticed a flattening surface at the bottom of the hill ahead, which opened into what looked like the bottom of a canyon.

Inches from Allora, the creature pushed off the powdery snow, flying forward. Tanner had to move fast. He brought his right foot upward, catching the snow on the edge of his board. Then he made a diagonal cut sideways.

The furry brown creature had Allora in its grasp when Tanner came soaring through the air, striking the creature on its side. It spun around in the air, crashed into the snow, and hit the base of a tree. Tanner tried to land on his board, but his balance was too lopsided, and he fell on his back and tumbled down the remaining incline. Allora also lost her balance and caught the sharp edge of her ski in the snow. The ski departed from her foot, and she followed Tanner as they both cascaded down the rest of the mountain in a flurry of white.

The creature stuck its foot in the snow, corrected the direction of the rest of its body, and continued the pursuit. Allora and Tanner made it to the bottom of the mountain and managed to land on the flat surface, but they began sliding toward the middle of the wide opening. They tried to move, but the surface was completely iced over.

"What do we do?" Allora yelled, slipping on what seemed to be a frozen river.

"You have to hit it with a burst!" Tanner insisted.

Allora tried to pull her hands up to focus, but she kept slipping.

"Now!" Tanner yelled, just as the creature planted its feet and jumped in the air.

Seventeen

Aftermath

The shadowy creature flew above the flat area, and the two waited for gravity to bring it down on top of them. Allora saw the panic in Tanner's eyes as a brown blur flew through the air and hit the enemy creature roughly in its side. The two furry masses hit the surface with a mighty force; the impact sent shockwaves through the ground, and water exploded upward. Both creatures were knocked into the forest on the other side of the river and disappeared into the dense trees.

The surface where Allora and Tanner lay broke apart like glass. Tanner instinctively grabbed Allora's hand and pulled her up, then swung her body to the edge of the ice. Allora glided along the surface, reaching back for him.

She screamed his name, but he fell out of view and into the cold river below. Allora ignored the screams coming from Katie, who was almost down the hill. Desperate to save Tanner, she hurried along the edge, looking for a stick or anything she could use to pull him out. She ran down the riverbank, sweeping the snow from the ice. Tanner had been pulled under the thick top layer of ice by the undercurrent, so she knew she had to act fast.

Allora pulled all of her emotions into a central location, and her body exploded in fire, which escaped from her hands. A huge stream of flames glided along the ice, melting it instantly. Tanner came into view, his body bobbing in the river. The fire burned out, but Tanner still moved down the rapids uncontrollably.

Allora couldn't move her body, and when her legs failed her, she collapsed into the snow.

Something swam through the water down in the canyon below. Tanner's body lifted out of the water and moved upstream.

Katie finally made it to Allora, who was getting back enough energy to lift herself up. Tanner was limp, but his body drifted on top of the water, and he finally came to rest on the bank, right in front of the two wide-eyed girls.

At that point, a creature pulled its head out of the water with the sunset to its back. The creature moved out of the water and out of the glare of the setting sun. Once the two girls were able to see, they looked upon the strange creature with amazement. It was a humanoid figure with the skin of a jellyfish, and its eyes were mesmerizing, bright crystal blue, with no iris. It stepped onto the snow bank and knelt down next to Tanner. "He isn't breathing," the jellyfish man said in a deep, calming voice. It then put its hand on Tanner's chest and closed its eyes. Its body began to glow blue, and blue veins covered it, pulsating and glowing in the dimming light of the sun. The blue veins began to snake their way toward the creature's heart, then into its hand with a jolt.

Tanner's body pulled upward, and he arched his back as if he'd just been shocked. A second later, he opened his eyes and pulled himself to a seated position, coughing up water.

Allora and Katie jumped on him, and his shivering body convulsed as they held him. Both girls ignored the creature standing in the water to their left and pulled off Tanner's soaked ski clothes. He was in his boxers when Dax came crashing through the snow above them.

"Hey!" Dax yelled, falling face-first into the snow bank. "Where is he? I'll kill him."

"Too little too late," Katie said, taking off her coat. "You missed it."

Dax pulled his head out of the snow to see a nearly nude Tanner in front of him and realized the girls were also pulling off their clothes. "Whoa, man. Am I interrupting something here? I can come back," Dax said in his usual joking manner.

"Shut up, you idiot, and help us warm him up," Katie yelled at her brother as she pulled her jacket over Tanner's arm. "He fell in the water, under the ice."

Hearing the seriousness in his sister's tone, Dax pulled of his boots and pants. "I don't think he'll fit in those, sis," Dax said, handing his ski pants to Katie.

Katie sneered at her brother and snatched them quickly.

Even after he was fully clothed in dry garment donations, Tanner couldn't stop trembling. "Th-thank y-y-you," he said, his teeth chattering.

Dax finally noticed the jellyfish man standing on the edge of the river. "Uh, what's with the creature from the Ice Lagoon over there?" he whispered, pointing at it with his thumb. "Who is he?"

Katie opened her mouth, but she couldn't get any words out before a brown, furry creature leapt over the river, right at the group. Everyone except Tanner, who was still shivering, jumped into the defensive stances Aunt May had so expertly trained them to use. Allora created a ball of purple of hadrons in her hand. She felt a cold yet soothing hand upon her wrist and looked over her shoulder at the jellyfish man.

"It's all right," the creature said in a soft but powerful voice. "I believe that's only your friend, Sas."

"How do you know for sure?" Allora asked.

"Trust me. I know."

Allora looked into the warlock's eyes and recognized the emotions of worry and fear, and she knew she was looking at Sas. Allora put down her hand, and the ball of hadrons disappeared, sending a shower of sparks down to the snow.

Sas moved with purpose, unlike Allora had ever seen before. "Is Tanner all right?" he asked, stepping onto the bank where they stood.

The creature stepped forward. "For now, but we must get him to a safe, warm location soon."

"Thank you, Baymar," Sas replied.

"Baymar?" Allora asked. "Are you the one that untied me from the flagpole at summer camp?"

The blue creature nodded.

"Can you create a short portal?" Sas asked. "I'm afraid I'm far too drained to summon one up."

Baymar thought for a brief moment. "Only one for the river's edge, the only spot my eye can conceive that is close enough to town."

"That will have to do then," Sas said. "We have to get out of here. That shifter is hurt, but he will definitely be back."

Baymar nodded, then swirled his hands, pulling up the water beneath his feet. All around them the water shot up, as if it were a marionette being pulled by a puppeteer. Baymar tucked in his hands, then thrust them out toward the bank of the river. The snow swirled around, as if in a blender, then pulled itself to the middle of the circle.

"Everyone through the portal now," Sas said.

They picked Tanner up and dragged him to the portal, then jumped in. After being pulled through the snow bank, they popped out and landed in the river. Tanner was now in agonizing pain from the reintroduction to the piercing cold water. Allora held him, but she slipped on the rocks. Dax caught both of them, and they all made it onto the riverbank, without Sas and Baymar, who hadn't come with them. Allora knew where they were, as it was the same location she went to whenever she was upset. They made their way up through the forest and back onto the familiar street.

The walk back to her house was long because they had to drag Tanner's weak, shivering body with them. Finally, they arrived at Allora's house and crashed through the front door in exhaustion.

"What the hell happened now?" Aunt May asked as they landed on the floor at her feet.

Too tired to speak, they sprawled on the carpet gasping for air. They were soaking wet, half-dressed in their ski clothes.

Milly sprinted down the hall, followed closely by Bell, and her eyes darted back and forth, contemplating the scene. "Tell me you were not up at that mountain," Milly said sternly, standing over her daughter with her hands on her hips.

Allora had more pressing issues to deal with. "No time, Mom. We were attacked. Tanner... river... hypothermic..." Allora stuttered between shivers and breaths.

Milly turned from a mother to a barking general within seconds. "Dax, take Tanner into Allora's room and strip him down. Allora, blankets. May, mirror glue. Bell, I need hot water."

Milly made a large fire while everyone did exactly as she had instructed. Dax was able to get Tanner under the sheets while his body convulsed. The girls put the blankets over him, and then went to the showers to warm themselves. Bell made tea, then went to Allora's room to spoon-feed the warm liquid to Tanner. Milly walked into the room minutes later, carrying a red bottle.

Tanner's skin was pale blue, and he was still shivering, even with six blankets over him. Milly grabbed the spoon from Bell and poured the contents of the red bottle into it. Red, yellow, and orange poured from the bottle, swirling around in a strange elliptical pattern. Milly fed Tanner from the spoon, and instantly Tanner's skin turned the colors of the liquid, then returned to its normal shade. He stopped shivering, turned his head, and fell asleep.

Bell's mouth dropped wide open in amazement as Milly displayed the bottle to her daughter.

"Fire juice. Your aunt made it years ago. It's pretty potent stuff," Milly said, getting up from the bed.

"No way! What is it made of?" Bell asked, completely consumed by curiosity.

"Mainly dragon saliva. You'd have to ask your aunt what the rest of the ingredients are," Milly replied.

"Dragon saliva!" Bell exclaimed, giddy with excitement. "We so need to get a pet dragon. You said that they're only the size of a big dog, right?"

"Sorry honey. Only chance of that would be on Sonora."

"So, when are we going?" Bell asked as Milly went to the kitchen to pour tea for everyone else.

Allora turned on the faucet, shivering as she sat down in the tub, too exhausted to stand. Beads of warm water hit her face, stinging her skin as she sat with her arms around her knees. Now, in the safety of her home, she could reflect on the past few hours. Her mind raced as she thought about the power that had come from within her. The amazing display of fire had been exhilarating, but she couldn't get over the powerlessness she felt afterward. The terror of watching Tanner's body floating down the river had almost been too much. Tears escaped from her eyes, but she couldn't distinguish them from the water streaming down her face.

With all the showers running at once, the hot water didn't last long. The girls and Dax exited at the same time and put on the clothes that Milly had laid out for them. Everyone met in the living room, dreading the explanation of their disobedience. The room was warm, thanks to the fireplace on the far side. They all sat together, staring into the fire silently.

A moment later, Milly brought them tea. She sat down with the rest of the group and gave them a stern look that told Allora she was really in trouble. Milly took a sip of her tea, placed it on the table next to her armchair, and said, "Now, who is going to tell me exactly what happened?"

Katie and Dax sat attentively, listening to Allora recount the events from hours earlier, shocked at the details of what had happened on the mountain. Milly was taking a sip of her tea when Allora mentioned the conversation at the riverbank. "Sas said a shifter attacked us."

Milly dropped her cup on the floor, shattering the porcelain mug. She stared at her sister, who glanced back with an equally fearful look on her face. "Then what happened?" Milly said, picking up the remnants of her teacup from the floor.

Allora continued the story, telling her about how Tanner had become submerged under the ice and what she had done to try to free him.

Milly remained silent while her daughter told her about the river of fire. When Allora was finished, Milly sat back in her armchair. "I don't think you know how lucky you are to be sitting here," she said. "If Sas hadn't been there…" Milly turned away at the thought of what could have happened.

Aunt May leaned in toward her niece. "What did the shifter ask you in the trees?"

"It asked me for the map," Allora said.

"How do they know about it?" May asked her sister.

"If they're asking questions about The Eye, they must know Allora is Sonoran. It also means they know we're looking for it." Milly paused for a minute, contemplating the potential consequences. "I don't like this," she said, "not one little bit."

"I don't either, but what can we do?" May asked.

"We can act. We need a hunting party."

The worried mother spent the rest of the night on the phone, informing the other parents and Sonorans in town about the day's events. They all agreed that it best to keep the children at the house.

Tanner was asleep in Allora's bed, so she set up sleeping arrangements in the living room. Exhausted, everyone went to bed with their thoughts.

Allora lay down on the couch and stared up at the ceiling. Although she was exhausted, sleep evaded her. Her mind raced through time, and one question crept in with every memory, *Why is this happening to me?*

Before that year, she'd practically begged for something new and exciting. Now, she could only hope for some sense of normalcy. Even the mundane tasks of her past would have been a welcomed reprieve from the life-threatening days she was living.

After a few hours, she finally drifted off to sleep. Her dreams took her to a wheat field. She walked forward. In the distance, a short, brown-haired man stood with his hands behind his back. Allora stepped through the wheat, gliding the straws through her hands as she walked. She could actually feel the texture of the wheat as it rolled with the wind. The man became clearly visible ahead. Allora walked along the top of a hill toward the man, who was standing on the edge of a cliff, where the ground dropped off to a large body of water. Stopping next to him, Allora gasped at the familiar face staring into the distance.

A peaceful smile hung above his chin as he turned to the young girl. "Hi, Allora," he said.

"Uncle Ben!" Allora responded, grasping him around the waist. Her embrace was tight, as if she never wanted to let him go. The reunion felt so real, and even the familiar smell of his aftershave was present when she buried her face against his chest. Flooded with emotion, Allora held on for dear life. He was the embodiment of a past filled with joyful memories, and when he died, her life had changed significantly.

"Beautiful, isn't it?" he asked, his calm voice flowing through the valley like the wind.

Still holding on to his waist, Allora turned and looked upon the beautiful scene reaching to the setting sun. The two stood for what seemed to be hours, watching the sun dip into the water.

"How are you here?" Allora asked.

Uncle Ben pulled his chin down his chest and stared lovingly at his niece. "I never left you," he said.

"I don't understand," she answered. "You died."

"I will always be with you. You must understand that you have all the answers you need. Trust yourself, Allora, and you will find the path you seek."

As he said those last, insightful words, his body faded away like fog, then disappeared into the wind.

Allora awoke from her dream and sat up. Bewildered, she remained stuck in one spot, frozen by thought. She finally got up and walked into her room, only to find Tanner standing in his boxers. The sight caused her to shuffle back and forth awkwardly.

Tanner smirked and almost laughed.

"Sorry, I, uh… I forgot you were in here," Allora said, grabbing the door-knob. She closed the door behind her and leaned against it. She couldn't help but smile at the thought of his perfectly toned six-pack, biceps, and long, muscular legs.

"What are you doing?" Bell asked, walking into the hallway.

Allora jumped as if she'd been caught doing something she shouldn't be. "Nothing!" she whispered harshly. She stepped into the bathroom and shut the door on her sister.

After breakfast, Allora's friends went home, and Bell scurried off to Aunt May's room. That left Allora alone with her mother, who was drinking her coffee and staring at her daughter.

"I know, I know. You're gonna yell at me for an hour about how irresponsible I've been, and now you're gonna ground me for a lifetime," Allora said, rolling her eyes.

Milly kept sipping her coffee and tapping her fingers on the table. "No, Allora, that isn't what I'm going to do. No matter what I do to protect you, eventually you are going to have to experience life and the consequence of your actions."

Allora had already created a rebuttal, but now she just sat there, confused by her mother's lack of emotion. Milly had conceded the fight before it even began.

Milly set her coffee mug on the kitchen table. "I think it's time you hear how your uncle really died," she said, her eyes gazing forward.

Allora remained silent.

"Ben and Swan learned about The Eye of the Titans from our mentor, and leader of the keepers, during the onset of the Rebel Wars, which led us to come here. They intended to use its power to change the course of the war, but the other side unfortunately had the same idea. They found the first piece in Shangri-La in Nepal."

"So, the place is real," Allora said.

"Yes, it's very much real. Shangri-La is the capital headquarters for the guardian organization on Earth," Milly said. "Sas claims someone in the guardian order betrayed Ben and gave away their location, which led them back here. The king sent a shifter, like the one you encountered yesterday. That shifter learned of our community and had intended to report back to the king. Uncle Ben caught up with it and prevented that from happening."

"By paying with his life," Allora said, thinking back to the night when she was ten years old and her hysterical mother told her about Ben's demise.

"Yes," Milly said, holding her daughter's hand. "And this family has never been the same. I just don't want you to make the same mistakes he made. You're almost an adult. Pretty soon, you have to start taking responsibility for your own life, and I won't be around ground you."

"So, does that mean I'm not grounded?" Allora asked as her mother left to do the dishes.

"Oh, no. You're still grounded."

Allora furrowed her brow and got up from the table. After grabbing her ski clothes, she went to the garage, and shoved them in a duffel bag. She tried pushing it against the wall, but since the zipper wasn't completely closed, a beanie fell out. As she picked it up, her eye caught sight of the box on the ground, the one containing her uncle's belongings.

She sat down on the garage floor and pulled the cardboard flaps open, then began to sift through old documents, sports memorabilia, and other possessions. She pulled out the old Oregon Ducks hat; Ben had worn it so much that the bill was perfectly molded to the shape of his head. He'd taught Allora that the best way to do that was to wear it in the shower, then bend it in a half circle until it was perfect.

She found her uncle's old coffee mug, the one that always used to sit on the kitchen table in the mornings. It was made of transparent, royal blue glass and had his name etched into it. Allora slowly turned the cup over in her hands while she thought back to their morning sports talks over breakfast.

She rummaged around in the box, pulling out object after object, until she finally reached the bottom. There was a small, worn, tattered book lying against the edge of the box. The binding was made of leather, and on the cover was a picture of what looked like an armored warrior, with the words "The Iliad of Homer" engraved in gold leaf. She flipped through the pages until a folded piece of paper dropped out of the book. Allora placed the book on the concrete floor and picked up the document. She unfolded it carefully and began reading:

Dear Allora,

I'm writing this to you in hopes that you will receive this book on your eighteenth birthday. I gave instructions to your mother to give it to you when you are old enough to realize who you really are. I don't think I'll be there with you by then. There's something I must do, and it may be the key to our survival. I don't expect you to understand right now, but I hope you will in the future. The next few years may be hard on you, and I can't imagine the hardships you'll face, but Allora, you must push forward. You are the key to a grander vision that I can't quite see myself. I know the weight of responsibility can be trying. Just lean on those around you for support. I will try to make it easier on you. I believe I've found what I've been looking for, but it will be the reason for my absence. Remember, Allora, never give up hope. It is the one thing that they can never take from us.

Your Uncle,

Ben

When she finished, a lonely tear dripped from her chin and landed on the paper. Allora sat for almost twenty minutes staring at the words, rereading each one until she memorized it. Wiping the tears from her cheeks, she placed the book back in the box, closed her eyes, and clutched the note against her chest. For a minute, she sat idle. Then she took one last look at the box, placed the note in her pocket, and shut out the light.

Eighteen

PLANNING

February arrived with a flurry of snow showers. Blankets of white powder and ice covered the roads, causing the cancellation of school. It wasn't long before the snow subsided and school closures ended, and Allora again found herself walking into her history classroom. She was relieved to see a familiar face looking up at her. "Mr. Swan!" she exclaimed and ran up to hug him.

Mr. Swan stumbled back, caught off guard by her excitement. "It's nice to see you too," Mr. Swan said, surprised at the girl's overt enthusiasm.

Allora let go and looked up at her teacher. "I'm really glad you're back," she said. "I need to talk to you about something important."

"Me too," he said.

"I have—" Allora began.

Mr. Swan cut her off. "Not now. Come back to my room after school, and we'll talk," he said, turning around to begin the lecture for class.

After school, Allora dashed to Mr. Swan's room and shut the door.

Before either of them spoke a word, he put his finger to his lips and proceeded to expand silencing glue to cover the room. "I've had to be extra careful lately," Mr. Swan said, moving toward the far wall to retrieve an object from its secret location. "Are you okay? I heard about the shifter attack."

"Yeah," Allora said, putting her head down. "I guess I'm fine."

Mr. Swan pulled the object from the wall and walked over to his somber student. "Hey," he said, picking up her chin, "what's wrong?"

Allora took a while to ask the question. "How well did you know my uncle?"

"I guess your mother told you what happened then." Mr. Swan walked over to the window and looked out on the patches of melting snow. "You know, I grew up in the hills. A place called Malhalla, a few hundred miles outside of Titanis. It used to snow there too." He paused for a moment to turn and lean against the windowsill. "That was where I met your uncle. We grew up together." Mr. Swan's eyes rolled down, and he laughed. "Your uncle used to get me in so much trouble. One time, we captured a dryad, put it in a box, and gave it to Milly as a birthday present. When she opened the box, the dryad jumped out and attacked her. It was one of the funniest practical jokes I'd ever seen."

"What's a dryad?" Allora asked.

"A type of tree nymph. They are small, shy creatures, but if you provoke them, they can be especially fierce. Your mom had a few scratches on her face. Not too happy about that."

Allora laughed. "Well, I'm sure Mom didn't like that one bit."

"Heh. I think your mom still hates me for that one." He chuckled. "Your Uncle Ben grew up to be an amazing man, and he saved my life."

Allora could see tears forming in her teacher's eyes, so she didn't dare interrupt. Mr. Swan wiped his eyes and continued. "After we got out of preliminary school, what you'd call high school, we both joined the Royal Guard. We seemed to be cut out for it and quickly moved up the ranks, until the wars began. We were arrested, but your uncle managed to escape. When he found out that I was scheduled to be executed a couple weeks later, he cooked up an elaborate plan to free me. We barely made it out of there alive, and I told him he was an idiot who could have gotten himself killed. Do you know what he said to that?"

"No, what?"

"He said, 'Swan, you were going to be a pretty ugly corpse without that head of yours.'" Mr. Swan laughed. "Your uncle was a real hero, Allora."

"Why did the king have you arrested anyway? Didn't you just say you were enlisted in the Royal Guard?"

"When we signed up for the Royal Guard, the man who was king enacted laws that gave rights to humans. That didn't go over very well with certain elitists and aristocrats. There was a coup, which was orchestrated by a power-hungry general named Salazar. He killed the king, and many of our friends."

"So that's why she doesn't like to talk about it."

Mr. Swan nodded. "This man also had your uncle assassinated, and he's looking to do the same to anyone who opposes him. Since you have the direct bloodline to the throne, you are his biggest threat, which is why your mother is so protective. And it's why he'll do anything to make sure you don't find the Eye of the Titans."

"I have a feeling that he won't succeed there."

Allora placed the orb in Mr. Swan's palm. He excitedly rolled it over, feeling the cold surface with his fingers. "You found it!" Mr. Swan exclaimed. "Your uncle would be so proud of you, Allora, just as I am."

"This is what he was looking for all those years?" Allora asked.

"I believe so," Mr. Swan said. "Let's give it a try.

He lined up the pieces of parchment and placed the orb along the top edge of the middle, then rolled the orb down along the edge while his palm glowed. As the orb slid along the perforated edge, it began melting onto the table, like pizza dough being rolled flat. Mr. Swan stepped away, and Allora watched as the melted orb flattened even more and the bright glow dissipated.

The parchment was finally one complete sheet, miraculously glued together, with no indication that it had ever been in three separate pieces. The last parts of the directions were clearly written in the same manner as the other parts of the riddle:

A water-bound mass of wizard's past
Where phantoms raise their Earthly mast
A witch's cauldron with secrets to bear
With stones you enter, but do beware

Allora read it through twice, just to be sure she hadn't missed anything. "Do you know what it means?"

"I'm not sure," Mr. Swan answered, and the two debated it for a few minutes before the teacher put it back in his safe. "While we try to concentrate on figuring it out, we can't leave it out to fall into the wrong hands. It should be safe here." As he stepped away from the wall, he looked at Allora, smiled, breathed deep, and shook his head. "All that research and all those years, and you manage to find the last piece to the puzzle. Thank you, Allora."

After Allora left the classroom that day, she headed straight for the library. The words of the riddle festered in her mind while she searched for books on magical places. For days, she spent all her free time in the library, searching the Internet and reading books on different places around the world.

Frustration boiled over after spending weeks among skyscrapers of stacked encyclopedias, fantasy novels, and research articles, with no progress. She went home, feeling defeated, flopped down on the couch next to her sister, and let out a discouraged sigh.

Bell didn't even flinch, for she was much too busy reading a book on molecular biology.

Allora pulled out the piece of paper she'd written the riddle down on. Staring at the words had no miraculous effect, no matter how many times she ran them through her mind.

Bell finished the page she was reading, then glanced over and read the first line of the riddle before Allora noticed. "'A water-bound mass of wizard's past'? What's that?" Bell said.

"It's nothing. Just some stupid riddle I can't figure out."

"Well the 'water-bound mass' is probably an island."

"Duh. I already figured that part out, kiddo."

"Just trying to help."

"I'm sorry, Bell. It's just that I have been looking at this thing for days, and the riddle just doesn't make sense. It's really frustrating me," Allora admitted, putting her hands over her face, and rubbing her bloodshot eyes.

"Don't you remember a place called Wizard's Island in the middle of Crater Lake? When we went there a couple years ago, I read the entire visitor's guide." With that, Bell got up and left the living room.

Allora pulled her hands down her face, and a bug-eyed expression began to form. "No way. It can't possibly be that easy," she said softly, slowly realizing that her little sister might have found the location of The Eye of the Titans without even thinking about it.

Bell walked back into the living room with a glass of milk in hand, and her big sister jumped up from the couch and grabbed her in a bear hug that caused her to spill milk all over both of them. "Hey!" Bell exclaimed. "What's the big idea?"

"Don't cry over spilt milk!" Allora said with a grin, then ran to her room, still covered in the white stuff but not even caring. She closed the door, grabbed the telephone, and dialed Katie's number. When she only got voicemail after a number of rings, she hung up and dialed again, and she kept right on dialing, with milk dripping from her hair, until Katie finally picked up.

"Okay, this better be important!" Katie yelled on the other end.

"Whoa! What's with the hostility? It's just me," Allora said.

"Sorry. I'm in the middle of painting my nails, and it's kinda hard to hold the phone while the paint's drying."

"Well, gee, Your Highness, I'm sorry to interrupt your all-important manicure, but I have some news."

"Go on."

"I found it!" Allora paused for dramatic effect, more excited than she'd ever been in her life.

"Shut up!" Katie said. "No way! Where?"

"I don't really wanna say over the phone," Allora answered. Paranoia had set in, mostly from reading too many spy novels, but also from being attacked by magical creatures from another world.

"Dax will get in touch with Tanner, and we'll all meet you at your house tonight," Katie said, blowing on her nails between words.

"Sounds like a plan," Allora said, then hung up the phone and headed to her room to do a little research.

Luckily for Allora, Milly had gathered quite a collection of information on Crater Lake, and what she couldn't find there, she was able to locate on the internet. When she Googled it, she quickly discovered an article that shocked her, a report on Sasquatch sightings reported decades earlier. "Sas was there," she said to herself while she sat at the computer. "It's gotta be the place."

Allora stopped reading the article when she heard Katie talking to her mother in the living room. She grabbed the others, led them to her bedroom, and closed the door. Once they were all safe inside, she projected a purple spark, struck a round, clear ball, and glue exploded onto the walls.

Katie opened her palms out and grinned. "I can't wait till I can do that."

Allora smiled and rummaged in her pocket till she found the piece of paper with the riddle scribbled on it. She passed it around to her three friends, who were sitting side by side on the bed.

"Is this the complete riddle?" Tanner asked.

"Yes, and I believe I know what it's referring to," Allora said with a smirk. She pulled out the book she'd been reading earlier and opened it to a panoramic picture of the beautiful Crater Lake. "There," Allora said, pointing her finger in the middle of the picture.

"What is it?" Katie asked.

"It's a 'water-bound mass' known as Wizard's Island. That rock formation over there is called The Phantom Ship," she explained, flipping the page and pointing to the picture of rocks jutting upward out of the water. "I think it has a lot to do with 'where phantoms raise their Earthly mast,'" she said, reciting the next line of the riddle.

The other three glanced back and forth between the pictures and the words, then looked at each other in awe.

"You found it, Allora!" Katie exclaimed, and they both screamed and hugged each other.

"I had a little accidental help," Allora confessed. "Bell reminded me of this place."

"I can't believe we've been so close to it all along," Dax said. "How come no one found it before if it's that obvious?"

"I'm not sure, but I found an article online that talked about Sas sightings near the lake many years ago. Maybe they looked there before and couldn't find the entrance. All I know is that we *have* to go down there."

"You know your mom will never sign the permission slip for that little field trip," Katie said.

"I think that she's coming around, but this might be a little too much of an adventure."

"Why don't we tell them we're going to Sas' for training?" Tanner suggested.

"Not sure that she's going to buy it, but why not give it a shot?"

"Good," Tanner said. "Then that will be our alibi."

"We also need supplies, like flashlights, camping equipment, food, water, weapons, and so on," Dax said.

"Right, but we need to be discreet. We shouldn't stock up on food and water till the day we leave, or else someone might get suspicious of what we're up to. I'm sure we can find camping equipment without having to buy a lot of it," Tanner said.

"I've got tons of flashlights," Katie said, prompting questioning looks from her friends. "What? So I'm a little afraid of the dark. Don't judge me. We all know there are some serious boogeymen out there, right?"

Allora chuckled. "We already have weapons too, but there's one small issue."

"What's that?" Tanner asked.

"We need the actual parchment from Mr. Swan's room."

"Why don't we just tell Mr. Swan about the location and have him come with us?" Dax asked.

"He's have to tell my mother," Allora said. "He's been ordered not to help us anymore with this. Too risky asking him for help."

"Why do we need the parchment anyway. Mr. Swan guards that thing like it's his baby," Katie said, "and we have no way of accessing his safe."

"I asked my Aunt Lizi about the wall trick, and she told me it can only be accessed with a specific hadron signature. That means only Mr. Swan can open it," Tanner explained.

"I know. I asked my mom the same thing, but we need the parchment because it has important information on the back. I saw the numbers when I originally got the parchment from Sas. I'm assuming there are more on the other pieces, a combination of sorts," Allora said.

"Then how are we supposed to get it?" Dax asked.

"I've already figured that out. We just need to make a duplicate, then ask Mr. Swan to let us see the parchment. While Katie distracts him, I'll make the switch. He'll put the decoy back in the safe, and we'll have the original," Allora said.

"And exactly how do I distract him?" Katie asked.

"I don't know. Get creative. Flash him if you have to," Allora said.

"What!? Ew, Allora. He's like... forty. Gross," Katie said.

"Well, it would do the trick," Tanner said shyly.

While they all had a good laugh at Katie's expense, she just crossed her arms in protest and stuck out her bottom lip as if she was pouting.

Allora hurriedly went back to the subject at hand. "Spring break is in a couple weeks. That will be a perfect time to go down there."

"When should we tell our parents?" Tanner asked.

"We should probably wait till a day before so they don't have time to check with Sas."

"Good idea, Dax. I'll drive," Tanner said.

"Okay. It's settled then. We'll create the duplicate this week, make the switch next week, pack up the car, tell our parents, and head out the next morning," Allora said.

"Sounds like a good plan, but I'm not flashing anyone," Katie said.

They all laughed again, then hurried out of Allora's room to get a snack before they left.

* * *

The next day, Katie and Allora went to the craft store on Main Street to find some parchment paper that would look authentic.

"I know this cool technique where we can stain the paper with tea to make it look even more worn and ancient," Katie said, and Allora agreed that it was worth a try.

Once they had the paper looking rather genuine, they spent days trying to copy the inscription. Whenever they got stuck, Allora asked Mr. Swan if she could see the parchment again. She worried that he might be getting suspicious that they were up to something, but he seemed proud that she was so interested in it.

Meanwhile, the guys worked on accumulating a large stockpile of camping supplies, which they stored in the back of Tanner's car.

"Okay, do we all know our roles?" Allora asked everyone while they were standing outside the school.

"Yes!" they all said at once.

They walked into the school together. It was lunchtime, the perfect time to pay Mr. Swan a visit, but just as they were rounding the corner, Allora bumped into someone.

"Hey! Watch where you're going!" Kim said.

"Excuse me," Allora said in a sassy tone.

Kim glared back at her, then turned her attention to Tanner. She pushed Allora out of the way to get to him and purred, "Hey, Tanner," seductively touching his broad chest. "When are you gonna ask me out on a date?" She fluttered her eyelids in a flirtatious manner.

All Tanner could muster was, "Um… uh…"

Dax smacked him on his back.

"How about after spring break?" Tanner said.

Kim lightly dragged her hand along his body as she moved past him, then looked back over her shoulder and said, "I can't wait." Then she turned and strutted out the front door, swaying her hips back and forth in a wide berth, causing both boys to stare hungrily at her until she was out of sight.

"Dude, that girl is so hot!" Dax said, clapping his friend on the shoulder. "You are so lucky!"

Allora walked up and smacked Tanner on the back. "Hey! Can you two focus please? We've got a job to do," she snapped.

Allora opened the door to find Mr. Swan working on paperwork at his desk. "Hi, Mr. Swan," she said as they all walked into the room and shut the door.

"Hey, guys and gals," he said, sounding slightly surprised as he looked up from the papers he was grading. He put his red pen down on the desk. "What's going on?"

"I wanted to show these three the new part of the parchment," Allora said. "They haven't seen it yet."

Mr. Swan got up from his desk. "Of course! I haven't gotten very far with it. I've researched several places, but nothing really pops out as an exact location," he said, walking to the back of the room and sparking the wall to retrieve the parchment.

The object melted its way out and flew into Mr. Swan's outstretched hand, and he brought it over and placed it on the desk in front of the boys.

Katie moved toward the desk where the boys were and shoved her brother to the side so she could get a better view. When Dax accidentally-on-purpose pushed her over the desk behind them, Katie went flying, and she began an Oscar-worthy performance when she crashed on the floor. "Dax!" she screamed, then began to cry, rubbing her rump.

Mr. Swan ran over and knelt down to see if she was all right, and as he did, Dax moved his body to block Mr. Swan's view of the parchment. That gave Allora the perfect opportunity to pull out the fake and swap it with the real one. Once the quick exchange was made, she moved back a step and eyeballed Katie to let her know the diversion had worked.

Katie stopped crying, got up from the ground, and shoved Dax just to sell it to her audience. They examined the fake parchment for a few minutes to sell the ruse, then they handed it back to Mr. Swan, who immediately rushed over to put it back inside the wall.

"Thanks, Mr. Swan," Tanner said.

"Anytime. If you think of anything that might help us find The Eye, please let me know."

After they all thanked Mr. Swan again, they hurried out of the building with the genuine parchment snugly tucked away in Allora's sleeve. "We did it!" she said, spinning around to hug Katie. "You really sold that fall. I had no idea you're such a good actress."

"Whip out the red carpet, Hollywood, 'cause here I come," Katie said.

Dax rolled his eyes. "Personally, I thought it was a little over dramatic," he said.

"Yeah? Well, you didn't have to push me so hard. I'm gonna have a bruise on my butt because of you," Katie said, pushing her brother with one hand.

"I had to make it look real," Dax replied, pushing his sister back. "Besides, if your butt wasn't so big, maybe it wouldn't have gotten in the way."

"Hey!"

"C'mon, you guys. Check it out," Allora said, unfolding the parchment and turning it over. "Look at these shapes." She pointed to small black smudges with distinctive abstract lines. "What do you think it means?"

"No idea, but we shouldn't look at it here," Tanner said, taking the parchment and rolling it back up. "We don't want anyone else knowing we have this. Mr. Swan isn't the only one we have to worry about, remember?"

As he walked to the car and placed the parchment in the back with the rest of the supplies, he filled them in on the rest of the plan. "We leave tomorrow morning. Make sure to tell the adults about Sas' overnighter as soon as you get home. We'll meet up at Allora's house like we always do, but I'll park my car up the street so we can get to it from the woods without anyone seeing us. We'll stop off at the grocery store, and then we'll hit the road. Sound good?"

They all nodded in agreement.

"Crater Lake, here we come!" Allora said.

Nineteen

Road

Allora slid out of bed before the alarm rang, then marched to the shower with a strange, determined energy for so early in the morning. As she readied herself for the road trip, she felt a sense of frightened anticipation, something like waiting in line for a rollercoaster, only far more intense.

Milly walked into the kitchen to see her daughter wide awake, eating breakfast, and was quite shocked. "Dressed already? At this hour of the morning? Who are you, and what have you done with my daughter?"

Allora tilted her head and lifted her eyebrows. "Huh? I've gotten up this early by myself before," she said.

Milly walked over to the coffee grinder to begin her usual morning routine of caffeinating herself. "Not since Christmas morning when you were five, you haven't," she said, placing the cap on the grinder and starting the machine.

Allora ignored her mother and went back to eating her cereal.

The others arrived right at seven o'clock.

Milly, of course, put them through her regular interrogation to make sure they were actually going where they said they were going. "Sas is expecting all of you, correct?" she asked, then sipped her coffee and looked over the rim of the cup at them.

"Yes, Mother," Allora replied.

"And you all are staying in the cave all night right?" Milly asked.

"Yes, Mother," Allora said. She gave Milly a reassuring smile and a hug and grabbed her bag. "Stop worrying so much. We'll be fine."

Milly walked them all to the backdoor and leaned out. "It's my job to worry. Make sure you don't divert from the path. It's the only safe way through the woods."

"We know, Mom!" Allora yelled back, as they crossed the field and disappeared into the forest.

They walked a few hundred feet up the path before Tanner turned right. He knew the way to the road because he'd done some preliminary hikes through the forest to memorize the route.

After weaving through the thick forest, they found Tanner's car about a half-mile down an old, abandoned dirt road that had once been used by lumberjacks. The warm sun shone upon them, and excitement spread quickly among the group. Even with the task ahead, they were all smiles as Tanner drove the car onto the highway and headed southwest. When they arrived at the grocery store, they exited the car carefully, scanning the parking lot for any familiar folks; they all knew that if they were spotted, it'd compromise their clandestine trip.

"Who's got the shopping list?" Tanner asked, looking at his friends expectantly.

"I made it last night," Allora said. "We need to get food, water, batteries for the flashlights, bug spray, and anything else we can think of."

Dax handed Allora a pen.

"What's this for?"

"Add beef jerky to the list please," he said, grinning from ear to ear. "Can't camp without it."

Allora rolled her eyes and ripped the list in two so shopping would go faster. Once they were done buying their supplies, including plenty of beef jerky to keep Dax quiet, they packed up the car and hit the road. Tanner took Mt. Hood Highway until he got to Boring, Oregon. Then, he turned onto Highway 211, which took him to the onramp to I-205. Twenty minutes later, they were on I-5, heading south.

"Are we there yet?" Dax whined after a while.

"What's the matter?" Katie asked, mockingly. "Do you gotta go potty or something?"

"Calm down, kids. Looks like we've gotta go about four hours south to Roseburg, then east on North Umpqua Highway," Allora said, sitting in front with the map. "A couple hours later, we'll be there."

For the most part, in spite of Dax's complaining and he and Katie bickering in the back seat like third graders on family vacation, the car ride down was jovial.

Allora felt strangely at ease, regardless of the fact that she had no idea what they were actually driving into. Being with her friends on a road trip felt normal and fun, a stress release from the threat of death, another life in a strange world, and a responsibility she didn't understand or want. She put her head out the window and closed her eyes. The wind hit her face and tossed her long, brown hair against the window of the car. The sun pierced through the scattered white clouds, warming her skin. Spring had arrived, offering a bountiful display of colors, definitely a nice change from the rainy, gray, snowy, cold gloom of winter.

They reached Roseburg sooner than they expected. Tanner pulled over to gas up the car, and the others took the opportunity to use the bathroom before they reconvened at the car.

"I got front this time!" Dax said excitedly.

Allora conceded and hopped in the back with Katie, then pulled out the parchment, which they'd tucked into plastic for safekeeping and protection from the elements. As Tanner drove out of the gas station and headed east, toward the lake, Allora unfolded the sheet and rested it on the seat between her and Katie. She turned it over and gazed at the symbols, arranged in a neat line down the left side. In the middle were seemingly random numbers, though they were arranged sequentially, and one word ran along the edge. "Credo," Allora read out loud.

"What's that mean?" Katie asked.

"Mr. Swan told me it means, 'I believe,'" Allora answered.

"Wonder how that plays into it?" Katie said.

"I don't know, but I'm sure we'll find out," Allora said, staring out the window.

Tanner turned the car south, onto Crater Lake Highway. Tall pines, still covered with patches of snow that hadn't gotten the memo that spring had arrived, lined the road to the lake. A natural perfume of fresh pine and floral scents filled the air. A vibrant green peeked from the snow-covered trees.

When Tanner pulled the car onto Rim Drive and circled the lake, they looked out the left-hand window, crowding against the glass. Tanner had to push Dax back so he could maintain his grip on the steering wheel. Mounds of snow lined the road as they zigzagged through the forest on top of the ridge.

At the end of the road, the visitor center appeared at the end of a large parking lot, a grandiose building made of oak, built on the edge of the ridge.

They scurried out of the car and ran to the edge of a steep canyon. The picturesque landscape seemed surreal. They were standing on a rocky outcrop, hanging on to a wood fence, looking down a steep vertical incline that dropped hundreds of feet below. At the bottom of the bowl-shaped canyon was a majestic, crystal-blue lake, sparkling in the sun.

Allora focused on one particular monument on the left side of the lake. Wizard's Island jutted out of the water like a miniature volcano, rising from the deep abyss below. She jumped up and clung onto Katie briefly. Allora was sure The Eye of the Titans was somewhere on that island, and they were so close to finding it. The excitement subsided as she realized the gravity and pressure of their next step. "This isn't gonna be easy," Allora said.

"That's okay," Tanner said. "We're used to doing things the hard way by now, right?"

Allora cast a sideways grin and then returned her eyes to stare out at the imposing task before them. "Right."

"What now?" Dax asked.

"We wait," Allora said, pressing her lips together and scanning the area. She pointed down to the boat dock at the bottom of the canyon. "That's where we'll set out from. We'll have to hang around until dark, and then we'll 'borrow' one of those small boats to get over to the island."

They all turned around and headed for the car.

"'Borrow'?" Dax said, lifting his eyebrows.

Allora smiled mischievously. "Just for a little while. We'll give it back… if we can."

"Grand theft boating, huh? That's gonna be a difficult thing to explain if we get caught," Dax replied as they walked back to the car. "Sorry, Officer. We were just borrowing the boat so we could sneak over to that island and find an alien artifact to help us defeat mythological beasts who are trying to kill us."

"Well, when you put it that way, it sounds totally believable," Tanner said.

Laughter followed as they all got back into Tanner's dirt-covered Bronco.

He drove to a secluded area of the woods down the road, a flat, dirt clearing on the edge of a cliff on the southeastern side of the lake. The view was amazing, so they pulled out some chairs and set them up to face outward, over the cliff. It was around three o'clock in the afternoon, so they had to kill some time before sunset.

After eating some snacks, they sat and thought about the voyage across the lake. After about an hour of discussing possible meanings of the strange markings on the back of the parchment, Dax and Katie went on a short hike to clear their heads. Tanner went to the car to retrieve the equipment they needed for their expedition, leaving Allora alone to marvel at the sun descending into the western horizon. The evening sky was clear, bursting into a rainbow of violets, oranges, and reds.

Tanner walked up, dropped the supplies in the chair, and moved next to Allora. "Wow," he said.

"Beautiful, isn't it?" Allora said.

"Yes it is," he said, gazing at her.

Allora twisted around and realized he didn't have his eyes on the sunset. Confused for a moment, she glanced up at Tanner. Their minute of gazing upon each other felt like days. Allora caught Tanner's motion toward her hand. She felt the warm touch of his fingers, inching their way past her palm and curling in the crevices between her fingers.

Nervous warmth flowed throughout her body, permeating her cheeks. Tanner knocked down her walls with the touch of his finger. When he stepped closer, Allora's eyes fluttered, still gazing into Tanner's. Her heart beat faster with every inch of space that closed between them.

Just as the sun submerged into the background, Tanner's lips neared Allora's, and his chest lightly touched hers. His body was warm, his heart beating in rhythm with hers.

"Whoa! Am I interrupting something here?" Dax said, coming out of the woods.

"You always have great timing, buddy," Tanner said.

Allora let go of the embrace, embarrassed by the intrusion.

Katie walked up behind Dax and slapped him on the back. "I told you to wait!" she said.

"It's no big deal," Allora said, trying to play it off. "It's not like we were doing anything," she lied, glaring at Tanner and silently demanding that he back her up.

"Yeah," Tanner said awkwardly, "nothing happened."

"Dude, you're a horrible liar," Dax said.

Allora shook her head. "We don't have time for this. We've got a boat to steal... er, borrow."

They all took her lead, altering their moods to a more serious demeanor. As much as Dax wanted to harass the two, there were more important matters at hand. Allora reverted back to her usual guarded personality. Even though the three were her best friends, she was embarrassed and confused by her feelings for Tanner. Her mind and body began to swim with exuberance as she recalled their near-kiss and the closeness of their bodies beneath that glorious sunset, but the logical side quickly took over. She shook her head, changing her thoughts to the unemotional operation that required her complete attention. She moved with a purpose while everyone else hurried to keep up.

"Hey," Tanner said quietly, "I just wanted to—"

Allora interrupted before he could speak his mind. "Not now, Tanner."

Tanner slowed down, unsure and a bit hurt that she was being so abrasive.

Katie sped past him and ran up alongside Allora. She didn't say anything, as she knew her best friend was in no mood for girl talk.

Dax patted Tanner on the shoulder. "Women," he said, shaking his head. "They're like the universe."

"The universe?" Tanner questioned.

"Yep. Vast, treacherous, and unexplainable," Dax said, laughing at himself and stepping past his bewildered friend to follow the girls down the hill.

Tanner marched forward, knowing he had to keep his wits about him for what lay ahead.

Night was fast approaching. They rushed down the ridge to the water's edge, moving along the rocks silently, inching their way to the docks ahead.

Allora pointed to a small boat with an outboard motor attached on the end. As they reached the back of the equipment shed at the base of the dock, they heard footsteps. Allora stopped and held up her hand, causing Dax to slip on a rock, and crash into the water.

The splashing sound initiated a response from the park ranger, who'd been about to head back up the crater. Allora motioned for everyone to scurry under the dock. The park ranger knelt down and shined his flashlight around, scanning the shore and the rippling water.

Pinned awkwardly against the back of the dock, the four pushed each other closer, trying to become invisible. The rocks were wet and slippery and reeked with the stench of dead, rotten fish. Katie audibly gagged, causing the light to jump from the water to the back of the dock, and Allora was certain they would be caught. The light scanned the rock they were hiding behind, then suddenly retreated.

Next, they heard the muffled sounds of someone in the distance.

"Let's go, Harry!" the voice said. "What's taking so long?"

"I thought I heard something," Harry answered.

Allora looked up between the cracks of the wood planks at the puzzled face of the park ranger.

"Meh, it's probably just an animal," the other ranger said. "I'm not about to miss out on my wife's meatloaf so you can investigate a ferret sighting."

The park ranger ignored his buddy and continued scanning the area. A moment later, he gave up and finally headed back up the cliff.

The four let out a collective sigh of relief when they heard the man's footsteps disappearing up the dirt path. They stayed under the dock for some time, until they were sure the nosy ranger was far enough away.

When they finally crawled out, covered in mud and debris, Tanner untied the boat. "We should probably pull it along the bank so they don't see us paddling out into the middle of the lake," Tanner whispered.

"Good idea," Dax said.

Trekking along the edge of the water took a long time. The moon was high in the night sky, beckoning them forward, like a guiding light to their final destination. Stars glittered in the sky, scattered majestically in their usual patterns.

With each passing rock, their task became more real and arduous. At certain spots along their journey around the lake, they were required to get in the boat and paddle along the edge of the water. Allora's foot slipped on a mossy rock, plunging it into the glacial waters, causing a sudden spasm of pain. When they reached the point in the lake where the span of water between them and the island was shortest, they headed out.

The hard-trekked journey was forgotten as soon as they reached the island. Allora put her left foot on a large boulder to hold the boat steady so the others could disembark safely and dryly. Tanner helped her pull the boat onto the sandy bank, while the other two looked around.

"Witch's Cauldron is at the top of the island," Allora said. "That's where the directions say we should go."

With only the moon to guide them, the group hiked up the steep incline. They weaved through trees and occasionally had to crawl up small, rocky hills, tripping over branches here and there. Dax flipped on his flashlight after stumbling on a fallen tree.

"Hey, no flashlights," Tanner said, prompting Dax to shut it off. "That ranger could still see us from the top of the crater."

"Fine, but if I twist my ankle, you're carrying me outta here!"

Katie laughed. "I would love to see that."

When they reached the top, Allora pulled out the parchment. "'A witch's cauldron with secrets to bear,'" she said, repeating the riddle she'd read numerous times, "'with stones you enter, but do beware.'"

"What the hell does that mean?" Katie asked, surveying the barren, rock-filled crater.

Witch's Cauldron wasn't anything spectacular, and since the incline of the bowl-shaped crater at the top of the hill gradually sloped, they steadily walked down the rocky surface to the middle, where a collection of boulders and rocks littered the floor. Small shrubs sprung from the ground, but no sign of an entrance of any kind. They were all perplexed and a bit frustrated by the normality of the landscape.

"I don't get it," Allora said. "I thought it would be clear when we got here."

"Yeah, well, I think we all thought the same thing," Katie said sympathetically.

They spent almost an hour searching through the dirt and rock, to no avail.

"I think it's time for a break," Dax said, sitting down on a boulder.

Allora plopped herself on another rock beside him, and the other two found stone seats of their own. Tanner had packed sandwiches, a bottle of water, and an energy bar for each of them, and the midnight snack was nice compensation for all of their physical exertion. The moon hung overhead as they chewed.

Dax opened his bottle of water and drank about half of it, then placed the bottle next to him on the rock in order to finish his sandwich. The rock wasn't flat, however, so the bottle tipped over, spilling the remainder of his water all over the boulder. "Oh, come on!" he said, getting up from his seat. "Sis, I'm still thirsty. Can I have some of yours?"

"Um... no," Katie replied. "You always backwash in it."

"Pleeeease," Dax begged. "I'm so thirsty."

"Maybe you shoulda been more careful then," Katie said, grabbing her water from her lap before Dax could snatch it.

While the two siblings wrestled for the bottle, Allora noticed something. "Hey, guys!" she said, pointing to the boulder where Dax had spilled the water. "Look!"

The siblings stopped fighting, and both rotated their heads to see a thin light shining off the slanting edge of the boulder. The water had washed away some of the dirt that covered it, exposing some sort of reflective surface. The moonlight hit the mirrored surface, bounced off at a hundred and thirty degree angle, and hit a spot on the ground about ten feet from the boulder.

Allora walked over and dumped the rest of her water on the boulder. "Do you have an extra shirt or towel in your bag?" she asked Tanner.

Tanner unzipped his backpack and withdrew a towel. "I guess this is as good a time as any to use this," he said, handing it over.

Allora wiped the dirt, revealing a shiny black surface below. When she stepped back, a bright stream of moonlight reflected off the rock, only to stop at a specific spot on the ground about twenty feet away, like a marker of some sort.

All four Sonorans walked over and began digging into the ground. After a few minutes of excavation, Allora brushed the dirt away to reveal a magnificent black stone, a little dusty but radiant nonetheless. No one knew what it was or what to do with it, but Allora pulled out the parchment and turned it over. When the moonlight hit the surface, it exposed a compass, etched in silver. The same silver ink surrounded five distinctive shapes that covered the back of the parchment.

"Whoa!" Katie said, huddling closer to Allora. "Did you notice that before?"

"No. It just appeared," Allora said, staring like the rest of them. "It must have something to do with the moonlight or this area or something. I'm not exactly an expert on magic parchments. Anyone got any suggestions?"

"Maybe we have to arrange the stones according to how they correspond with the compass," Katie said, pointing at the first symbol. "See? This symbol and the rock are the same shape."

"Nice work, Katie. Let's try it." Allora positioned the parchment with the "N" facing the North Star, silently thanking her mother for forcing her to join Girl Scouts. *Didn't sell all those cookies for nothing, I guess,* she thought.

Next, she turned the black stone counterclockwise. As she did, she could feel the stone grinding against the circular rock underneath, and the stone moved as if she were winding up a toy. As soon as the rock was positioned like the picture, they heard a *clink*. The circular rock, along with the black stone, sank into the ground, and the four scooted along the gravel, crawling backward to escape the sinkhole that was forming.

When nothing further happened, Allora turned back to the parchment. "There are more symbols, so I guess that means there are more stones. Pour some water on those boulders outside the cauldron and wipe them down."

They each chose a boulder and began cleaning it, until five beams of light angled from outside the cauldron in every direction, crossing in the middle. Next, the boys dug up the stones, while the girls arranged each one according to the position on the parchment. "This rocks!" Dax joked, drawing eye-rolls from everyone at his horrible pun.

When they got to the last stone, Allora paused before turning it. She looked up at her three friends in anticipation. "Here goes nothing."

Twenty

Island

Allora turned the stone to its correct position, according to the diagram, and the round rock sank into the ground like the others. Again, she scurried backward to avoid the sinking ground. To everyone's surprise, even after the rock sank farther into the ground, nothing happened. They hoped for some sign of what to do next, but even the air remained eerily still. The cold air escaped their mouths in puffs of mist against the moonlight. A sense of frustration and disappointment came over the four, like lighting a wick on a firecracker that doesn't explode.

"Talk about anticlimactic," Dax said against the silent night.

Katie stood in the middle of the cauldron then suddenly fell backward and disappeared into the ground.

Allora yelled, crawling to the edge of a deep hole. All she could see was a foggy mist escaping from the black void. "Give me the flashlight!" she yelled to Tanner. When he tossed her a Maglite from his bag, Allora shined it around, but the dust blocked any visibility. "I can't see her! What do we do?" she cried.

"We go after her," Dax said, folding his arms.

"Dax, wait!" Tanner yelled as Dax jumped into the hole. Tanner looked after him with a frightened yet determined stare. "He's right. We didn't come this far just to give up now," he said, dropping into the dark hole behind his friend.

"You guys are crazy!" Allora yelled, but no one was there to hear her. She paced back and forth, debating about what she should do. "Right. Jump down into the creepy, dark hole, Allora. That sounds like a great idea," she said out loud.

After thirty seconds of self-doubt, though, Allora took a deep breath, folded her arms, and plunged into the unknown. A rush of cold air blew her hair back as she fell through a circular tube, spinning around and picking up speed along the way. It smelled of Earth and mildew. Then, the surface of the tube angled itself toward her, and she felt herself sliding. The surface was completely smooth and slippery, as if she was on a waterslide, only there was no water.

Her screaming continued as she rocketed through the dormant volcano. The tube bent, forcing a hard right turn, and Allora coiled around, moving at an alarming speed. All she could do was try to keep her body straight. The steep angle of the slide eventually leveled out, and she progressively slowed down. The end of the tube flattened out, forcing her body to reduce speed, and someone caught her as she slowed to a stop. Her hair shot out in every direction from the wild ride, but her eyes glistened with hope and gratefulness when she saw Tanner standing there at the end of the tube.

Tanner grabbed her hand and helped her up. "Took you a while."

Allora smiled, happy to be alive. "I'm never doing that again."

Dax came bouncing over. "Are you kiddin' me?" he said, grinning from ear to ear. "That was the best ride I've ever been on, and I didn't even have to buy a ticket! I say we find our way out and go for another spin!"

"Count me out," Katie said, hugging her dizzy friend.

"I thought you were a goner," Allora said, exhaling and embracing Katie tightly.

"That makes two of us," she replied.

Allora gazed around the large, circular room. It was the size of a high school gymnasium, covered entirely in reflective obsidian. The floor and ceiling were etched with intricate hieroglyphs, and in the middle, a stone basin, filled with flames, illuminated the room. Allora turned to Katie for an answer.

"It was like that when we arrived."

The light from the fire bounced off the walls, creating dancing shadows, but their next obstacle overshadowed the magnificence of the room. Sixteen doors lined the walls of the circular room, precisely the same distance apart from one another. Above each doorway was a Roman numeral, carved into the black stone.

Allora pulled out the parchment from inside her coat and unfolded it carefully to look at the back, holding it up in the light of the guys' flashlights. "I guess the numbers on the back correlate with the Roman numerals on top of those doorways," Allora said.

"You guess?" Dax said. "Don't you remember what it said? 'Heed the warning of the path you take, for one false choice will be the last you make.' My guess is it's a bad idea to guess."

"We just need to think this through. The numbers are eight, five, three, two, one, one, zero," Allora read out loud.

"I've got it!" Dax said, much to everyone's surprise. "We're screwed."

Katie stepped to her brother and punched him on the shoulder. "You're no help!"

"Yeah, thanks, Dax," Allora said. "Like we need the pessimism right now."

Meanwhile, Tanner was staring at the numbers intently. "Wait!" he suddenly said. "I've seen this exact arrangement of numbers before, in geometry class. This is a Fibonacci sequence." He glanced up to see puzzled expressions on his friends' faces. "Don't any of you pay attention in math class?"

"Ew. I hate math," Allora said. "It's my worst subject."

"I never really got along with my math teacher," Katie said.

"Don't look at me," Dax said, gesturing to himself and shrugging. "You know I suck at math."

Tanner could only smile and shake his head. "The answer is thirteen," he said. "That's the doorway we need to go through."

"How sure are you?" Allora asked.

"About this sure," Tanner replied, as he sauntered over to the black doorway and stepped backward as he smiled.

Allora stomped her right foot and scowled. "Why does everyone keep doing that?"

Katie and Dax just shrugged.

"Fine, but I'm not going last this time," Allora said, following Tanner's lead and stepping into the black doorway with her flashlight pointed in front of her.

She felt a pulling force, as if every molecule in her body was being stretched, and then she landed on a flat stone surface. "That was... a portal," Allora said between struggling breaths.

She swiveled her head up to see a long cave of majestic, glowing blue, and her mouth dropped open. The ice tube looked like frozen waves of glass, stretching a hundred feet and then curved to the right. Immediately above them, stalactites hung, dropping down beads of minerals onto the multicolored ground. In the midst of such an unimaginable sight, Allora ignored the siblings, who arrived seconds later. She walked along the sides of the crystal-blue tunnel and felt the walls of cold ice. The ceiling above curved in a half-circle; there was a wave pattern to it, as if the current had been frozen in time. The blue water around them seemed to radiate light.

"The lake is... above us," Tanner said. "But how is that possible?"

"You tell me, Mr. Geometry," Dax said.

As they inched into the ice tunnel, the ground became rocky. They pushed forward, still gazing up at their surroundings, which were like nothing any of them had ever seen before. At one point, Allora saw a fish swim up to the cave wall, then dart away. Mist created an unusual ambiance throughout the cavern, and Allora felt a slight chill as they moved deeper into the tunnel.

They walked about two hundred feet, until the blue ice opened up to a dark, expansive cave. Dax lit the torches that hung on the wall to either side of them, projecting light across a reflective surface. The floor was obsidian, but it was carefully arranged, like perfectly square tiles in a bathroom. Allora's eyes rolled upward to the numerous sharp, pointed stalactites hanging above the cavern.

"Well? What do you think?" she said, stepping onto the different block of obsidian.

"I'm not so sure we should walk out there just yet," Tanner said, gliding diagonally behind Allora.

The expansive field of black tiles seemed too easy. A slight sheen reflected the flicker of light from the torches. Squinting, Allora tried to see across the expanse, but she had no luck, and there didn't seem to be any way to go but forward. "What choice do we have?" she said, stepping onto the tile in front of her. "See? It's no big deal," she said over her shoulders to her friends behind her.

Just as the words escaped her mouth, she felt a strong pull from behind. Allora was yanked backward as one of the stalactites shattered the tile she'd just been standing on. Tanner had seen the impending fall and was able to grab the back of her shirt before the sharp tip of the calcium spear skewered the unsuspecting girl.

Tanner grabbed her shoulder and stared down into the black abyss with wide eyes. "Whew! That was close."

Allora breathed heavily, feeling a chill run up her spine as she thought about what could have happened.

"Yeah, you can say that again," Dax said, staring down through the space where the tile had been. "Look!" He swirled his flashlight down through the hole. "Either it's a long way down, or there are marshmallows at the bottom, because the thing still hasn't even made a sound."

"'One wrong move will send you deep,'" Katie said, hanging over her brother's left shoulder. "Pretty literal with that one."

"Now what?" Allora said, still a little frazzled.

"I think we should all run across at once," Katie suggested. "Those things on the ceiling take a few seconds to fall. We can make it."

"But how do we get back across after we're done?" Tanner argued.

Katie scratched her head. "Didn't really think about that."

"I saw something weird happen when you first stood there," Dax said, moving toward the reflective surface Allora had started from before she stepped forward.

"Watch my reflection," he said, stepping onto the platform. Suddenly, Dax's mirrored image split into many different ones, drawing gasps from his friends. The multiple reflections launched themselves forward in all directions, as if all the mini-Daxes had minds of their own.

The other three moved closer.

"See?" Dax said, twisting his head around. "I thought I was crazy at first, but I guess not."

"Which one do we follow?" Allora asked.

"Do you guys remember Mr. Swan talking about Hermes?" Dax paused for a moment as his friends all looked at one another, dumbfounded. "You know, the messenger of the gods."

Still, no one had an answer.

Dax shook his head. "Well, this guy had winged shoes that he used to fly around. The instructions say, 'Be careful to step with feathered feet,' right?"

"Right," Allora said, nodding.

"Well, if you look at that reflection of me," he said, pointing to the tile diagonally to his left, "it has wings on his shoes." Feeling confident with his theory, Dax stepped onto the tile.

Everyone looked upward, half-expecting the stalactite to fall, but nothing happened. Dax kept following his winged reflection, hopping from tile to tile.

Allora went next. She was about to step on the same tile as Dax, but she pulled up at the last second, noticing that her own winged reflection had jumped to the diagonal tile to her right, not the left, confusing her. "Hey, Dax," she said.

He stopped and spun around. "Yeah?"

"My reflection went the other way, to the right."

Dax thought for a second. "The instructions are simple," Dax said, jumping to the next tile. "Follow the feathered you."

"If you say so," she said, stepping onto the right tile cautiously.

Their paths diverged, sending them in random directions. The light of the torches dimmed as they reached the end of the tiles. Flipping on the flashlights, they saw the slight shape of a large doorway in the distance.

As they approached the wooden doors, the design work came into focus. Intricate drawings of warriors and gods were carved into them, with gold plating adorning the edges. Bulky copper rings the size of tires hung where the two doors met. Tanner and Dax each pulled a ring backward, straining their muscles from the weight. The hinges creaked loudly, as if they hadn't been exercised in ages, and a cloud of dust burst from the opening crack between the doors.

Allora walked forward, fanning the dusty air with her hand, then stepped into a grandiose room. Once their feet touched the strange yellow floor, small, round orbs lit up the room. Gigantic gold statues seemed to greet them as they entered, standing majestically, grand, and proud, like watchmen standing guard.

Awestruck and fascinated, Allora proceeded slowly along the corridor. Behind them, normal-sized gold men were evenly spaced along the wall. Half of the statues stood upright, sunken into the wall, while the rest stood in full form, frozen, with long spears at their sides. Allora joined the others in the middle, and they all walked down the corridor together.

"This is amazing," Katie said, spinning in a circle. "I think I've found my new home."

"Can you imagine how long these took to make?" Tanner said, walking up to one of the giant golden statues to their right, a mostly naked bearded man holding a trident and wearing a loose robe. Tanner took notice of his long beard and flowing hair. "This must be Poseidon."

"It took me an entire week just to make a stupid mug in pottery class," Dax added.

Allora was gawking at another statue that looked familiar, like something she'd seen in one of her history books.

Katie came up behind her. "Well? Who is it?"

The female statue wore a toga that came down to her lower thighs, her hair was in a tight braid, and along her chest was a sash that held a quiver of arrows against her strong back. Her chin pointed proudly, and an expression of strength had been molded perfectly upon her face.

"It has to be Artemis," Allora said, touching the feet of the statue.

Katie moved to the next statue, the goddess Demeter. She was dressed in an even longer, flowing toga, and there was a crown upon her head. A staff was angled up, held in Demeter's grasp.

"C'mere, guys!" Dax yelled. "This one's got wings for feet," he said, pointing at a thin, naked statue of a man wearing a helmet. "It's gotta be Hermes."

Something caught Allora's eye while they stood there. Turning to the left, she saw a light shining on a flat podium in the distance, and she stepped toward it, drawn to it like a bug to light.

"Where are you going?" Katie asked.

Allora didn't say anything and only quickened her pace.

The other three forgot what they were doing and ran after her.

She slowed down, moving up the steps to the golden podium. It was spotlighted by an orb hanging in midair, high above. Allora stepped on the platform where the podium sat and looked upon it. Nothing was there but sand on a plain stone tablet, a humble artifact that seemed strangely out of place in the elegant, golden, sparkling room. The sand was piled in a pyramid and occasionally sparkled in the light of the hanging orb.

"Where is it?" Tanner asked, moving up alongside Allora.

Katie got up to the platform. "Maybe somebody else found it first."

"You mean we came all this way for nothing?" Dax shouted from below. "I say we go back and ride the slide again."

"Hush!" Katie scolded.

Allora pulled out the parchment again, motioning everyone to be quiet. The instructions weren't very specific, but she remembered the Latin word on the back. "Credo," she said out loud.

Nothing happened.

"Well, you guys look like you have this covered," Dax said, storming off to one of the golden men on the wall. "I'm checking out some of this-uh-artwork."

Allora ignored him and kept thinking, wondering why it hadn't work. *Did I miss something?* The questions swirled around in her mind, but there didn't seem to be any clear answer. The harder she thought, the farther away her mind traveled.

Meanwhile, Dax was busy trying to yank one of the golden spears free.

"What are you doing?" Katie said, descending the stairs to yell at her brother.

"What does it look like?" he said, pulling at the golden spear.

"That isn't yours!" Katie crossed her arms.

Dax paused momentarily, staring up at the golden eyes of the statue. "I did not steal a boat, ride a crazy waterless waterslide, and play stalactite hopscotch to go home empty-handed. Think of it as a souvenir."

"That's it!" Allora said softly, dropping the parchment. "I believe." She placed her hands, palms up, over the tablet and closed her eyes. They all looked at her like she was crazy, but Allora didn't care. Somehow, she knew what she had to do. In a whisper, she said, "Credo, credo, credo, credo." She repeated the word over and over again.

Dax ignored the group and went back to prying the spear from the golden man's grasp.

Allora kept her eyes shut and kept repeating the word, imagining what she sought. Her hands began to glow as the hadrons in the room flowed into her body. All of a sudden, the sand from the tablet began to filter through the gaps between Allora's fingers, and even more of it relocated to the air over the palms of Allora's hands. The sand hovered an inch above, distributing itself into a glowing circle, spinning into a core like gravity forming a new planet. Particles of sand condensed into a ball, and then the whole thing caught on fire and released a powerful burst of light that expanded throughout the chamber. The light withdrew, speeding back into the core, imploding into a solid ball of black rock.

"I got it!" Allora said, holding up an orb of obsidian.

They heard a loud *clank*.

"I got it too!" Dax said, holding up his prize.

Just then, a decrepit skeletal hand burst out of its golden shell and grabbed Dax by the wrist. Dax screamed and dropped the golden spear, then moved back to the platform while the creature started to break through his gold casing. A deafening screech came from the former statue. Suddenly, all around them, the golden men broke from their metallic prisons. The creatures looked like skeletons, except they had translucent skin with a slight shimmer. In their eye sockets glowed red, pulsating fiery eyes. They seemed neither alive nor dead.

"I told you not to touch it!" Katie said, backing into the platform.

Golden shards crashed onto the floor, echoing loudly throughout the chamber.

Securing the orb inside her coat, Allora prepared herself for a fight. "Baykok," she said, fascinated by the weird creatures. "Mr. Swan told me about them."

"Uh, we don't really have time for a Sonoran biology lesson," Tanner said, pulling Allora, and jumping down to join the others. "Run!"

Gold spear flew across their path as they sprinted down the long corridor. The army of baykok had freed themselves from the golden casings and were quickly pursuing the intruders. Allora shot a purple hadron burst, knocking one of the creatures into the statue of Poseidon.

At the edge of the large wooden double doors, two baykok stood in their path, blocking their escape. Allora rotated on a hundred-eighty degrees, then shot two purple balls into the creatures' chests. Both baykok flew back, striking the half-open wooden doors, crumpling into a pile of bones. They hurried across the dark cavern, the beams of light bouncing erratically as they got to the edge of the tiled flooring.

"I guess it's time to test out your original idea, Katie," Allora said between breaths.

They all ran ahead, darting across as fast as their feet would take them. Behind them, they could hear the progressive crash of stalactites breaking the tiles.

Katie slipped, fell, and slid along the ground. Dax stopped, grabbed his sister, and pulled frantically as the rock missiles crashed down sequentially on the tiles at Katie's feet.

"Move it, you two!" Tanner yelled as Allora and he reached the safety of the cavern opening.

After a few more clumsy steps and near missteps, Dax and Katie leapt in the air and landed on the ledge, just as the last of the stalactites crashed into the tile floor. They breathed heavily, coughing occasionally from the dust cloud.

Across the deep chasm, the baykok stopped at the edge, helpless to get across the deep opening since all of the tiles had crashed into the abyss below.

Breathing hard, Dax and Katie stood up from the dirt floor.

"That's it. I'm tired of close calls," Katie said, shaking out her shirt.

"Looks like we might have to deal with a few more," Dax said, pointing across the chasm. "The bony brigade seems to be... changing."

The baykok had started forming multiple arms that grew out of their torsos, enabling them to crawl on the walls like spiders. They scurried along the cavern ceiling.

"Let's get outta here!" Allora said.

They all turned and darted into the ice tunnel. Dax hurdled a boulder and helped his sister over.

Tanner reached the obsidian cave first and took a good look around. "I don't see an exit, guys."

They all scanned the walls, searching desperately for some kind of way out, and they collectively held their breath when they saw small skeletons leaping over rocks in the distance. Red eyes glowed under the blue mist, and it was clear that the baykok were moving fast. The four teens stood in a line, bracing for the inevitable attack.

"Now I know how General Mustard felt," Katie said to the puzzled audience standing next to her.

"What?" Allora said.

"You know, Mustard's last stand, surrounded by Indians."

"Custer," Allora corrected. "General George Armstrong Custer."

"And you call me an idiot," Dax said, pointing to himself.

"You *are* an idiot!" Katie yelled. "This whole thing is your fault! Why'd you steal that spear? I oughta take the thing and shove it up your—"

"Guys! We don't have time for the blame game," Tanner said, pointing at the baykok that were within a hundred feet and closing fast. Tanner grabbed Allora by the arm. "We need those hadrons of yours!"

Allora stepped forward, took a deep breath, and pulled in the hadrons like Aunt May had taught her. Focusing the energy, she generated one large purple hadron ball around her chest and sent it shooting down the ice tunnel. Baykok flew left and right as the sphere blasted through. The hadron ball burst, causing shockwaves of energy that knocked them over.

"That doesn't look good," Dax said, pointing to the large cracks forming inside the tunnel.

The force from the hadron burst had fractured the stability of the tunnel walls. The cracks grew, and an eerie snapping sound echoed into the cave. Suddenly, a wall of water crashed into the tunnel, surging toward them.

"Oh god. What have I done?" Allora said.

The rushing water sounded like a freight train. Allora and Katie embraced each other, assuming they had only seconds left to live, awaiting their watery grave.

Out of sheer desperation, Tanner moved in front of the rest and performed the series of motions Aunt May had shown him. Blue hadron energy circled in front of him. Tanner closed his eyes, feeling the cold of the water pushing toward him. The circling blue energy changed, turning into water within his palms. Allora looked up to see the wave of water reacting to Tanner's movement with his hands, and just as the roar of the wave burst through the cave opening,

Tanner thrust his body forward, releasing a shockwave of energy that knocked him back. He tripped over the huddled girls, and collapsed from exhaustion.

Allora opened one eye after a few seconds of silence, and the two girls sat up in disbelief. Even Tanner was wide-eyed, staring at what he had done. The rushing flow of the water was frozen.

"You did it!" Allora said, jumping on Tanner and giving him a hug. "And you're a Fermion like me!"

Tanner was caught off guard by Allora's affection, but he didn't mind it.

Dax walked around the large ice sculpture, staring at a baykok frozen in the wall of ice. He stared at the red-eyed skull and tapped the ice, and the creature's eyes spun around. Dax fell backward, putting his hand down to regain his balance. "Uh, guys, we should leave," he said, moving away from the mound of ice. As he made his retreat, he noticed a crack in the far wall.

Katie was on the other side, trying to find a way out. "And how do you propose we do that, genius?"

"How about we try this way," Dax said, squeezing himself into the wall.

Allora and Tanner got up quickly, and they all rushed over to the far side of the cave to find Dax shimmying sideways up small, narrow stairs. The crack was wide enough for them to scurry between the sides of the rock.

As Dax ascended, the walls widened, and the stairs became larger. About twenty yards up, Dax was able to climb normally, and he looked up to see a daunting ascent ahead. The others followed him for a painful climb, but the relief of escaping the caves reenergized them. The rock walls were slanted and increasingly taller as they climbed, and Allora's legs began to burn.

"This is harder than soccer practice," Tanner said. "That hadron burst took it out of me too."

"I know how you feel," Allora said, remembering that last time she had produced fire.

"If Coach Hale knew about this, he'd bring us down here for a pregame field trip," Dax said.

The boys continued talking about their soccer season while they hiked, but Allora was too busy with her own thoughts to pay any attention. She couldn't stop thinking about the orb resting against the inside of her coat.

"What do you think, Allora?" Tanner asked, twisting around. "Allora?"

She looked up, snapping back to reality. "What? Oh, sorry. I was thinking about something. What did you say?"

"Are you okay?" Tanner asked.

"Yeah, I'm fine," Allora said. "I'm just a little tired, that's all. What's up?"

"Dax was saying we should stop in Roseburg and get some food. You down?"

"Yes! I'm starving," Allora said, and the thought of food caused her stomach to gurgle in agreement with the plan. "I could really go for a cheeseburger."

"I second that," Katie said.

"Hey, Dax," Tanner said, trying to find an end to their ascent, "how much further is it?"

When Dax squinted and finally noticed the end to the steps, he said, "I think I see the top, maybe ten more minutes."

That said, they continued upward. Their leg muscles were throbbing, and every step was daunting, every movement more painful than previous one. The last ten minutes turned into twenty as their pace slowed to a crawl. Dax reached the last step and collapsed on a flat, level surface. One by one, they all reached the top, only to look at a wall of rock. Allora glanced back down the dark stairs, relieved that none of the baykok had escaped their icy prison.

"Great. We've traded one dead end for another," Katie said, frustrated. "Only this time, we scaled a mountain for it."

Tanner felt around the wall with his hands. There wasn't that much space, so it was a small area to search.

Dax walked over next to Tanner, followed by Allora and Katie. "I was really looking forward to that cheeseburger too," Dax said, leaning against the wall.

To all of their surprise, he didn't hit rock. Rather, he kept falling sideways. Tanner tried to grab him, but Dax's momentum pulled them both through. Katie tried to grab Tanner, but the weight of the boys was too much for her, so all she could do was swing her arm around and grasp Allora by the coat.

After all four passed through the rock, just as they had done in Sas' cave, they emerged in bright sunlight. Allora continued falling sideways, and then slid down a large boulder, on her back. She had no room to turn around, since sharp rocks jutted up on both sides of her. Finally, when the rocks parted and she had room to twist her body, she flipped onto her stomach right before reaching the edge.

Allora screamed, then fell into a bush, bounced off, and landed on a body. Dax was at the bottom of the pile, moaning. He had taken the weight of everyone dropping on top of him. Finally, she rolled sideways and landed in the dirt.

They remained still, lying on their backs, while a tour group stood in a state of confusion a few yards away, pointing, whispering, and snapping a barrage of photos with their cameras and phones.

"Are you guys alive?" Katie finally asked.

A chorus of guttural moans and grunts followed, the only acknowledgment they could muster.

Allora could see the visitor center through a small gap, between the curious tourists. "We made it," she said.

The night was over, and morning had come. Allora closed her eyes, basking in the feeling of the warm, soothing rays of sunlight upon her face. It was a beautiful spring day, without a cloud in the sky. The Eye of the Titans was now in their possession.

"Let's go home," Allora said.

Twenty-One

Eye

The forest was darkening as the sun set against the western ridge. A spring rain drizzled down from the foliage, allowing her to step silently through the underbrush. Her eyes darted across the plain of vision, scanning the area for movement. Her prey was elusive and far superior in evasion. Her hair and clothes were damp, allowing a chill to permeate her body. A twig snapped in the distance. She stopped moving, and squinted her eyes. There was a mass moving through the leaves of a bush. It was dark brown, and large. Allora smirked, and moved quickly, maintaining her silent footsteps as she got closer to the intended target. Rounding a tree trunk, past the edge of the bush, she pulled her stick up to strike.

Her eyes grew wide as the target turned. "Got ya!"

A large brown bear sprung up, standing on two legs and growling angrily. Allora wheeled backward, tripping on her own foot, and flopping down into the mud. The enormous beast clawed forward, snarling as it barreled down toward the terrified girl.

Just then, another presence laughed profusely, popping out from behind a tree nearby.

"I see you met George," Sas said. "Come here boy!"

The bear almost smiled, and bounded off toward the warlock, jumping up onto Sas' shoulders, licking his face.

Allora's eyes were wide and her mouth dropped. "You have a pet bear named George?"

"Nah, George is more of a friend. I've got a special kinship with the life of these woods. They are my eyes and ears. This guys is one of my favorites though."

The bear dropped down, got a good head rub from Sas, and stomped off into the night. Sas helped Allora to her feet, and they hiked back up the hill toward the cave. Allora had successfully convinced her mother of her farce, and went to Sas' place to make sure that the lie was convincing. There was also another purpose for her trip.

"I've got a question," Allora said as they trudged through the mud. "Do you know why my uncle wanted to find the Eye of the Titans so badly? Do you know what it could be used for?"

"Well, my father said that it had a specific link to the Titan Wars," Sas said as they got closer to the cave entrance. "Somehow it was one of a few items that was used to power some kind of weapon."

"You mean there's more than just this one artifact?" Allora asked, rubbing the round orb that she had zipped up in her interior coat pocket.

"Yeah, it was supposed to be a part of a set of keys meant to unlock a power greater than anything on this world or Sonora. You can see why the other side wants it so badly."

Sas led her toward the cave, opened a portal to her backyard, and she jumped through.

Milly was sitting in her usual spot in the kitchen, not too far from the cof-feemaker. "Hey! Welcome back. How was training?" she asked.

"It was… fine," Allora said, pulling off her dirty shoes.

"Nothing eventful happened?" Milly said.

Allora zipped through the kitchen and headed for her room. "Nope."

She closed her door softly, got her gear from outside the window, and put it in her closet. She tucked the orb in the far corner of the closet, then placed a bag in front to conceal it. It wasn't the ideal hiding spot, but it would do for the time being.

* * *

April had arrived, bringing the downpour of Oregon rain. Allora met up with her friends, and went quickly to Mr. Swan's classroom. Dax closed the door while Allora motioned for Mr. Swan to get out one of his silencing glue. As soon as the jelly-type material covered the walls, Allora pulled out the orb from her coat.

Mr. Swan's face went white, and he looked at the object. He opened his mouth to speak, but none of the words dropped out. He kept cocking his head up from staring at the orb, as if he wanted one of them to acknowledge that it was real. Even when Allora nodded her head, he still couldn't believe it. "How... where... when...?" was all he could stutter.

All four nodded their heads proudly and smiled at him.

"But you... you're just kids. The stories of The Eye say it was hidden among difficult, nearly insurmountable obstacles that would test even the strongest of Sonorans."

"Well, the stories were right," Tanner said. "It wasn't exactly easy."

"It would have been a lot easier if my knucklehead brother over here hadn't tried to steal that gold spear," Katie said, sneering at her brother.

"Hey, how was I supposed to know it would wake up an army of evil golden demons?" Dax said.

"Oh, I don't know, maybe you should have read the last part of the parchment a little closer," Katie snapped.

"Guys, let's focus," Mr. Swan said, motioning with his hands. "Where was it?"

"Allora's the genius," Tanner admitted, wrapping an arm around her neck.

Allora blushed and shook her head. "I can't take all the credit. Technically, my little sister figured it out. It was at Crater Lake, below Wizard's Island in the middle of the lake."

Mr. Swan smiled and shook his head. "You never cease to amaze me, Allora," he said. His proud demeanor changed when he thought of them going alone. "You should have told me of your plans. Any one of you could have been killed."

Allora spoke up in the middle of the awkward silence that followed. "We knew if we told you, you would have tried to stop us. You always talk about stepping up the challenge of responsibility, so we did exactly that."

Mr. Swan stared down his student with a furrowed brow. "That also means taking on the consequences that come with that responsibility. Would you have been able to live with the consequence of Katie being killed? Or Tanner?"

Mr. Swan let his words sink in, but before he could speak again, Dax said, "What about me?"

Mr. Swan looked at him with a perplexed expression. "Excuse me?"

"You named everyone else but me? Is it okay if I die or something?" Dax asked, crossing his arms.

Everyone chuckled.

"All right, let's take a look at this orb," Mr. Swan said, placing it in his palm.

They moved around beside the teacher so they could finally see the object that had been so difficult to retrieve.

"So…" Katie said impatiently.

Mr. Swan laughed. "You ready?" he said, pointing his finger.

A small spark exited his index finger and shot into the orb. As soon as it hit, Mr. Swan launched backward, only to crash into the wall of the classroom.

"Whoa!" they all yelled, then ran to their teacher and helped him up.

"You okay?" Allora asked.

Mr. Swan shook his head, barely conscious. "Yeah." His eyes fluttered. "Wow! That little thing is powerful." He staggered to the orb on the ground, picked it up, and handed it to Allora.

"Won't it be safer with you?" she asked.

"Obviously not, if you so easily tricked me and took the parchment. Besides, I don't think I was meant to possess it. Give it a try."

"No way!" Allora said, trying to give it back.

"Just trust me. I think that it's only going to respond to the hadron signature of the one who found it."

Reluctantly, Allora pointed her finger at the obsidian orb, and winced as she shot a hadron spark into the object. The purple light swirled into the interior of the orb, and grayish purple smoke spun around in the shape of an eye within. Then, the shape dissipated. Mr. Swan raised his eyebrows and smirked.

"We need more information about this thing before we try and use it. In the meantime, if you're going to hold on to it, you need to know how to create your own hiding spot."

Mr. Swan walked over to a blank wall and turned to face them. "First, you have to place your hand on the spot where you want to hide the object. Focus a small amount of hadrons to the palm of your hand. Once you feel the hadrons pulsating, twist your hand and stop when you want to. Remember which way you twisted your hand and at what angle you stopped," Mr. Swan instructed. "It's like the combination lock on your lockers. You spin your hand one way, then turn the other. When you're satisfied with the combination, let go." Mr. Swan did so, and the wall started to swirl. He took the orb and placed it into the wall, then sparked the wall, making it solid again.

"And how do you get it back out?" Allora asked.

Mr. Swan placed his hand on the wall again. "Do the same combination with your hand," he said, twisting his hand the same way as before. "Make sure to spark the wall while rotating." The orb slowly melted out of the wall when he was done. "Also, very important, make sure to guard this with your life. Got it?"

They all nodded in acknowledgment.

Mr. Swan knew he had to start preparing them for what they were inevitably going to face, and the four teens would have to grow up faster than most. The Sonoran rebellion was relying on them to lead the onslaught of Titan aggression that had plagued their past, and now they had the one tool to shift the balance of their campaign.

As Mr. Swan watched them leave his classroom, he thought back to the night that had sent him to Earth. The painful memory had always lingered in the back of his mind, just at it had in the minds of all who had witnessed the atrocities of that evening and thereafter.

Mr. Swan watched as Allora looked back and smiled before she left. He knew the outcome of the future lay in the hands of his star pupil, and guilt engulfed him when he noticed the innocence still glowing on Allora's face. He had set her destiny in motion, and there was no stopping the coming events.

Tanner, Dax, and Katie went ahead, stopping in the lobby in front of Kim.

"Allorrrra," A voice whispered. It was soft, yet powerful. She hesitated, feeling the energy emanating from the Eye of the Titans. She pulled the round object from her jacket pocket, she stared at the misty eye swirling inside. The artifact's beauty and mystery was mesmerizing. Suddenly, microscopic pores opened up on the surface of the obsidian orb, and a cloud of purple smoke exploded outward, like an aerosol spray. Allora was engulfed by the cloud, and coughed uncontrollably, dropping the orb back into her pocket. The cloud of purple mist evaporated quickly. She stumbled, falling against the locker, blinking profusely as her vision clouded, while her feet lumbered around erratically.

"So then, you'll go to prom with me?" Kim asked.

Tanner looked back and forth, unable to answer. Truthfully, he didn't really want to go with her. Not until Dax shoved him in the shoulder did he blurt out, "Uh… sure."

Allora's mind faded. The toxic chemical agent moved through her body, affecting her nervous system.

Kim stood with a big, sappy, victorious grin on her face, like a candidate who'd just won an election, and then left after giving Tanner a kiss on the cheek.

"What is going on?" Allora asked, holding her head against the tide of pain that pulsated with each thought.

"What was I supposed to say?" Tanner said, throwing his hands up. "She cornered me."

"I think I'm going to be sick," Allora responded, not even comprehending anything because of the excruciating pain that filled her body.

Dax jumped in to his friend's defense. "Personally, I'm happy for him. I'm just pissed she didn't ask me first."

"Seriously?" Katie said. "That girl is crazy, don't you guys see that?"

"Prom really isn't that big of a deal," Tanner said.

"This is wrong," Allora said, staggering out of the school.

"I don't understand why you're so mad at me," Tanner said, shrugging his shoulders.

Dax shook his head. "Man, I'll never figure women out. They make less sense than those red-eyed goons we ran away from the other day."

"Maybe that's because you have the emotional capacity of a robot," Katie said to her brother.

"Allora, wait, let's talk about this," Tanner said, following her out the main double doors into an empty parking lot. Dax and Katie weren't far behind. The gas completely consumed Allora's cells, her body seized up, and she collapsed, falling hard to the concrete.

Twenty-Two

FEVER

The rain was heavy, falling in a torrent in the spring air. Allora glanced around. Her vision was hazy, but clearing. The forest was familiar, yet felt eerie and dark. She looked down and wrung out her soaked shirt. The cold crept in like the coming of a fog. The wind came up from the ground, like a vent on a city street.

She walked forward, listening intently to the constant drumbeat of the rain dripping down from the canopy. Her heart was beating faster as the trees closed in, slowly lowering their branches.

"Run," A voice whispered. The old and raspy voice was the same voice she heard in the hallway at school.

Planting her back foot, she sprinted through the brush, swiping aggressively at the branches that tried to lasso her limbs. The rain beat back against her face. From the ground, skeletal hands sprung up, grasping at her ankles as she ran. From the foliage, numerous large spider-like creatures crawled down, just like the one from the ape caves.

Baykok broke with the mud, pulling from the ground to join the pursuit. The downpour of rain increased, accumulating in puddles, and slowing her pace. Fear consumed her as the puddles turned to a river. From behind, a rushing wave of water barreled through the forest. Her arms swung wildly as she trudged through the deepening river.

She glanced behind as the cresting wave crashed down, spinning her body wildly. Bubbles blew from her mouth, forced out from the impact. A light shone from her right. Without breath, she scrambled toward the light, pulling at the heavy water. Just about to break from depths, the surface froze. Her hands searched hysterically, trying to find a hole. Her mind was dropping from consciousness. Instinctively, her hands burst with fire, melting the ice above. She sprang with her last strength, and erupted from the depths, coughing and vomiting the liquid she had swallowed.

Sharp, pointed teeth bit down on her torso and limbs, pulling her from the water. The world spun around, and gravity switched, dragging her down through piles of snakes. She tried to scream, but her throat was still sore from almost drowning. The emotional anxiety caused her entire body to convulse.

* * *

"She's having a seizure!" Milly yelled, trying to hold onto her daughter's body as it shook.

Aunt May rushed into the room, holding a grey bottle. She squeezed her niece's cheeks as Milly tried to hold her wrists tightly against the mattress. Dax, Tanner, and Katie burst into the room, and helped to control Allora's other limbs. Aunt May poured the substance from the grey bottle down the throat, and closed the mouth, holding her nose and under the chin. Allora's body stopped shaking, and eased back down into the bed.

"The Talman juice will help with the seizures, but her fever is at one hundred and eight degrees," Aunt May instructed. "Any more than that and she could run the risk of serious brain damage."

"What could have caused this?" Milly asked.

"It doesn't seem to be a normal flu. She could have been poisoned or exposed to some sort of bio weapon. You know we used a few in the Rebel Wars."

"Did you three see Allora with or around anyone that might have done this?"

They shook their heads in unison.

"We need Ferris on this one," Milly instructed, staring down at her daughter's pale face.

"I'll be right back," Aunt May said, leaving the room.

* * *

The sunlight glinted off the window of a tall skyscraper, blinding Allora as she sat alone on a park bench. Raising her hand to shield the light, she could see the surrounding landscape. A lush green park encircled by towering buildings. Kids pushed each other on a swing set, dogs were running for tennis balls, and a woman was shaking a small stuffed bear in front of her baby who was lying in a stroller next to her. The air was a mix of hot dogs, exhaust, and bark dust.

Across the playground and through the grassy field, a man stood staring her way. Allora squinted in the sunlight, noticing the familiarity of the distant man.

"Uncle Ben," Allora said softly, standing up from the bench.

Just then, the ground shook as she ran through the playground. Allora stumbled, catching her hand on the metal swing post, watching the surrounding skyscrapers sway in the sky. Cars honked and crashed into each other. A water main burst, showering the streets. The earthquake grew in strength, shattering windows in the buildings. Glass rained down onto the streets, and screams echoed into the park. The ground beneath Allora lifted and split apart. She hung onto the metal beam as the ground shifted, leaning to one side.

Allora tried to plant her feet to get leverage to jump across the opening chasm, but the angle and shifting dirt was slippery. All she could do was watch the carnage and chaos. Buildings collapsed under the extreme vibration, fire exploded from broken gas lines, and water filled the streets as the sea crested over the ports.

She stared at the young women clutching her crying baby. The fear in her face broke Allora's soul. The sound of concrete splitting drowned out the constant rumbling of the earth. The skyscraper was splitting near the top, and dropping down onto the playground. Allora could avoid it, but the woman with the baby wouldn't make it. Allora pushed off from the slanted slab, leapt over the crevice and rolled on the bark dust toward the park bench just as the building

was a few feet from crashing to the ground. She put her arm up, focused hadrons, and created a shield above herself and the woman.

The weight and pressure was overwhelming. The ground beneath cracked
and she broke through it, falling into a dark abyss. The woman and baby disappeared. She was alone, falling through a never ending tunnel. Shifting her
weight, she moved through the air toward the side of the tunnel. Below, a distant
orange glow appeared, giving some light to the tunnel. As she got closer to the
side, shapes formed. Dead faces appeared with closed eyelids. Allora dropped
her legs, moving away from the tunnel's sides as the eyes popped open, and
hands sprang forward, trying to grasp her falling body.

Then, the walls of the tunnel closed in. The only escape was the orange
glow beneath. She tucked her chin to her chest, hugged her sides with her arms,
and dove head first. Heat hit her face as the orange circle grew. The tunnel was
collapsing, and dead hands got closer. Allora's body burst into a purple fire as it
rocketing toward the lava below. She hit the fingertips of the dead hands as she
sprung from the bottom of the tunnel into an open cavern of magma.

* * *

"Oh Zeus, she's crashing!" Milly yelled, feeling the faint pulse on her
daughter's wrist and watching Allora struggle to breath.

Mrs. Ferris rushed into the room, pulled up the girl's shirt, and placed
three round stickers on her chest. Suddenly, Allora's body raised up from the
bed and dropped back down. Tanner's fist pulsated with frustration, watching
helplessly from the corner of the room. Mrs. Ferris pulled a vial and a needle
from her brown medical bag. Placing the needle into the main vein in her arm,
she injected the grayish fluid into her system. Then, she pulled back the girl's
eyelids to see small purple veins throughout the sclera and iris of the eye. After
checking the pulse and temperature, she grabbed an old leather-bound book
from her bag.

"Carpetalius Mothkramaticalus," Mrs. Ferris said, closing the dusty tome.
"Also known as Serpent's Sight. Nasty stuff. It contains a certain hallucinogen

that'll test the minds strength. Learned about it in my PhD program at Titanis University. Comes from venom of an extinct ground snake in the upper mountains of Avalon."

Aunt May put a hand over her mouth and dropped her warm eyes to her niece. "Is there a cure or antidote of some kind?"

"Not that I'm aware of," Mrs. Ferris responded. "I believe that the only cure is time, and Allora's ability to overcome her own fears."

"How did she get exposed to it then?" Milly asked.

"Unless someone synthesized the formula, which I doubt because of the extreme complexity, she'd have to have been exposed to something older. An artifact most likely. This stuff was used as a way of keeping ancient artifacts from being found by unworthy suitors. Excalibur, holy grail, and numerous other items were imbued with the stuff."

Tanner and Dax had slipped out of the room.

"We have to tell them," Tanner insisted.

"Would something like The Eye of the Titans have this same stuff imbued in it?" Milly asked, stepping backward into the hallway, staring down the two boys.

"Busted," Dax said.

"Get me Swan right now!" Milly demanded.

* * *

The fire was immense. It scorched Allora's clothes, burning intensely and shearing off scraps of fabric as her body continued to fall toward the lava. She closed her eyes, feeling the power from the fire, and absorbed the energy into her cells. A shockwave burst from her naked body with the strength of a nuclear explosion. All of the rock and magma was dissolved, leaving Allora to fall onto a field.

She wore a tight black battle suit, kneeling in front of a masked man with a hooded black cloak. In her hands were two katana swords. She got to her feet and waited in the dark mist of the night. The masked hooded man pulled a sword from a sheath attached to his back. Allora ran forward, swinging around with her two swords. Steel met as the swords connected. Sparks dropped to the damp field, and the sounds of clanking metal echoed into the void of the dream.

The masked man thrusted the blade forward, slicing the suit and ripping into Allora's side. She winced and parried, striking down with one sword and thrusting with the other. The man blocked the first strike and spun around to avoid the second attack. Allora saw an opening, slid past the man as he tried again to thrust forward. She flipped the sword to point backward, and drove the sword into the man's back, piercing the suit. Then she swung around and sliced the man's wrist. He dropped his weapon, and reeled back.

"Take off your mask," Allora demanded, pointing a sword toward his face. The man reluctantly pulled off the hood, then the battle mask. "Tanner."

Allora's eyes popped wide, wanting an explanation.

"You killed me," Tanner said, pulling his hand from the wound, and placing a palm out to show her the blood. He inched closer. Allora dropped her swords. Before she could react, Tanner pulled a knife from the hidden compartment on his belt, and stabbed her in the gut. She screamed and leaned forward against her attacker.

"You will fail," a voice said, this one female. The blade was pulled from her abdomen, and the attacker stepped back. Allora grabbed her gut, trying to keep pressure on the wound. She looked up to see her own face smirking back at her. "And everyone you care about will die."

* * *

Mr. Swan rushed into the bedroom, breathing heavily.

"How is she?" He asked, coming around to the end of the bed.

"How is she?" Milly exclaimed, stepping up from next to the side table. "She's got an extreme fever and her heart almost stopped, so you tell me!"

"Milly, I never approved them going down there. They did it on their own."

"Only because you kept pushing them after I explicitly told you not to!"

"This is how it was supposed to happen though. The Eye is meant to test the warrior in the three pillars of life. It tests them physically, emotionally, and mentally. Mind, body, and soul. The worthy shall prevail."

Milly lunged across the room, wrapped her hands around Swan's neck and crashed into the armoire, breaking it into pieces. "I'm going to kill you!"

* * *

Allora was shocked. She was staring at herself. So caught up in the moment, she took a deep breath, calming her mind and focusing her thoughts.

"This is not real," She said to herself. "You are not real. This wound is not real."

She kept repeating the words until the blood stopped gushing, and the apparition of herself faded.

The sun rose out of the darkness, filling the field with light and expanding till there was nothing but light.

Allora lifted her head up from the pillow, awakening from the dream. Her fever had dissipated, and the effects of the Serpent's Sight had dissolved from her cells.

"What's going on?" Allora asked, confounded by the oddity of her mother strangling her teacher with her friends trying to pull them apart from all directions. Her room was a complete mess. "Is this another hallucination?"

Everyone stopped moving, and glanced up. Then, her friends leapt onto the bed, smothering the girl.

"Told you she'd come through," Mr. Swan said, receiving a raised eyebrow from Milly as she pulled her hands from his neck.

"Are you alright?" Milly asked, sitting down in the bed, and checking over her daughter.

"My whole body is sore," Allora said, pulling at her clothes. "And I'm drenched in sweat."

"Can you guys give us a minute?" Milly asked, prompting the others to leave the room. "I know about Crater Lake. Do you know how stupid that was?"

"Mom, I've got to follow this path. I know you think I'm crazy, but I know what I'm doing."

"Are you sure?"

"I don't think I'll ever be sure of anything, but I've at least got to try."

"Even if you die?" Milly said, gently swiping her daughter's bangs from her face. "You are more important than you realize. You are the rightful heir to the Titan throne, and if you die, Salazar wins."

"If I don't continue with this path, he'll win anyways," Allora said, staring straight into her mother's eyes confidently.

Twenty-Three

PROM

Brushing her long, brown hair in a furious fashion, Allora sat in front of her mirror, dreading the evening's events. Prom was only hours away, and she'd had to reluctantly settle for Brandon as a date since no one else had asked her. He wasn't the worst guy in the school, but Allora had definitely had her heart set on walking into the prom on the arm of a suit-clad Tanner. She smiled when she imagined him in a tux, but her smile quickly faded when she thought of Kim hanging all over him during a slow dance.

She stopped brushing her hair and sat back in her chair with a sigh. Looking across the room, she stared at the wall where the orb was hidden. Allora got up from the chair, walked to the wall, and performed the combination to open the hiding spot. *Why is this piece of rock so important?* She asked herself, twisting the orb in her palm. A black glint sparkled against the dim light. Staring into the almost-liquid interior, Allora felt a surge of energy flow into her hand.

The bedroom doorknob twisted, and Allora quickly shoved the orb in her purse right before Milly opened the door.

"You sure you want to go to this?" Milly asked.

"Yes mom, I want to go," Allora said rapidly. "I'm good. No more fever and I feel good."

"It's just that a few days ago you almost died, so I completely understand if you…" Milly just stared at her daughter for a moment.

"Mother…" Allora said, tilting her head and raising her eyebrow.

"Well, you should probably get ready. Everyone will be here soon," Milly said, closing the door.

Allora slouched forward, letting out her breath. Katie showed up while Allora was putting on her dress, and she walked in with her own white dress in hand, along with more makeup and paraphernalia than any one woman could use in her lifetime. "Oh my god! Allora, you look hot!"

"Shut up," Allora said, pulling up the middle of the short, strapless purple dress. The bodice was tightly wrapped with a purple band that fit snuggly around her waist, and the outfit beautifully accentuated Allora's long, muscular legs. Open-toed black heels finished the ensemble, with a web-like pattern over the heel and a strap across the top of her foot.

Katie hiked up her tight white dress while looking in the mirror. "You look amazing. Brandon's gonna love it."

"Yeah? Well, he's not the one I'm trying to impress," Allora said, looking at her reflection in the mirror and pulling the sides of the dress down to eliminate wrinkles.

"If it's Tanner you're worried about, don't. He's gonna be so jealous and feel like a fool for being there with her instead of you," Katie said, pulling up her dress. Like Allora, she had rented a strapless, short dress that flowed outward. It was white, with a satin sash that tied in the front, and it perfectly matched Katie's personality. She had never really liked clothing that inhibited her ability to run.

Allora ignored Katie's comment and went to the bathroom to put on her makeup. Part of her wanted Tanner to be jealous. She knew it wasn't the right way to go about getting his attention, but Allora was hurt that he was taking Kim, of all people. She applied her lip gloss and a few other minor cosmetics, then joined Katie in the living room.

Katie noticed her friend pulling at her dress. "What are you doing?"

"I hate thongs," Allora said, tugging on the fabric. "Who invented these things anyway? I don't know how you ever convinced me to wear one. It's like I've got a constant wedgie."

"You never know what might happen tonight," Katie said with a wink.

Allora turned to Katie, who was smiling widely. "I know what's *not* gonna happen."

She pointed her finger at her friend and sent a small purple spark in her direction, shocking her.

"Hey!" Katie yelled. "Quit zapping me."

Allora grinned. "Serves you right."

"Girls, your friends are here," Milly said as she walked in from outside. "Oh my!" she said, catching a glimpse of her daughter and Katie. "You both look beautiful, though you went a little heavy on the makeup, didn't you, Katie?"

"Even the *Mona Lisa* was painted," Katie said with a wink, then rubbed her side while she greeted her classmates.

The first to arrive were Jenny and Tanya. Allora couldn't believe two of the girls she despised in the beginning of the year were now going with her to prom. Behind Jenny, Brandon strutted in, dressed in a black and white tuxedo and a black bowtie.

"You look amazing girl," he said, walking up to Allora, tugging at his collar as if he was very uncomfortable.

"Uh... thanks," Allora responded without much enthusiasm, never one to take compliments very well.

Katie's date, Kyle, was dressed in an eighties-inspired retro red suit. He walked through the door with a huge smile on his face and strolled up to Katie, who was holding her hand to her mouth, unable to believe his outfit.

"Are you kidding me?" Katie exclaimed.

"I know, right? I saw it and had to have it," Kyle said, holding his jacket sides outward and spinning around. "Awesome, huh?"

Allora couldn't help but burst out laughing, and Katie sneered in her direction. "Yeah, it's totally, uh... rad," Allora joked.

Jenny's date to prom, Robert Mondrach, came in a few minutes later, looking incredibly handsome. Robert was dressed in a black Armani suit with a matching black vest, a silver tie, and polished black shoes.

Tanya's date, Chris, the starting center for the football Pioneers, came in next. He was six-five and looked a little uncomfortable in his undersized black suit.

Dax came in with his date moments later, a girl Allora recognized as Erin. She was a sophomore on the cheerleading team, and she'd been at the rock quarry the night of the rover attack. She looked as incredible as any of the other girls in the room. Her dress was pink, tight, and flowed at the bottom.

"Hi, Erin," Allora said, assuming the girl might be nervous about being one of the youngest in the group.

"Hey," Erin responded. "That's an amazing dress. Where'd you get it?"

Allora looked down. "This rental?" she joked. "Found it in Portland."

The adults congregated in the kitchen with their cameras in hand, and Milly appeared around the corner to address everyone. "Okay, guys, picture time!" she said, holding up her camera.

"Hey, we're missing someone," Allora said, looking side to side. "Where's Tanner?"

Dax popped his head forward. "He texted me and said he's already with Kim and that he'll meet us there."

Everyone filed through the front door. When they congregated outside, they huddled up with their dates, boys in the back and girls in the front. The rhododendron bushes were blooming behind them, which made for a great backdrop.

Allora grabbed her stomach, feeling queasy. There was something wrong.

With every flash of the camera, she caught a glimpse of Tanner being beaten and tortured, and over time, the flashes became more intense. Her heart began to beat faster, her mind swam in her skull, and a tingling sensation made her limbs feel funny.

She closed her eyes and heard a scream come from within, *"Allora!"* from a voice that was unmistakably Tanner's. The second the adults were done with the photo session, Allora sprinted to the bathroom.

Katie was the only one who noticed the quick departure and ran after her, wondering why she was so upset. Katie rounded the corner to see Allora over the sink, splashing water on her face. "Don't! You're gonna to mess up your makeup," Katie said.

"I don't care," Allora snapped.

"Look, Allora, I know Brandon's not Tanner, but he obviously tried to look nice for you, and you should give him a chance. It's rude to leave him standing out there just because—"

Allora grabbed Katie by the shoulders. "It's not that," she said.

Katie had never seen her friend so upset before. "What is it then? What's wrong?"

"I can't really explain it, but I need to go check on something."

"What do you mean?" Katie asked.

Allora let go of Katie. "I need to borrow your car. My mother is leaving soon to help with the prom setup. I need to leave as soon as she's gone."

"But what am I supposed to tell Brandon and the others?"

"I don't know, Katie. Think of something. Just tell them I had to take care of something. Please do this for me. It's... important."

Dax came around the corner to go to the bathroom.

"Allora is leaving for some reason," Katie told him, then turned back to Allora. "What about dinner? And where are you going?"

After a long pause, Allora said, "I have to go check on Tanner."

"C'mon, Allora! Can't you just let it go this one night?" Katie said.

"I need to make sure he's okay."

"He's probably just getting some pre-prom nookie," Dax teased, smiling.

Katie turned around and smacked her brother on the shoulder. "Why do you always have to be such an insensitive jerk?"

Allora ignored the twins and snatched Katie's purse from her grasp, but Katie was too busy lecturing her brother to notice. Allora removed the car keys and dashed out the door while the sibling rivalry raged on.

Milly gave her daughter a goodbye hug, then left with the other adults to go help with the setup and serve as chaperones. The second her mother was out of sight, Allora jumped in Katie's driver seat and turned the keys.

Suddenly, the passenger door opened.

"I need to go, Katie," she said, but the individual who hopped into the seat next to her wasn't Katie.

"So what are you waiting for? Let's go," Jenny said.

"Huh? You don't even know where I'm going," Allora said, confused.

"I overheard you talking to Katie. I don't trust that Kim girl either. Something's not right with her, and I still care enough about Tanner to want to make sure he's all right. A girl like that digs her stilettos in a guy, and who knows what she'll do."

"I have to do this alone," Allora responded, frustrated that Jenny was holding her up.

Jenny crossed her arms and glared at her sternly. "Don't make me call your mom. Let's go."

Allora thought about it and realized her mother would have preferred she go with someone anyway instead of running off on her own. Besides that, she knew she didn't have time to argue with Jenny. Without another thought or any more debate, she threw Katie's car in reverse and sped out of the driveway.

Allora weaved through traffic, pushing down on the gas pedal. The house where they'd dropped Kim off before wasn't that far away. Allora pulled the car into an area that couldn't be seen, and then both girls crept along the road, till they found a row of hedges that gave them a perfect view of the house without exposing their whereabouts. Allora knelt down next to Jenny, placed her purse on the ground, and they waited, not knowing what lay behind the dark red door of the Nelson house.

A loud, and obnoxious ringing erupted from Allora's purse, breaking the silence. Frantically, she fumbled around the purple bag.

"Hello?"

"Where are you?" Katie asked. "We're about to leave."

"I'm at the Nelson's place," Allora answered just as the front door of the house crept open. "I gotta go." Katie's frantic voice trailed off as she ended the call.

Jenny tugged on the purple fringe of Allora's dress. They both ducked down and watched Kim strut out of the doorway. As they gazed between the branches of the bush in front of them, they saw Kim carefully scanning the front yard from side to side, like a sentry. They remained silent, waiting impatiently.

Slowly, Kim stepped off the porch. The *crunch* of leaves beneath her feet grew louder, then stopped at the edge of the bush. Both girls held their breath as they looked down at Kim's shiny red heels through the twigs. Suddenly, Kim's feet snapped around, like a soldier on patrol. After a few agonizing minutes, she went back to the house.

Jenny popped her head up in time to see Kim lock the front door, turn, and walk out onto the road.

They peeked around the bush to see her rounding the corner. "Where the hell is she going?" Allora asked.

"I don't know, but I love her dress," Jenny said.

"Really?"

"Can't fault the girl for having good fashion sense."

"Where's Tanner?" Allora asked, scanning the windows of the house. The question hit Allora right in the gut, and her breath escaped at the thought of anything happening to him. Panic stricken, she became more determined. "We have to get inside that house."

Jenny had to hike up her long yellow dress to keep it out of the rain-soaked lawn of brown, thick grass that no one had cut in far too long. They inched toward the side of the house and stood on their toes to see inside the window. Flakes of paint peeled away from the windowsill, as Allora lifted herself up to get a closer look.

"Does anyone even live here?" Allora asked, dropping back down into the mud.

"I don't know, but I saw her lock the door. How are we gonna get in?" Jenny whispered.

Allora confirmed it by trying to twist the doorknob. They tiptoed around the porch, searching for an access point. The floorboards creaked and shuddered under their weight as they walked carefully across them in their mud-covered heels and made their way to the back door.

With every minute, Allora's stress level rose. The pained images of Tanner being tortured kept flashing in her mind. Frantically, she scanned the windows on the first floor. One window was opened slightly. "Jenny, give me a boost. I think I can squeeze through," Allora said, after muscling the rusty window up another inch.

After removing her heels, Allora stepped onto Jenny's clasped hands, and then shimmied through the small opening. As Allora crawled across the top of a washing machine, her dress caught, and she pulled awkwardly, ripping the synthetic fabric down the side. Off balance, her hand slipped from the edge of the appliance, sending her crashing to the linoleum.

"You all right?" Jenny whispered through the window.

"Yeah, I'm good," Allora answered, examining the tear on her dress. "I'm not sure my mom's gonna be too happy about losing her deposit on this dress though."

Jenny wiped off her muddy heels the best she could, then walked inside, and both girls tiptoed through the kitchen and into the living room. A layer of dust covered the shelves and cupboards, and huge cobwebs hung in the corners like drapes. At the bottom of the stairs, they caught a whiff of a putrid, nauseating stench wafting down from the second floor.

"Oh my god!" Jenny whispered, squeezing her nose shut. "What is that?"

Allora shrugged her shoulders, plugging her nose as well. The two moved cautiously up the steps, trying not to make a sound. Jenny's heel got stuck, causing her to fall forward, and the sound reverberated against the filthy, dusty walls. Allora cringed, snapping around, and Jenny looked up with an apologetic look.

They continued their ascent, being more careful this time, and finally made it to the top step. They stood and stared intently down the darkened hallway, as if expecting a ghost to appear. The shutters on the window were closed, and the air felt cold and dank. The sickening smell lingered, but everything was eerily quiet. A chill shot up Allora's spine, causing her to shake.

Allora grabbed the doorknob of the closest room and twisted the brass handle. The rusty knob clanked and squeaked. She bit down on her lip, knowing that if anyone was in the house, they certainly would have heard that. The house was old, and none of the hinges had been oiled in years.

When the wooden door opened into the master bedroom, an inescapable stench blew out. The bed was in the corner, and there were lumps under the sheets. Even when Jenny tried to pull at Allora's arm, and even when her legs grew heavy, as if they were made of lead, she kept going. Every step increased a dreadful feeling of trepidation, but she had to know if Tanner was there.

As Allora apprehensively grasped the sheet that covered the bed, Jenny moved closer. Curiosity had beaten out her fear, and she walked to the edge of the bed and gave a nod. Allora swallowed hard, then yanked back the sheet. Both girls jumped, and Jenny tried to move her hand to her mouth to hush the unavoidable scream, but it still echoed in the stillness. Allora, on the other hand, was too grossed out to move.

Lying in the bed before them were Mr. and Mrs. Nelson, decomposing as if they'd been dead for a while. The grotesque image was burned into the forefront of the girls' minds, and the smell of death overwhelmed their nostrils with a noxious odor they would never forget. They ran out of the room, and Jenny gagged as if she might vomit.

In the hallway, they heard what sounded like a groan coming from one of the other rooms. Unsure of the source, Allora walked down the hallway with her ears trained forward. As she walked, the noise grew louder. The dark hallway was only illuminated by the light that shone through the slits in the shutters.

Jenny was still behind her, bent over, with her hands on her knees. "Where are you going?" she asked.

Allora didn't say anything, for she was too busy concentrating on the noise from the room.

Jenny finally managed to stand up straight when the dry heaves stopped. "Allora, we've gotta call the police!" she whispered. She hurried over to Allora. "We have to go!"

"No!" Allora said, shifting her attention back to the closed door. This time, she swung the door open quickly, bracing herself for what she might see. Instead of a corpse under a sheet, she found a boy sitting on a chair with his head down. "Tanner!" Allora ran over and hugged him. "I thought you were dead."

Tanner slowly picked up his head and looked at her. His hands were bound behind the chair, and he couldn't speak because of the rag tied around his head and mouth. When Allora removed it, he let out a breath he'd been holding for far too long and blurted out, "I'm sorry."

Allora shuffled behind the chair to untie his hands.

"I shoulda listened to you. I just... I..."

He was still in his tuxedo, but it was cut up and dirty. Around his neck, a bowtie hung loosely. Blood trickled down his cheek, and his right eye was blue and swollen. His hair was damp and disheveled.

"Tanner, what did she do to you?" Jenny asked, finally making her way into the room.

Both girls frantically pulled at the rope, but the tight knots took a while to get loose.

"We've gotta get out of here before she comes back. That girl is psychotic," Jenny said, pulling the last of the rope away.

Tanner rubbed his wrists as he got up. "Tell me about it."

The three were about to leave the room when they heard the front door open. Fear stopped them at the doorway, and they froze, not sure what to do.

Tanner grabbed Jenny's arm and closed the door as quietly as possible, then swung Jenny to the other side of the room. "The window," he said. "It's our only chance."

He unlatched it and yanked it open, then held Jenny's hand and helped her up onto the windowsill. She stepped onto the roof and slid down the shingles to the gutter. Allora clutched her purse, and stepped onto the roof. Tanner pulled his body up, and swung his feet around as the brass doorknob turned.

Twenty-Four

STORM

The door swung open, revealing two figures. The rover from the rock quarry stood next to the girl in the red dress, whose eyes grew wide as she stepped into the room.

There was a moment of pause. Time stopped. Kim's body became tense, her eyes turned cherry red, and she shook in an unnatural spasm of anger. Allora recognized what her next move would be, but she couldn't communicate it in time. Kim pulled her hands to the sides of her body, and a red glow grew at her waist. Allora pulled Tanner down the roof just as Kim sent the red glow shooting into the wall. An explosion of wood and glass shot out, propelling Allora, Tanner, and Jenny into the air. They hit the grass of the yard, and rolled. Jenny landed awkwardly and twisted her ankle.

Allora's purse flew from her shoulder, landing somewhere in the corn field. Splinters of wood and shards of glass rained down. Kim and the rover appeared from the blown out, burning hole in the top floor. Allora focused, absorbing hadrons, and shot a burst toward the house. The purple ball of energy exploded into the roof, forcing Kim and the rover backward. That gave Allora and Tanner enough time to help Jenny up so they could run off through the cornstalks that filled the back yard.

They weaved through the brown, withered corn, zigzagging away from the house, toward the forest. Jenny limped through the pain, wincing at each step. The sharp edges of the dead corn kept cutting their arms, leaving long slits of red. Once they made it to the edge of the farm, they stopped, allowing Jenny enough time to catch up.

"Do you have your phone?" Tanner asked.

"My purse," Allora said, frantically scanning around, realizing the worst. "Oh, no! I had the Eye in my purse. We have to go back for it."

"No way. Not safe. You've got to get to the school and call someone," Tanner instructed. "It should just be up through these trees."

Jenny was on the ground, holding her ankle and wincing in pain. "Guys, just leave me and save yourselves," she said in a pathetic gesture that was almost comical. She winced and rocked her head back. Jenny's ankle was bruised and ballooning to the size of a cantaloupe, probably broken. "I'm finished."

Tanner rolled his eyes. "Take her. I'll distract them."

"Be careful," Allora responded, grabbing his hand.

Tanner held the tips of her fingers, smiled, and then moved back into the stalks of corn.

Allora scurried into the woods ahead, listening to Tanner yell behind her. The light from the sun was dimming, but the girls pushed through the darkening forest. Their dresses were ripped and painted in mud.

In the distance, thunder filled the air, and the ground vibrated with every *boom*. Ahead, the trees opened up to a bright, unnatural green turf covering the ground ahead, illuminated by the surrounding field lights. Rain pelted down as they struggled up the last incline. They were almost out of the woods, quite literally, when they heard a branch crack behind them.

They broke through the edge of the forest to feel the soft turf beneath their feet. Allora turned her head in time to see the streak of red, and her movement sent Jenny flying to the right, just in time to let the red ball shot between them. Allora landed on her arm, and the impact knocked the wind right out of her. Jenny rolled to a stop near the goalpost.

Allora tried to pull herself up to defend against the next attack, but it was too late. She recognized the dark figure approaching, the same maniacal creature that had attacked them on Halloween. His dark, sinister, red eyes glowed as he pulled his hands to the side to fire again.

The wraith leapt out of the forest, firing another burst. Jenny jumped in front, taking the full impact of the attack. The hit knocked her back into Allora, and both of them slid along the wet turf. The wraith grabbed Allora's dress and flung her back toward the forest. She flailed around, dropping hard into the turf. Again, Allora's breath escaped. She managed to get up on all fours, gasping for air, and caught a glimpse of the dark black, bleeding wound on Jenny's abdomen. Allora couldn't tell if she was alive.

Allora got to her feet and focused two purple hadron balls in her palms. The wraith mimicked her move, attacking in kind. The hadron missiles detonated, exploding like a burst of fireworks. The force pushed Allora back, but she braced her right foot behind her to get traction and then ran forward, readying herself to strike. The dark creature sent another shot, and Allora angled her body, twisting around like a gymnast performing a floor routine. The red streak missed by mere inches.

Launching her own attack, Allora fought the wraith, punching and kicking in short bursts. The wraith flipped around to avoid Allora's high-swinging leg, and that gave him an opportunity to attack, which he capitalized on, punching Allora hard in the side. She pulled her feet back in order to evade the creature's next move, but she slipped. The kick hit her hard in the head, knocking her down.

A red burst exploded into her body, lifting her off the ground. The pain was so intense that she almost blacked out. A hazy figure ran from the forest, and a wave of water hit the wraith from behind. The black form of the wraith tumbled along the turf and then instantly froze. Allora blinked profusely. Water dripped down her face. Between the beads of rain, she saw Tanner get hit by a hadron burst, and he flew to a stop next to her.

She felt a forceful hand grasp the back of her dress. Whoever it was pulled her up and slammed her against the metal goalpost. Her vision was blurred, but images began to come into focus. A hand seized her neck and clenched, causing Allora to choke. As she struggled for breath and blinked her eyes, the figure of a short, black-haired girl in a red dress came into focus.

Kim kept a firm hold on her neck with one hand, and used the other to focus energy against her arms to keep her immobile.

The rover came around and put his reptile-like hand on Allora's forehead. Small suction cups stuck to her skin. After a long minute, the rover's eyes grew wide and sinister, as if he'd finally found a treasure he'd been seeking.

"Is it her?" Kim asked, glaring at her prey.

He pulled back and declared, "Yesssssssssssss." His tongue slithered out, licking the side of Allora's right cheek.

"Send a gateway relay to Titanis, and inform them that we found Princess Aurora."

"My name is Allora."

"Silly girl. So naive. Now, where is the Eye of the Titans?" Kim asked, squeezing the girl's neck tighter.

Allora flexed her neck and scrunched her face. "You'll never find it."

"What about thisssssssss one?" The rover asked, kicking the side of Tanner's unconscious body.

"Tell us where the Eye is princess or he dies," Kim demanded. Allora glared into the red eyes. A few seconds passed. Allora stayed quiet. "Kill him."

An energy grew within the core of Allora's chest. Her hands closed down into tight fists, and her neck flexed. From the forest, a bright glow illuminated the darkness, moving at great speed, distracting the rover. The glowing object flew through the air, and struck Allora in the chest. The increase of energy was instantaneous, filling Allora's slight form with an incredibly amount of hadrons. Electricity shot from her fingertips. She swung forward, launching a purple burst into the girl with the red dress. Kim screamed as the ball of energy hit her stomach, launching her back into the canopy of the trees.

The rover sprang over Tanner's waking body. Allora swung around, striking the rover in the chest with another burst, sending him flailing into the bleachers. A familiar voice echoed from the dark forest as Tanner got to his feet.

Katie and Dax popped up from the incline and ran over, brandishing weapons and a purple purse.

Katie hugged Allora. "You've looked better," she said, noticing Allora's bird's-nest hair, protruding in all directions, the cuts all over her body, and the tears in her dress. "You definitely need this little accessory," Katie said, handing her a bow.

"Thanks," Allora said.

"Is that Jenny over there?" Katie asked, noticing the limp body on the field.

Allora thought back to Jenny's unselfish act of bravery. "Yeah, she saved my life."

"Is she…" Katie asked, unable to say the word.

Tanner ran over, knelt down, and placed two fingers on Jenny's neck.

"She's got a pulse," he said, ripping part of his shirt to place on the girl's bleeding wound. "We need to get her to a hospital."

"We need reinforcements first," Tanner suggested. "Its not safe."

"What's going on?" Katie asked. "We went to the Nelson house, and it's destroyed."

Dax gave Tanner his sword. "Yeah, we saw the Nelsons dead in their bed. I don't even wanna know what happened there. Looked like a horror flick."

"I found your purse in the back yard there," Katie said, handing it over, "and then this round, glowing ball shot out of it and flew into the forest. We followed it, and it led us here. Was that the Eye? Did you bring it with you?"

"There isn't much time to explain," Allora said, strapping the quiver of arrows on her back. "Kim killed the Nelsons, and we think she might be one of the assassins sent here to kill us."

"Yeah, dude, she's evil," Tanner said, grabbing his sword from Dax.

Dax twisted his staff around. "Damn. Why do all the hot ones have to be psychotic killers from other worlds?"

Just then, the ice containing the wraith shattered. An arm swung out, as the wraith broke free from the icy enclosure. He pulled a short stick from the clasp on his back, and pressed a button on the shaft. Two sharp blades extended from either end. Then, he ran at them, swinging the bladed staff in circles.

Tanner ducked, and spun around with his sword outstretched. Dax was able to block the wraith's downward swing, which almost cut Tanner in half. Dax shifted his feet for a better position, pulling the staff around his body and clipped the wraith on the knee. His leg buckled, and Tanner went high. The wraith pulled his weapon up, blocking Tanner's strong downward strike.

Allora notched an arrow, looking for an opening as Katie sprang forward to join the fight. Every move the wraith made was blocked and countered. Allora couldn't find an opening, so she tossed the bow, grabbed a sword, and joined the others.

Lightning illuminated the sky, and rain pelted the four as they stabbed, sliced, and blocked. The addition of the girls was too much for the wraith. They had him surrounded, and when he tried to escape to the other side of the field, Katie blocked his path. Dax saw the opportunity and swung his staff around, knocking the wraith on his upper back. Tanner came in with the final blow and thrust his sword into the creature's stomach, which instantly caused it to go limp. Finally, the wraith was dead. Its red, glowing eyes faded and became as black as its skin. Suddenly, the wraith turned into ash, melting into the turf with every drop of rain.

A heart-stopping screech came from the forest behind them. The sound of breaking branches echoed into the field as Kim exploded from the foliage, and landed on the turf. She was breathing hard, and immediately changed, expanding to twice her original size. Her red eyes burned brighter, bursting into balls of flames. Her teeth grew sharper, and her bones protruded outward. She also grew two more arms that jutted out from her sides.

"I guess that's why they call 'em shifters," Dax said.

Kim didn't waste any time and ran right at them. Allora pulled back a purple burst and sent it streaming toward the shifter, but the creature deflected it as if it were nothing. Then, swords clashed. Tanner took the blunt force of the creature's first strike, which sent him backward.

The shifter hit Dax with a quick hadron burst, propelling him into the four-foot wall at the base of the bleachers next to the gym. Katie made an acrobatic turn and swung her katana. The strike sliced off one of the creature's arms, triggering the shifter to hit Katie with a free arm. Katie flew back and hit the same wall as her brother, then slumped on the track, unconscious.

Allora initiated her own assault and sliced off another one of the creature's arms. The infuriated shifter bellowed from the injury, then swung around to hit Allora, but she was able to roll out of the way. Tanner gained his footing and ran back into the fight, just in time to save Allora from a swinging sword. The shifter dropped the sword, crossed one arm underneath the other, and hit Tanner with a hadron burst to the chest. Tanner soared through the air and plummeted to the ground. His body didn't move.

"You will never win," the creature said in a low, frightening voice. "No matter what you do, you will die. We are too many."

"You're wrong!" Allora yelled back through the constant beads of rain that pelted the ground, even louder than the thunder that roared overhead.

"It's only a matter of time!" the creature shouted back. "All of your friends and family will die, and this world will be ours."

Allora couldn't take it anymore. "No!" she screamed. A bubble of energy expanded under her feet, and launched her high into the air. Energy filled every cell in her body, and flowed down into the sword that she pulled up behind her head. Purple fire surged from the steel, creating a trail of light, like a comet shooting through space. The shifter reeled back, modifying her position for the assault, and pulled her sword up. Allora's enflamed blade cut through the creature's weapon like a knife through butter, and then down into the head of the shifter, slicing it in half. The blade smoldered on the ground as the creature's severed body fell lifelessly onto the turf.

Allora keeled over in complete exhaustion. She looked up to see Katie and Dax stirring. With what was left of her strength, Allora turned her head to see Tanner's body to her right. She picked herself up and sluggishly crawled to him, then fell weakly at his side. "No, Tanner. Please. You can't be dead," Allora said, shaking him. There was no heartbeat. "I-I need you." She bent over his body and put her head on his chest. Her tears blending in with the drops of rain.

Dax and Katie limped across the field, and both knelt at Tanner's feet.

Allora's skin began to glow. The glowing light that had filled her body with power escaped her chest, and the light dropped into Tanner's body, illuminating him from within. Then, the glow floated out, forming into a ball. The light quickly dissipated, and the orb fell to the ground. Tanner's hand squeezed Allora's, jolting her upward. His eyes flicked open. She jumped on him, hugging his body as hard as she could. Tanner winced in pain, touching the bleeding wound on his blackened chest..

The rover leapt out of the bleachers, heading toward the forest. The four had no chance of chasing him. Rovers were known for their speed. The creature looked back, grinning at the thought of coming back with reinforcements. He leapt into the forest and was gone.

"We have to go after him," Allora said.

"We'll never catch him," Dax said.

"But if he gets away—" Allora began to argue, but her words were cut off by a sudden commotion in the woods.

Sounds of battle ensued, followed by yelling. The young warriors sluggishly limped to forest's edge. Two blurry creatures sailed over their heads. Sas pulled the rover down, making sure the creature didn't break apart and escape. He slammed the rover to the ground and pinned every limb down.

The creature wiggled and jerked to get loose, but he was trapped. Finally, the rover gave up fighting and stared up at them. He began laughing. "You have no idea what lies ahead for you. You may defeat me, but they know. Oh yessssssssss, they know!"

Sas couldn't stand to hear another word. He lifted his leg and stomped down on the rover's head, crushing him. After a few seconds, the rover dissolved into the ground.

A crowd of people erupted out of the woods. Allora had never been happier to see her mother. Behind her were Aunt May, Tanner's Aunt Lizi, Bell, Mr. Swan, Principal Winters, Mrs. Ferris, Sheriff Newton, Jarrod, and Maureen.

"Oh, thank Zeus," Milly said, running over and hugging her daughter. "Are you hurt?"

Family and friends exchanged hugs with each other, and all the parents worried over the cuts and bruises they saw.

Allora was worried about Jenny, but Aunt May was already on it. She was alive but badly hurt. Mr. Swan picked her up, then vanished through a portal that Aunt May created.

Milly checked her daughter to see if she needed immediate medical attention, then decided it would be best to get them out of there, before Sheriff Newton had to officially call it in. There was so much death and destruction that it couldn't be covered up completely, so they all hurried through Aunt May's portal.

Allora was pulled inward and reappeared in the field behind her house. The nightmare was over. She was home.

Twenty-Five

BEGINNING

A searing pain greeted Allora as she trudged into the hallway, still in her pajamas. Every time she moved, her muscles fought back. The bruises on her body were becoming much more accentuated, and she could still feel the stinging cuts littering her torso. Her legs were stiff, which made walking out to the living room difficult.

Katie sat up on the couch, wiping the sleep from her eyes. Allora searched through the couch and found the TV remote between the cushions. Aunt May entered the living room as Allora turned on the television. Milly was nowhere to be seen.

"May, where's Mom?" Allora asked her aunt. "She's usually making coffee at this time."

"She had to run out to take care of a few things," Aunt May replied.

Allora turned on the morning news and listened to the report.

"Thanks, Jim. In Sandy, police found Barbara and Randy Nelson deceased in their home. The couple allegedly kept to themselves, and initial reports claimed the couple died from an apparent gas leak during the night. Sources report that they didn't have any children or close relatives," the woman said.

"So unfortunate, Mary. In other local news, the Sandy High School Pioneers will be playing on a new field sooner than they thought, and all students will be able to take advantage of a new gymnasium. It is unclear whether this has anything to do with the state soccer championship, but the project was originally slated to break ground at the end of the school year. Principal Jodie Winters says other factors have enabled it to start ahead of schedule, but the remodel will not affect graduation. Now, let's take it to Pete for a weather report."

Aunt May disappeared into the kitchen without looking at her niece.

Rushing to follow, Allora winced at the pain her steps caused. "How is that possible?" Allora asked.

May started to answer, but Milly came trudging through the back door, took off her shoes, and went straight to the kitchen.

"So I'm guessing you saw the news," Milly said, preparing her morning coffee.

"Mom, how did you do that?" Allora asked, with raised eyebrows. "The field was destroyed, not to mention the Nelson house."

Milly poured water into the coffee machine, then directed Allora into the living room, where Katie, Dax, and Tanner were now wide awake. Sunlight beamed through the window, casting a yellow glow over the living room. Allora sat down to wait on her mother and took another look at the paintings that adorned the wall. They each seemed to take on a new shape, as if they were no longer far-off lands but portraits of a world that seemed closer than ever.

Milly leisurely sat down in her armchair and took her time to sip at the warm coffee. "First of all, I'm so glad you four are all right. Luckily, Katie called me before she got there." Milly paused. "I thought the worst when I heard you scream, Allora. We must have gotten to the Nelsons' when you killed that shifter. I'm honestly very proud of all of you. Not many can take on a shifter, let alone a wraith and a rover at the same time. I knew this day would come, but I was dreading it all the while." Milly changed her focus to Allora. "I guess it's time for me to start treating you more like an adult now. You will always be my baby though." Milly blinked quickly against the tears that were forming in her eyes.

"Mom…"

"Sorry." Milly pulled her tears in and rubbed her eyes. "We have contingency plans in place for this kind of incident, as similar things have happened before, albeit not this… brazen." Milly paused, wondering if it was going to get worse.

She already knew the answer, but she didn't want it to be true. Forces in Sonora had no care for order and peace. They wanted Earth for their own, and they would stop at nothing to conquer all.

"What about Jenny? Is she okay?" asked Allora.

"She's in the hospital, but only as a precaution," Milly explained, glad to be distracted from her ominous thought. "The doctor says she'll be fine. I was just there."

"You know, she saw almost everything," Allora said. "How did you——"

"Keep her quiet?" Milly said, interrupting her daughter. "Sheriff Newton took care of it. We have methods to keep humans from knowing the truth."

Allora looked to Tanner, who seemed to be thinking the same thing. "Can we go see her?"

"You should," Milly said. "She's probably pretty upset right now."

Allora ran to her room and dressed in a hurry.

"Take my car," Milly said, tossing him the keys. "Remember, Allora, you can't let Jenny think you know more than you do."

Allora nodded, and they left the house. Tanner had borrowed some of Allora's uncle's clothes, as the shredded tuxedo would have looked bad. He almost looked like Uncle Ben in the oversized sweatshirt, baggy, ripped jeans, and well-worn baseball hat. They hopped in the minivan and took off to the hospital.

Sheriff Newton was in the front entryway. He motioned them over, and whispered a story in their ear. Then, he left and the two headed into the hospital to the check-in area. Jenny was in intensive care on the second floor, and her parents were already in the room with her. Tanner gave them a hug, and then the adults left to give them some privacy.

Jenny was wearing a sullen, confused expression, and as soon as her parents were gone, she erupted with words. "I feel like I just woke up from a horrible nightmare."

Allora began to say something, but Tanner took the lead. "Are you okay?"

"I'm fine," Jenny answered. "A little sore, but I'll live. How are you guys?"

"Recovering," Allora said, trying to think of what to say next.

"Sheriff Newton told me what happened," she said, glaring up at Tanner and Allora as they sat awkwardly on the bed.

Jenny sat up a little more. "I can't believe we got into a car accident on the way to prom." They nodded. "I don't understand why I can't remember."

"You hit your head pretty bad," Tanner said.

Jenny stared back as if contemplating the plausibility of the explanation. "And Kim?"

Tanner nodded with pursed lips. "Yeah. She didn't make it."

"It was awful," Allora added.

They remained in the room for a few more minutes, discussing the fake car accident. Then, Tanner and Allora left the room, exhaling while they walked down the hospital hallway.

"Do you think she bought it?" Allora asked.

"I'm not sure," Tanner responded. "I just can't believe that they wiped her memory."

When they got to Allora's house, Milly let them know that Katie and Dax had gone home, and Tanner had to take off as well, since he hadn't seen his aunt since the night before.

Once Tanner was gone, Allora confronted her mother. "This isn't over, is it?" she asked, even though she already knew the answer.

"No, Allora, it's not." Milly placed her hand on her daughter's shoulder.

Allora looked up from staring at the floor.

"I just want you to know that I'm very proud of you," Milly said, embracing her daughter.

Allora reciprocated, holding onto her mother tightly and remaining there for a few seconds longer than normal.

* * *

Weeks went by without incident, and all the students at school believed Principal Winters' announcement about the renovations. Jenny continued ask questions, but she didn't give any indication that she remembered the real events of the night.

Allora, Katie, Dax, and Tanner went to the graduation ceremony, reveling in the fact that they were now seniors. After graduation, they decided to pay Sas a visit. It took them a while because Sas's cave was so far up the mountain, but when they finally arrived, they found him talking with Aunt May.

"Hi, guys and gals!" Sas said, running over to give them all a big hug all at once.

Squished together in his furry arms, the friends tried to reciprocate, but they couldn't get their arms free.

Sas let go and stepped back.

"Nice to see you, too, ya big, furry ape," Dax said, sucking in air.

"We just came up here to thank you for what you did at the school," Allora said. "We never got the chance earlier."

Sas's mood changed when she said it, as if he was offended that they felt the need to thank him. "You four are like family to me, and I'd never be letting anything happen to you. I don't think Aunt May would either."

Leaning on her staff at the perch on a large boulder, Aunt May said in her usual monotone voice, smiling slightly, "You all performed brilliantly. I couldn't have asked for any better."

The six of them talked for a while as the sun dipped into the western sky. Tanner, Dax, Katie, and Allora hiked to the lookout at the top of Sas's cave to watch the sunset. The four of them stared in silence at the beautiful landscape, relishing the peaceful serenity of the moment. The familiar orange orb dipped into the western horizon, and the warmth subsided. They knew there was a fight ahead, but somehow it seemed less scary knowing that they had each other.

The dying sunset glowed with a purple hue, soon replaced by a dark blue night sky. In the distance, they could see a dark cloud hanging low, like a spy waiting for the right moment to strike. Though the evening was clear and the storm had passed, another was brewing in the distance. It was a storm like no other, fueled by the events of the past and aimed at the unsuspecting town residing in peace at the base of the mountain.

THE END...

63610997R00123

Made in the USA
Lexington, KY
12 May 2017